CARRY THE ONE

CARRY THE ONE

CITY OF ANGELS SERIES

Sailor Penniman

DARROW PUBLISHING — LOS ANGELES | *AEQUALITAS*

This is a work of fiction. Names, characters, businesses, applications, merchandise, places, events, websites, and incidents are the products of the author's imagination or are used in a fictitious manner. Any resemblance to actual businesses, applications, merchandise, places, events, websites, incidents, or persons, living or dead, is purely coincidental.

Carry the One

Published in the United States by Darrow Publishing.

ISBN: 978-0-9993487-1-0

1 2 3 4 5 6 7 8 9 10

For tent-dwellers everywhere

Other books by Sailor Penniman

Then Came Michael
The Ugly Post

∞ CHAPTERS ∞

∞ 1 ∞

REPO MAN

TOBIAS HAD NO FRIENDS LEFT. It had taken five months, but they were all gone.

It started the day he stood in the parking lot of the high school where he taught algebra, geometry, and calculus and watched the repo man leave with the last regular roof he had had over his head.

It hadn't been a luxurious roof, one that belonged to a Mercedes or a Lexus or a Cadillac, outfitted with satellite radio, seat warmers, and an iPod docking station. It was a Honda with cloth seats, cupholders, and a functioning heater, but that hadn't mattered. The mortgage on his tiny condominium had adjusted in the bank's favor, and his paycheck had *not* adjusted, which worked in the school district's favor. Tobias had landed in the middle—of the street, mostly—after foreclosure on his home and an auction of it to the highest of the low bidders.

His Honda had provided the last layer of insulation between him and the outdoors, and it had kept him on the fringes of normal, where his friends lived. Its repossession was, in a sense, a second foreclosure on his home, and it had closed the door on normal and evicted him into a friendless place with no boundaries on trouble— all of outdoors.

He had tried to stop it, but with little energy. He was tired. "That's my car," he had said to the repo man. It was all he could think of to say.

"I know. That's why I'm here."

It was third period, Tobias's preparation period. He had headed to his car to "go home for lunch" just in time to see the repo man hitch the vehicle to his tow truck. And with the car, the repo man had taken from Tobias everything that floated around in the passenger area and rolled around in the trunk: his meagre wardrobe, a blanket, a lifeless pillow, a few books, some photos he hadn't put in storage, a plastic cup with a lid and straw, a flashlight, his toilet articles, a small cooler, a couple of receipts, six flares, and his spare tire. He had one bit of good luck. It had rained that morning, rare for Los Angeles, even in January, and Tobias had used his umbrella to walk to his classroom. It was the one thing the repo man didn't get.

The second foreclosure, on the Honda, had been, in many ways, worse than the first one, although Tobias never deluded himself about the first foreclosure, on his condo. It had been ugly and filled with shame, a moment elongated into interminable misery by letters and threats and notices to vacate the property and a humiliating public sale, of his three bedrooms and two bathrooms and closets and kitchen and places to maintain junk drawers. The auction and moving his belongings into a storage facility had been the wickedest thing to happen to him until they took his car on that dank Tuesday morning, which officially started the clock on his having nowhere to go.

After the ache of seeing his car leave the lot dulled a little, Tobias stared at the empty parking space and cried, in the rain, quietly. He felt no shame in crying. His Honda was worth the tears. It had given him someplace to be every night, a universe not much bigger than he was but which he controlled. His car made him look and feel ordinary and regular when he drove down the street in it, along with everybody else who lived ordinary and regular lives. In his car, he appeared to go somewhere and therefore felt he *went* somewhere.

And his car kept craziness at bay as he settled in each night, with the radio off, to save his battery, and silence and regrets of the year gone by, and the seventeen years gone before *that*, moved in. It let him read by the right half of the overhead light just long enough to forget his problems before he crawled into the back seat for six hours of cramped slumber.

Sometimes, he parked on the edge of a park and envied people he watched as they strolled home, some enjoying the luxury of owning a dog they walked on a leash, or he found an empty bit of curb down a suburban side street lined with houses full of comfortable people and remembered how it had been to be one of them, or he hid in plain sight in a parking lot and gained a new neighbor every fifteen minutes, couples who bickered about how long they would take inside the store, pubescent children who fought over whose turn it was to sit in the front seat, yappy canines that barked their objections to being left in the car. He failed to notice that these routines had normalized life in the Honda. Over time, he accepted a slow slide into mediocrity, and, later, destitution.

Living according to aftershocks had been a flaw Tobias had carried with him his whole life. He had no internal system that warned of disaster or tipped him off that a tsunami was headed his way. He easily solved math problems, where one step logically led to the next and the result was preordained by Pythagoras. Without that map, he struggled to see how current actions led to future pain.

Back when, he had left for college with a scholarship and no real plans beyond that, hurt by a family that shunned him for being gay. He had come out and stormed out and let his natural gift for math determine his destiny instead of aiming for something. Much later, as his misfortunes multiplied, he had pushed the limits of his means and made bad decisions that were the incremental steps to his life becoming a large problem with an answer that had a negative sign in front of it.

It had started during the impending foreclosure, when he had begun to factor into his operation his bank's overdraft fee system. If he went over a little, they covered him at thirty-five bucks a pop. Little by little, the pops added up, and he began each pay period digging out of his overdrawn hole. Each cycle, the pit was a bit deeper, the hole bigger. Finally, it got so that half his paycheck went toward bringing him to zero.

By the time he moved into his car, legal bills from the foreclosure on his condo and late fees with every creditor stacked up. Most times, the late fee was all he paid. Collection agencies called often.

The storage facility put a lien on his belongings for falling behind in his payments by more than a month and eventually sold his things—dishes, fancy linens, bobbleheads, books, everything— all to cover *that* tab. What they couldn't sell, they tossed, even his personal photos. The key was to not reward him for being a deadbeat by letting him have the things no one wanted that could be described that way because they were so personal, they mattered only to one person, Tobias.

Finally, he skipped a car payment and then could only afford some of the next payment and none of the late fee. He paid less and less each cycle. Then the bank had sent the repo man to the only valid address on file for him—his workplace.

And from there, it had gotten worse. Without a car, he couldn't stray far from his job. So, he slept there and showered mornings in the boys' locker room. On clear nights, he slumbered in the bleachers of the football field, on the visitors' side, which was obscured from the line of sight of the main part of campus. If it rained or was too cold to fall asleep, he stayed one step *behind* the custodians and spent the night in his classroom once they had finished with it, but that was risky. To minimize the danger of getting caught, he seldom did it. He reserved that luxury for the bitterest of cold nights.

On the off nights, he sometimes paid for a movie ticket, which was expensive but cheaper than a cheap motel, and slept in his seat until the movie ended, or he sat in the bookstore until it closed, or he hopped a bus to the nearby mall to review lesson plans in the food court and browse for clothes and gadgets he couldn't afford. He just needed somewhere to pass the evening before he was turned out for the night. He endured the stares of mall employees who wondered about the weird guy with the backpack who never left.

Being dead even with and not *above* suspicion caused him for the first time in his adult life to dislike that boyish air his light brown hair, dabbling of freckles, and trim physique gave him. He wasn't bony or skinny, but something about his lean, healthy weight implied that youthful baby fat hadn't been too far in his past, even though it had been. His young-looking countenance didn't help him when he needed to look his thirty-six years and like a responsible man who'd once had a mortgage, instead of the twenty-eight-ish he presented that could be twenty-five and that sometimes caused people to think he still lived at home with his parents, which somehow translated into his being more capable of engaging in shenanigans.

He subsisted, but the inability to put together one good night's sleep cost him his concentration in the classroom, and life turned bad exponentially from there.

He had replaced just a few clothes he lost in the Honda repossession and wore the same thing to work every few days. It meant his clothes weren't always clean. He caught colds more often, but he reported to work sick to have shelter for the day. He was moody and treated the students with an air of crankiness. He had nowhere reliable to grade homework and even less time to do it since he used the hours directly after school to strategize for the night.

Once, he lost a set of exams at a diner. He had tucked them under a carry-away tray and nodded off at his table. While he dozed, a busboy had cleared his tray with a swipe of it into a large tub and had taken the exams with it. The contrite man confessed, but it was too late. Discarded, half-chewed food, dirty napkins, coffee, unnatural condiments blends, and lipstick-lined straws mingled with everyone's math. Tobias gave every student an A. Parents of the C-or-worse students didn't complain. Parents of the A students who volunteered in their spare time, played a minimum of two sports and two instruments, obtained fluency in foreign languages, and forwent family outings and TV and *life*, all to win prime seats at prime universities, were outraged. His school principal was, too. Tobias erased the As and gave the exam again.

Tired all the time, he finally missed days at work here and there and eventually everywhere. He wasn't a tenured teacher, and he wasn't sure that would have helped him. It was a slow crawl to his finish, but they finally fired him for poor attendance, they said, officially, but he knew it was for being poor.

He had faced a fork in the road. He could have stayed in Los Angeles or gone home to his family in Florida. Returning to Florida amounted to no option.

Staying in L.A. wasn't much easier. Bunking with friends proved prickly. He loved L.A., as the song went, but it was a huge city full of isolated individuals. Everyone let everyone else "do their thing". Tobias was unwilling to move into someone else's world with no job or car or preordained move-out date or ability to solve for X, that factor of a known future.

Still, he had stayed in L.A. and moved downtown where he had access to some services and a twenty-four-hour neighborhood of sorts. He lived off a small unemployment benefit and had used his last paycheck to buy supplies and what even an extravagant camper would consider a luxurious tent. It was his new home.

It had a ten-by-ten-foot floor area and would let a six-foot-six-inch man stand at full height, more than enough room for Tobias, at five feet, eleven inches.

The tent was watertight with superb ventilation. It had front and back floor-to-ceiling zipper doors and four mesh windows, one on each tent wall, that he could seal closed with covers.

It wasn't always easy to guard, from people or creatures. He woke up the first morning to find three rats enjoying the warmth with him. He dipped into his absolute last money to buy four, small, battery-operated ultrasonic devices that repelled rats, and they never came back.

Humans weren't as easily fended off, and the sixty-eight pounds the tent weighed, plus his gear, made it miserable on him when the pressure was on from police or boorish neighbors and he had to move. The first three weeks, some force pushed him off his patch of sidewalk every other day. He had tried San Pedro Street, Sixth Street, Los Angeles Street, Maple Avenue, and San Julian Street, but it had turned out badly almost every night. He had two fist fights and barely held his own. He didn't think he would make it in the long run. He regretted buying the tent.

Desperate, he tried a different tack and moved a little west and north. After two more days of wandering, he had settled into a homeless reserve on Spring Street, two short blocks from Temple Street and several government buildings. The juxtaposition between City Hall, which towered in plain view on Spring, just two blocks away, the courthouses, and the tent neighborhood seemed peculiar, but the police allowed the coexistence, and the lack of retail establishments kept foot traffic low.

The tiny bivouac township spilled down the sidewalk, away from the buildings to the freeway overpass, and hovered right over the 101 Freeway. With a small group of other tent dwellers, Tobias had found a kind of permanence. He was king of his cloth castle. He tried to be happy with his tent purchase.

He didn't absolutely hate tent life. The white noise of the steady stream of vehicles below him on the freeway comforted him. The heat from the cars rose and kept him warm on cold nights. He tried not to think about what the carbon monoxide and other fumes did to his lungs.

On the other hand, it had been five months since his car had been repossessed, three since he had lost his job and moved into the tent. In the long, warm days of June, when the sun shone on the vibrancy of everyone else's lives well into the evening, he lived with another bitter truth: He was on his own.

It was a strange thought, for him—the notion of singularity— since he tended to think in exponents. They applied everywhere, he always argued. His joblessness provided a glaring example. He had gone from math teacher to ne'er-do-well with one job lost. He was an exponential loser, and each day of unemployment added several layers of failure to his life and compounded his problems.

That day, Tobias told himself he tried to solve them, even if his attitude didn't add up with the impression he had of his efforts. He was at the behemoth central branch of the Los Angeles Public Library on Fifth and Flower Streets, where patrons could use the Internet for free for one hour a day. He made a stab at searching for a job on the library computer, but the hunt for employment had offered no final kill. Because the school district had fired him, he stated honestly on every application TERMINATED as the "reason for leaving", which made him an undesirable candidate. Too, several creditors had sued him and won default judgments against him. His application was dead on arrival with any prospective employers who ran a credit check on him.

So, most days, he surfed the Web for a good chunk of the hour. If he ran out of time before he saved any changes to his resume, he didn't care. There was always the next day and maybe thousands of days after that.

His hour expired, and he left the library and walked east to Grand Avenue and headed north for the Music Center near Grand Park, an upscale area peppered with operagoers, theater wonks, and philharmonic fans, either coming from or headed to a swank eating establishment before their show.

It was a spot that had borne him panhandling fruit in the past. He thought he would try it again. He wanted to buy himself a drink he would nurse from a barstool like it was in the ICU, down to that dirty, half-warm, half-cold melted ice cube water, which had so little of the original drink flavor left, it tasted sour. He had showered at the mission that morning and didn't want to let being clean enough to sit in an air-conditioned bar go to waste.

An hour and a half later, it wasn't going well. He remembered that the opera and philharmonic seasons had ended for the summer, which cut his panhandling options down to the theater crowd.

By six thirty, he had solicited just four dollars and eighty-two cents, a small fortune for some things in the homeless world, but not enough for a mixed drink and a good tip.

He was ready to give up and go home to his tent and invest his small stash in breakfast the next morning.

Then he spotted a man wearing what looked like an accidental three-day beard, with the hairy spikes going every which way, and who looked as though he had been wearing his clothes for those same three days.

He was intoxicated.

Tobias openly stared at him. Underneath the disarray, he had smooth dark hair that looked natural in every way. He was fit and lean and seemed as though he'd be agile if sober, but he was clumsy at that moment and wore his problems all over his wobbly walk and dazed-looking eyes.

Forty-is-the-new-thirty-two, recently homeless, very clueless.

The man proved Tobias's last assessment. He reached into his pocket for something and moved a beat too slow. He operated at the speed of a drunk.

He pulled the object halfway out of his pocket, and a thief who looked as if he came up with the idea because the man was dumb enough to present the opportunity rolled down the spacious, smooth, glittery-stoned sidewalk on skates and swiped it from him.

It was a cell phone, probably the man's final connection to the functioning world. It was always the last thing to go, used up until the mobile company shut it down. The thief had simply sped up the process for the man.

The skating mugger hadn't been the only opportunist.

Two ruffians on scooters appeared.

While the man stared at his empty hands, baffled by the first strange larceny, the other two gangsters came to an abrupt stop and bookended him, one in front, one in back. The man had no escape.

Tobias couldn't hear what they said, but they had clearly demanded the man hand over whatever else was on him.

The man was too inebriated to obey the thugs. He weaved in place, and they tried to reach into his pockets.

The man had enough moxie to push them away without their hands landing in his pockets.

Tobias began a cautious but quick walk in their direction.

The man put up an unsteady fight, and the thieves dropped their original quest. They transitioned from the man's pockets to the man. The thief in front of the man punched him hard in the gut.

Tobias sprang into a jog, to help the man, who was doubled over in pain.

"Hey!" Tobias yelled.

The hoodlum behind the man reached down, squeezed the man by the back of the neck, yanked him backwards, and exposed his stomach and ribcage to the mugger in front.

The man's face was oddly serene. He didn't seem to know or care what happened to him. His earlier defense of himself appeared to Tobias to be instinct more than a logical step in the narrative of the attack. The man seemed to forget what to do on his side of the assault.

Tobias arrived just as the criminal in front rammed his fist into the man's sternum and the one in back shoved him to the ground. They hopped on their scooters and yelled epithets at the man, as though he had offended *them* for not allowing them to finish their mugging. They made quick getaways.

Tobias knelt by the man. "Are you all right? Let me help you up."

The man got up under his own steam and shrugged off Tobias. He stalked off walking a crooked line, propelled by the sheer oafishness of his inebriation. He took big, loping, unreasonable steps. He was on a mission to nowhere.

Tobias gave him a wide berth.

The man headed across Grand Park. From the Music Center, the park aimed downward over several long asphalt steps that were almost plateaus and that were adorned with flower beds. The steps formed a walkway alongside a gigantic fountain.

The man stumbled over the large steps and across the flatter cement terrain that came just after the fountain and jaywalked over Hill Street, which ran through the mid-way point of the park.

Tobias followed.

The man arrived at Broadway and abandoned the park and meandered south on Broadway and hit Second Street, where Broadway was closed for underground Metro repairs.

The man saw the barricades and stumbled to the closest storefront of an establishment that was closed the way many downtown shops were by that hour.

The man snuggled into the store's doorway notch. With knees pulled close to his chest, he dropped his head, and went to sleep.

Tobias saw trouble where the man couldn't. They were too far west of Main Street for an overnight stay on a store's stoop. Main Street ran north and south and was downtown's imaginary border between white collar life to the west and Skid Row to the immediate east. Everything to the west was off-limits to freer souls like the man in the doorway. The man stood a good chance of being arrested before daybreak and sent to an unintentional homeless shelter, Los Angeles County Jail.

Tobias approached the man and rousted him.

The man rebuffed him. He opened his eyes and talked to no one, in a cranky tone. "Wha? What the f—?"

"Ohh-kay. Okay. That's all. You're coming with me." Tobias wedged in behind the man and placed a firm grip on his upper arms. "Come on. Up."

The man had ceded enough willpower to whatever he had drunk and allowed himself to be hoisted to his feet, even helping by bracing on his own feet as he headed into a standing position.

"Let's go," Tobias said.

The man was the same height as Tobias. He turned and leaned close enough to Tobias to breathe spirits in his face. "Where we going?" His expression was suddenly full of whimsy.

"My place. Walk with me."

The man took two steps and stopped. He swayed a little. He looked at Tobias. "Wait." That time, Tobias caught a strong whiff of whiskey. "Do I know you?" the man asked.

"No. Let's go."

The man scrutinized Tobias with dull eyes that looked as if they sent information to his brain in slow-motion. He smiled. "Okay."

Tobias used the man's left arm to guide him. They took several shaky steps and settled into an awkward rhythm. A hundred feet up Broadway, they turned right onto Second Street, toward Spring Street. At Spring, they turned left and headed north.

What should have been a five-minute journey took them fifteen minutes, but finally they arrived at Tobias's tent over the 101 Freeway. Tobias led the man inside.

"Stand there for a second."

"Okay." The man rocked a little on his feet, but he managed to stand in one place.

Tobias opened the nozzles on his self-inflating air mattresses and pillows and unrolled his own sleeping bag and the spare he kept on hand for nights when it made more sense to zip two bags together because it was cooler that way. He guided the stranger to the sleeping bag designated for him and let him plop down. The air mattress below the bag offered a soft landing. Tobias removed the man's shoes.

"Go on. Get in."

The man crawled in without an argument. He lowered his head onto the pillow Tobias had tucked under the top of the sleeping bag and fell asleep before Tobias could zip the bag shut.

Tobias wasn't tired, but no longer able to leave with a houseguest to worry about, he undressed and slid into his own bag. Bored, he read for a while by portable lamplight. From time to time, he glanced at the man. After a couple of hours, he put the book down and stared at him. He slept like a stone. Other than his chest, nothing on him moved. He made no sound. He looked serene and as though he dreamt easily or not at all.

He's handsome.

And troubled.

Tobias turned out the lamp and rolled over to face the opposite direction of the man. He would get up early the next day, buy the man some coffee, and send him on his way.

∞ **2** ∞

STYROFOAM CUPS

Somebody shook Arthur. Somebody irritating. He didn't know who it was. He was only certain he was hungover and slept someplace snug. He wished the person would let him snooze.

"Hey. Wake up," the somebody said.

Wait, that's different. What a pleasant voice. Arthur wanted it to keep talking while he dreamt on an endless loop.

"Time to wake up. I've got hot coffee."

The voice is gentle and offering coffee. I'm not as irritated.

In a softer tone, the voice repeated, "I've got coffee."

Arthur smelled the coffee. Reality infiltrated reverie. The real world overpowered his sleep. He forced opened his eyes.

A face he presumed belonged to the nice voice stared at him.

It was a nice face.

It had the beginnings of a tan and a very few light freckles, no more than twelve or fifteen, dotted strategically on the cheeks and across the nose, as though someone had drawn them there after they chose the perfect spots on the face's smooth skin to place them.

"Where am I?" Arthur asked. He took care not to emit too much air. He hoped his breath didn't offend the person with the nice face and voice.

"My place. My tent, really. Someone stole your phone last night and roughed you up. Wasn't me." The stranger held up his hands in innocence. "I followed you though, after it happened. Brought you here, kept you from going to sleep on Broadway and waking up in County Jail."

Please say all of that again. I'd like you to talk forever.
Wait. Jail?

Arthur sat up straight and blinked his eyes several times to wake himself for real. Two seconds later, he bent over in pain.

"Agh," he said, at half-voice, to control the flow of any bad breath.

"I know," his host said, as though Arthur had aimed his "agh" at him, when Arthur still wasn't sure what went on. He only knew that what made him feel cozy was a thick sleeping bag that surrounded him. It seemed to be atop a soft and airy mattress. He sucked in his stomach and did a few limited-motion, pain-filled, mini-sit-ups.

"Whoo, that hurts." *I wish I knew why.*

"Probably will for a few days."

He seems to know why.

"That one guy was pretty rough on your gut."

Which guy? And, anyway, it's not too bad right now, with you talking, even if I'm very confused about who you are and why I'm here. I wonder what my hair looks like.

He did more sit-ups, and flashes of memory came to him. Scooters or skates and being pulled from behind and pushed to the ground.

"I think I remember," he said. "Some guys on skates, or something. By the park? And then I think I walked with you to some tents." He felt foolish. *Did this man just say that same thing?*

"This tent, yes. Would you like some coffee?"

The man handed Arthur a small Styrofoam cup of dark liquid. The man was not in a sleeping bag. He sat in a camping chair close to Arthur and looked as though he had been up for hours, possibly watching Arthur sleep. Arthur hoped he hadn't snored or drooled.

"I cancelled some plans I had last night," the man said, "and the cash I saved bought two smalls. I wanted to buy two larges, but four and change wouldn't do it. Sorry."

Arthur sniffed the coffee and closed his eyes. "No, this is perfect. Thank you."

It'll mask my morning breath, too, even if coffee's not much better. He used his free hand to finger-comb his hair. The movement hurt his ribcage, but he faked his way through the pain.

"I'm Tobias," the tent-owner said.

Tobias.

"Arthur."

Tobias nodded acknowledgment.

"Coffee's good," Arthur said.

"I'm glad."

They stared at each other for a prolonged moment. Arthur knew why he eyed Tobias. He wondered if Tobias watched him for the same reason. Gay men sometimes extended glances at other men into full stares, to see what was returned. An equally long stare could tell all. It wasn't always interest. Sometimes, it just meant *I'm gay, too*, a quick message before the person looked away, although in Arthur's mugged and hungover state, he feared the longer glance from Tobias meant *You look a serious mess.*

"Would I really have been arrested?" Arthur said.

"Probably."

"I can't thank you enough."

They drank in silence. Arthur took sips at slow intervals. He wondered why he wasn't in more of hurry. He felt self-conscious, sitting there beaten up and borrowing a place to sleep from a stranger, but he took his time with his coffee, as though he had scheduled breakfast with his friend Tobias in his tent.

"Where do you normally camp out?" Tobias said.

"Camp out?" *What does he mean?*

"Tunnel? Parking lot? Shelter?"

That's what he means. Go with it, Arthur. This is the first real conversation you've had in years.

He faked a chuckle. "Uh, yes, I'm everywhere it seems. I guess last night I was on Broadway."

"And now you're on Spring Street."

"Spring Street." Arthur went with the vein of the small talk. "You been here long?" he said.

"Homeless in general, about a year and a half, if you include the time I lived in my car and a couple of rough months in no man's land, living in the great outdoors in territory surrounded by all my creditors. Moved in here about three months ago. I did things backwards. Lost my house and car first. The chaos cost me my job."

"I'm sorry."

"Thanks. This," Tobias waved his hand to indicate the tent as a whole, "is my humble abode."

Arthur stared at Tobias and nodded momentously.

"What about you? Been out here long?" Tobias said.

Arthur panicked. He didn't have a good story. "Uh, no, just a short while." He changed the subject. "You're very generous, Tobias. You took a big risk bringing a stranger in here. For all you knew, I could have sobered up and beaten you over the head and taken your things."

They studied each other with quiet politeness.

"I look ragged," Tobias said, with a small smile, "but I'm only thirty-six. I've had my share of fights out here. I could have handled you." He chuckled. "Haven't you heard? Thirty-six is the new twenty-eight."

Arthur laughed. "I thought it was fifteen."

Tobias laughed, too. "I wish." Then he shook his head in pretend disgust and laughed again. "Actually, no I don't. Fifteen. No thanks. I'll stick with twenty-eight. Or thirty-six."

Arthur chuckled and rubbed his stomach from the pain.

"Careful," Tobias said, with light, waning laughter.

Arthur still laughed a little. He was in a great mood. "Either way, you don't look ragged. *You look twenty-eight.*" He smiled. "And don't count me out at forty-one, last night, notwithstanding. I could pass for thirty-two, thirty-three, somewhere in there, and you know it." He grinned wider.

"You could. I thought that myself," Tobias said. He grinned back.

"I've been lucky," Arthur said. "My hair has stuck with me. It helps." He sipped more coffee and felt Tobias's eyes on him.

"Yes, it does," Tobias said.

His tone made Arthur look up from his coffee.

They stared at each other through another long pause.

"I saw that thief take your phone," Tobias finally said, "and, well, the way those guys ganged up, you were kind of a sitting duck, bobbing and weaving on the street. I don't know. Every teacher has a bit of the school counselor in him. Or her. I guess I felt sorry for you. Don't take that the wrong way."

"No offense taken. I'm sure I was a sight." Arthur tried to laugh at himself again but couldn't muster the humor that time. Flashes of the mugging, and the three days that led to it, came to him, and he was ashamed and embarrassed and worried about what it all meant. He drank more coffee to divert his attention from unsettling thoughts.

"You're a teacher?" he said, to get even further away from his problems.

"Was, yes. Math." Tobias held up his hand. "I know. You always sucked at math, wish you were better at it, envy people who like it." He chuckled again and drank his coffee.

"Something like that." *Nothing like that*, but Arthur shrugged and offered a self-deprecating smile in apology for not understanding math. The shift in tone gave him the perfect opportunity to leave before the conversation turned to what *he* did.

"I guess I'll be getting out of your way." He drank down the last of his coffee and looked for a place to throw away the cup.

"I'll take that," Tobias said, and he reached for the cup.

"Thanks." Arthur smiled. As he plotted his exit, he realized he wasn't wearing his shoes. That meant Tobias had removed them for him. He hoped his feet hadn't smelled bad. On reflex, he finger-combed his hair again.

"Are you sure you don't want to stay? Those punks got off a couple of hard punches. There's plenty of room if you want to recuperate for a bit and head out later."

There *was* room, Arthur noticed, as he looked around the large tent. There was space, on either side of him, for Tobias's sleeping bag, which at the time was rolled up and stored in a corner, with an empty area that led to the tent walls. A few dishes and a tiny camping table made up a makeshift kitchen, and a duffel bag functioned as a large dresser drawer. A few pairs of shoes were lined up against the tent wall, including Arthur's. There was a second large camping chair folded up near the duffel bag.

Two-thirds of the way up on each wall, windows let in a cool breeze, and the entire space smelled like fresh air and a scent coming from some secret air freshener that Arthur guessed had a name like "mountain spring" or "crisp linen". He was vaguely relieved his shoes didn't provide the overriding scent. Out of it all, one thing interested Arthur. He wasn't sure why.

"Why do you have two sleeping bags?" he said, which caused his face to turn hot. He hadn't meant to blurt out the question.

"Sometimes, when I can figure out how to fumble with the zippers, I turn the two bags into one huge one. On warmer nights, a larger bag is actually cooler."

And sleeps two. "Nice."

"Like I said, you're welcome to stay, rest up, if you like."

"No, I've overstayed. I'll be okay."

"Are you sure?"

"I'm sure. But thanks."

"All right."

Arthur pretended to feel no pain as he worked his way out of his sleeping bag and began to roll it up. His full bladder threatened to ruin his smooth exit. He needed a bathroom badly. He remembered he had last used one well before he encountered Tobias in the park.

"That's okay. You can leave the bag," Tobias said.

"No, I got it." Arthur rolled up the bag tight and squeezed it into the attached compression sack. "There you go."

"Thanks," Tobias said.

Arthur reached for his shoes and quickly put them on, again relieved he didn't detect any unpleasant odors coming from them or the socks on his feet.

"So, where you going?" Tobias said.

Arthur had hoped Tobias wouldn't ask that. He was ashamed of the answer. "Back to where I came from." *Please don't ask more.*

"Where's that?"

I knew it. "Nowhere in particular. You know how it is."

He stood and ducked out of what appeared to be the front door of the tent. His ribcage muscles throbbed at him. He hid a wince and kept moving.

Outside, he bounced on his feet a couple of times, to give the impression of full fitness. It put excruciating pressure on his bladder. He thought it might explode. He noticed, though, that his discomfort didn't detract from the fact that in the crisp, morning light, Tobias and his faded freckles were charming.

Behind Tobias and up the street lay a row of tents and makeshift dwellings of all sizes. It took Arthur just a few seconds to see that Tobias had the largest tent in his mini-neighborhood.

"I can't thank you enough, Tobias. Really. I appreciate the save." He laughed a little and held out his hand for a shake. "Jail. That's pretty intense."

"Nah. No worries." Tobias returned the handshake and gave a warm smile. Arthur could have sworn he felt an extra stroke from Tobias's thumb across the soft part of his hand.

"Good luck," Tobias said.

"Thanks, and you, too."

Arthur walked away and headed south on Spring Street. Just after Temple Street, he turned west and cut through Grand Park, which bordered the back of the enormous courthouse that ran the length of that block of the park. There, Arthur was out of Tobias's sight, shrouded by the huge building.

If Tobias had had X-ray vision, he would have seen Arthur making his way through the park, across the backyard of the courthouse, over Broadway, through more park, then over Hill Street and up the slope, past the fountain and onto Grand, close to where he had been mugged.

He was relieved Tobias had normal vision and couldn't see where he went when he got to the end of the long strip of park and exited the other side. It was embarrassing.

$\infty\ \mathbf{3}\ \infty$

TIME IN A BOTTLE

"MR. DEWYNTER. YOU'RE BACK." ARTHUR'S administrative assistant, Kelly, stood up to greet Arthur, as though Arthur had caught *her* strolling into *her* job after going missing for three days instead of the other way around.

Arthur had told Kelly many times she could call him by his first name, but, at twenty-two, she declined the offer. She wasn't afraid. She had graduated college in three years and held her own with the trickiest people in Arthur's orbit. She was invaluable and a breeze to work with, and she talked to Arthur, in tone and content, as though they were on a first-name basis. She just wouldn't take the last step and use the name. She saw Arthur as ancient and old enough to be her father.

By all accounts, he looked great for his age—money, access to health food and the best skin care, and regular exercise with the proper amount of sleep had gotten him that—but at her age, he was still old. She had managed to make Arthur feel like his having a first name he unreasonably wanted people to use was his shortcoming, as though Kelly shouldn't have been bothered with old men who expected busy young people to allow them into their universe with things like a first-name basis. She had subconsciously filed him under FIFTH PERIOD TEACHER or MY DENTIST, and there would be no climbing out of that space.

"Yes," he answered. *I'm back.* He sounded as uninterested as he was. He was the owner and CEO of a boutique investment firm that netted him, *before* he added interest and other gains from his own investments, a personal income of fifteen million a year, year after year after year, so that he no longer cared how high the pile of money was, and it bored him stupid and lately had caused him to drink away the doldrums a little too often.

A problem was developing, he knew. Sometimes it worried him, as it had earlier that morning when he'd learned he barely dodged jail and a severe beating, but at other times, he secretly looked forward to the trouble. Trouble was at least interesting.

He walked into his nine-hundred-square-foot office and dropped into his throne-like chair.

"What'd I miss?" It was Thursday. He'd been gone since he had stepped out for coffee the previous Monday morning and had kept going.

Kelly followed him into his office and sat down in one of the two large visitors' chairs in front of his sizable, glass desk, a piece of furniture he found more absurd every year. It held no important papers and secreted no private files since it had no drawers. It was a showpiece, a prop in his role as an Established Man. A laptop, a phone, a notepad, three No. 3 pencils, and a pretentious lamp he never used because he never worked late were the only things it carried that hinted that he did any work there every day.

He did a great deal of work there, but he had been at it so long, so many years, he no longer needed the constructs of the hardworking investor. By that point in his career, those things were just emblems and not real tools. The work, and success, spilled out of the files and numbers he had maintained in his head for years.

"You missed your meeting with Tannover, but I rescheduled for next Monday. He needs you more than you need him. And since I had a feeling you weren't coming in, I called him and cancelled before he spent time getting here, so it wasn't a problem."

Masterful—and appreciated—diplomacy about my 'not coming in'.

"Almost managed to make him wonder if he was in your way, needing an appointment. I was nice though, don't worry."

"Thanks. I know you were. That's good work."

"And, I hope it's okay, but I kept today open. Nothing scheduled. Tomorrow either."

He rubbed his temples with his eyes closed. *Are you kidding? That's perfect.*

He said the same thing aloud. "Are you kidding? That's perfect. As you can see, I'm not dressed for meetings. Just came in to catch up on phone calls."

His head screamed. After he'd left Tobias's tent, he'd walked with a bulging bladder to the Biltmore, one of downtown L.A.'s most luxurious hotels, despite its location across from a rundown Pershing Square and its proximity to Skid Row, which was within walking distance if a person had fifteen minutes.

He had returned to the room he'd checked into the previous Monday. He relieved his aching bladder and his bowels and sent his pants and shirt and every undergarment to the valet to be cleaned. Despite how long he had been wealthy and comfortable around the support systems for those with money, having grown up with limited means, he never failed to marvel at what money would buy, including someone else to wash his three-day underwear and socks.

He shaved with hotel supplies and took an extra-long shower to let the hot water run over his sore abdomen and, with all his clothes gone, slept naked for two hours and dreamt he was in a castle made of tent material that had people in it with nice voices who roamed around with pillows.

He woke up sweaty and starving. He couldn't remember eating anything over the previous three days. All he had conjured up were pictures of himself drinking, in bars, on benches in public, in front of a sundry shop that had had a small selection of alcohol—he hadn't even waited until he was farther down the street; he had opened the bottle right outside the store.

And then there had been coffee with Tobias. That had been very different from what had come before it. He thought about coffee with Tobias for a long while, in his hotel bed, nude, with the television off and the drapes drawn. The only light in the room came from the sunlight that slipped in through the crack in the curtains.

He lay in the dark and remembered Tobias and no longer wondered if Tobias was gay because Arthur knew he was. He daydreamed about his overnight companion and fell asleep.

An hour later, he woke up and sat up. He donned a lush hotel bathrobe and ordered a large, personal brunch of eggs benedict, with extra Hollandaise sauce, cottage fries, lobster cream cheese, a side of fresh fruit, orange juice, and a pot of coffee. He read the *Wall Street Journal* they had left at his door that morning and perused the *Los Angeles Business Journal* on a laptop the hotel had rented him.

During brunch, the valet arrived with his clean laundry. After he ate, he took another ninety-second shower and dressed in his fresh clothes. Still, his head throbbed as he checked out of his room and Ubered his way back to his office in Century City, a swank Los Angeles business district adjacent to Beverly Hills situated on just one hundred and seventy-six acres. His Maserati had sat in his personal parking space in his office building's garage since the previous Monday.

He couldn't believe what an asshat he had been. He had finished a call on that Monday with another client he had just made three million dollars richer and told Kelly he was going for coffee.

Instead, he had walked down Avenue of the Stars, close to where his office was, until he was too far away to bother to walk back.

He took an Uber home to Beverly Hills and changed into clothes from the secret side of his closet. It wasn't the section that held the wardrobe worth hundreds of thousands of dollars that functioned more like a set of costumes he used to play the lead role of Successful Investor in a summer blockbuster movie. The clothes came from a corner of the closet that hid his favorite items—discount-store cotton slacks, thick sweats, navy-blue undershirts he wore as real T-shirts, socks without a gold-toe section, and casual loafers and old running shoes.

Dressed more comfortably, he took another Uber downtown, where he hoped to find trouble. He had been a hypocrite about it, though, and a bit of a coward. Before going on his devil-may-care, spit-in-wind, drunk tear, he had made sure to grab a thousand dollars in cash from his safe, to go with his limitless credit cards, and check into extravagant digs at the Biltmore.

Those were minor safeguards, though, and his behavior baffled him and signaled to him that he stood on the edge of catastrophe. He had lived a cautious life. He preferred buttoned-down to unleashed. If he went anywhere downtown where he could stumble upon clients, like the Music Center or upscale eating establishments, he made sure he looked like their trusted investor.

Yet, that Monday, he hadn't cared. He had wandered around downtown, by average-looking car and on foot, and presented a version of himself he didn't understand—and that he wouldn't want anyone to see, yet every passerby had seen him.

And Tobias had seen him, a fact that embarrassed Arthur. Worse was that Tobias had been right. Arthur *had* bobbed and weaved all over the city for more than two days. He catted back to his room and slept in his clothes the first two nights and wondered who drove by the places he meandered and spotted him.

And still he didn't care enough about the risk to his reputation to slow down and go home. He dove deepest into the bottle the third night, the Wednesday he had been assaulted. He had been too tanked-up to find his way back to the hotel, which had been a five-block walk down Grand Avenue, from where the thugs had jumped him, with no turns required, but still he couldn't find it and instead wandered around the edge of Grand Park. He had been fortunate Tobias had rescued him and brought him inside.

Tobias.

"Frank took some of your client calls," Kelly said, "and here are the messages from late yesterday, people who wouldn't take voice mail for an answer and insisted on talking to me." She stood up.

"Thanks, Kelly. I'll go see Frank, and Charlie, too, in a sec. Make sure you get outta here by three today."

"I can do that."

"Oh, someone stole my cell phone last night. Can you scare up a replacement?"

She turned back and gave him a blank stare, as though she didn't understand how a person walked around for several hours—*overnight*, in fact—with no phone and only mentioned it in passing. She stifled a verbal reaction with an exaggerated lift of the eyebrows that said, "Oh-kay. Uh, sure."

She said aloud, "E-mail me your account number, and I may need the answers to your security questions. I got it from there."

He knew not to fight her about giving her his information. He would only look silly. Already, she disapproved of his not allowing the firm to have a website or a Facebook page or any social media accounts. In that, he had been right though, even if Kelly doubted him. There were some things "twenty-two" didn't yet understand.

Not only would Arthur not allow any online presence for his firm, but he had paid a high price to a service that went through the pains of having Arthur's name—and the name of every employee—scrubbed from as many sites as feasible. He had been fanatic about no one googling anyone associated with his firm, not only for their privacy and safety with clients—when money was at stake, people sometimes behaved dangerously—but to keep the firm from appearing mundane and average.

He required all staff to blog and "like" and "favorite" and share and otherwise comment online in as nondescript a way as possible. Online videos that showed their faces were strictly out of the question. He allowed snapshots only and encouraged extreme discretion even there. None of them complained, not even Kelly, who thought it was all a bit silly. He compensated them well for their sacrifice of online fame. A few even appreciated the anonymity his restrictions gave them.

His tawdry behavior of the previous three days notwithstanding, he and his firm were elusive, exclusive, elegant, and not easy to get. He had painstakingly built his firm waiting for one wealthy client to refer him to another. As he had gained wealth, he quietly moved into the neighborhood of those he served and eventually out-earned, and they thought he had always been there. He was one of theirs. They didn't post testimonials about his financial advice for the world to gawp at. And they preferred not to place their financial futures in the hands of someone who could be rated on a five-star scale.

Arthur had explained to Kelly that there was run-of-the-mill, flash-in-the-pan money that flowed through investment firms all over the world. Then there was what he called granite currency, old solid money that wouldn't budge without a careful plan to get it to the next meadow of opportunity. He saw himself as Sisyphus and his clients' money as the boulder the Greek king pushed up the steep hill, otherwise known as the market. He owned each of them a little and had made a fortune getting their individual boulders to the tops of their personal mountains of desires and dreams without any of those great stones rolling over him as one had his mythical counterpart. He had no plans to stand at the peak of any mount and put that fact "on blast" with a website, even if, on his own time, he loved the Internet and used it every day. That was how he knew it would be anathema to his clientele.

The most he allowed was a monthly investment update he sent to his clients in the body of an e-mail as a half-newsletter he unimaginatively called *Dewynter*. It was one page and boring-looking and contained no images and included no links to anything or any mentions of any third-party websites, with the lack of website listed for Arthur's firm conspicuous by design. The whole thing was flat and read like a classroom handout, and his clients loved it. It communicated with them while requiring that they do nothing in return. He knew Kelly would one day understand his approach.

After she had left his office, he dove into his work. For two hours, he wondered who owned whom and felt like a different mythological figure, Prometheus, bound to his life of financial servitude by his Zeus-like clients who kept him chained. As he massaged them over the phone, flashes of what he had seen that morning in Tobias's encampment made him wonder if he could borrow from Prometheus and not so much steal fire from the gods for the sake of others but give some part of himself to change circumstances for people like Tobias.

Tobias.

∞

The strain of pushing boulders that day almost defeated Arthur. What kept him moving uphill was that it was the right thing to do. Frank, his junior partner, who had taken a risk and given up a coveted Wall Street opportunity to go with Arthur's claimed tried-and-true, old-fashioned boutique approach, and Kelly, who ran Arthur's life even when he didn't always remember to, and Charlie, the firm's Wall Street–watcher, numbers-cruncher, and overall liaison with the world, who managed a small team of five that kept their firm in line with everybody from future clients to the IRS, depended on his not tanking his business for the sake of three-day drunks.

Maybe four-day ones if he hadn't been thwarted.

Maybe a little stay in the hospital or a stint in County Jail that would ruin his reputation if he didn't take better care to…care.

Maybe a reservation at the county morgue.

His office in Century City had a view of downtown L.A. from a window that ran the length of the wall, just over the wall-to-wall built-in credenza. Most days, he barely glanced in that direction, but that day, during his phone calls, he stared at the skyline and wondered where the overpass on Spring Street, just north of Temple Street, might be in the panorama. It surprised him that he had slept like a rock all night there, in a tent, suspended over the 101 Freeway, with horn honks and the brakes squealing on buses as background noise.

He thought again about his overnight host.

Tobias.

He wondered what Tobias did that Thursday, what he did on Thursdays, in general, where he waited out the day and whether he did it alone or with someone not important or very important who had tacit dibs on Tobias's second sleeping bag.

Maybe they talked math with each other, Arthur thought, or solved equations over dinner, and had smart, hot sex afterwards in the tent, with the two sleeping bags joined together, if, *what had Tobias said?* he could fumble with the zippers. Maybe the someone knew how to figure out the zippers for him.

Tobias. Smart, sexy in a vulnerable, trusting way.

Arthur had half-lied to Tobias about his own smarts and regretted it sitting in his office as he wondered who might be dazzling Tobias with his own brains. Arthur was excellent at math, made a killing using it.

He *did* envy people who liked it. That part had been true. Arthur had a working partnership with math and nothing more. He had no affection for the sport of figuring. His only connection to math was what money added up to. He thought it a pity that someone who loved math enough to teach it was homeless while someone who used it for personal gain—a borderline castle in Beverly Hills he shared with no one, three cars worth six figures each, plus a few mid-sized spares for the domestic staff's use, travel by private jet, enjoyment of only the finest food and wine, and an office with a view of downtown—thrived.

He looked at his watch.

Two o'clock. *I should have accepted Tobias's offer to rest in the tent. I might still be there.*

Two-thirty. *Does he have enough money for lunch? He used his last cash to buy me coffee. Why didn't I tell him who I was and give him the five hundred dollars I had in my pocket?*

Three o'clock. "Kelly?"

She appeared in the doorway.

"Please go home. Don't worry about my cell phone. I made it just fine without it last night." *The finest I've been in a long while.*

She looked skeptical.

He smiled. "Seriously. I'm good. In fact, I'm leaving right behind you. I'm caught up."

She stared at him.

"I promise I'll be here tomorrow. We can deal with the phone then. Have a good one."

"Okay." The word had a tinge of doubtful sing-song in it. A few minutes later, though, she logged off, shut down, and left.

Arthur did the same.

Why wonder what Tobias is doing when you can go find out?

∞

Arthur parked his Maserati in his standalone, ten-car garage, hopped out of it without locking it, and trotted along the seventy-five-yard path that began behind his large manor and worked its way around to the front door of his house. He entered and quickly disengaged his alarm.

His bedroom was on the third floor. In the smaller foyer adjacent to the great entryway, he accessed a staircase that looked unending, like it disappeared into Emerald City. He took the steps three-at-a-time. He sailed past the second-floor landing and sprung to the top floor. When he arrived there, he broke into a slight jog, right and left and over and down long hallways to his room, one of several master suites in the house.

He went to his room-sized closet and clapped his hands. Lights and overhead music came on in synch. He reached for a clean pair of pants.

Then he remembered Tobias thought he was homeless. He stood near the last row of Brioni suits that led to his more casual clothes and wondered why Tobias thinking he was homeless mattered when he was no longer in Tobias's tent, enjoying his hospitality and drinking his coffee, as a rescued drunk.

Shouldn't I go back and tell him the truth and maybe even pay him for his trouble?

The answer that came to Arthur surprised him.

That answer was no.

It meant clean clothes, casual or not, wouldn't do.

He walked across the closet toward his hamper and hoped to find enough dirty clothes there to put together something to wear. He held out little hope he'd find anything. His housekeeping staff did his laundry in small loads a few times a week.

He opened the lid to the hamper and was out of luck. He had been gone three days. His staff had probably washed his weekend laundry on Monday, sometime after he had come home and changed and left for the Biltmore.

Then the obvious hit him. He was wearing the clothes he'd had on since Monday, the clothes he'd been mugged in, the clothes Tobias knew. The Biltmore had laundered them, but he'd worn them for a few hours. They were no longer fresh. Showing up in the same clothes Tobias had seen him in that morning would be the perfect way to appear homeless.

And Arthur was sure of it then.

He knew with certainty that he wanted Tobias to believe he was not only homeless, but destitute, with nowhere to go.

He told himself it would be for one evening, while he assessed the situation, whatever "the situation" meant, and that once he was on stronger footing with Tobias, he'd confess and even pay him back for his help.

Just for tonight. After that, I'll tell him the truth.

CHOPSTICKS

ARTHUR DOUBLE-CHECKED ONLINE MAPS to find his destination, using the courthouse on Spring Street as the best landing point to get him to Tobias's tent, and called for a taxi from his landline at home.

The long cab ride had gone smoothly until they were a few blocks away from journey's end, where Arthur came up against a downside to having money. If he made a request people thought wouldn't suit him, they wouldn't fulfill it.

He wanted to go to Spring Street. He asked the driver to take Sunset Boulevard out of Beverly Hills and into downtown, where it became Cesar E. Chavez Avenue and led to Spring Street via a diagonal cut-through, and drop him on the corner before the cut, which was really Broadway. It was close to Tobias's encampment but far enough away that Tobias wouldn't see him get out of the car.

"The GPS says to keep going. Spring's right there."

"I know, but don't keep going. I don't want you to drop me on Spring. Stop at the corner of Cesar Chavez and Broadway instead."

"But it's just another block."

The driver took the cut-through onto Spring Street and kept driving. The driver had seen Arthur's stately home in Beverly Hills and figured him for a man who didn't want to be inconvenienced, *dropped on a street corner and forced to walk,* even when he had demanded it, as if Arthur either didn't realize how bad the street corner was and would appreciate—and even require—the "save" by the driver, or as though he played at humility to appear to blend with the masses, with the tacit expectation in the farce being that the driver should ignore him since they both knew it was a game.

It never failed to strike Arthur as odd that, through money, he had attained a level of privilege manufactured out of thin air that led people with nothing to gain to help him maintain it. At any given time, there were two to three people focused on one, on him, as though he were the planet's customer, always entitled to good service.

Arthur spotted Tobias's tent and ducked.

"Keep going!"

"But we're here."

"Keep going!"

Arthur and the driver stopped quibbling at First Street, which was two, long, Los Angeles city blocks too far.

Arthur used the trek back to mentally rehearse the fake life story he had invented for himself. He didn't think he'd need it after that night. He hoped not to use it at all, that he and Tobias would reach a point in their conversation where Arthur could naturally confess his truth. He had memorized the story mostly in case the subject came up sooner.

He reached Tobias's tent and called out, as a way of knocking. There was no answer. He was disappointed.

He figured it served him right. It was rude of him to assume Tobias had nowhere else to be—or that he wouldn't have a guest or be asleep or inside listening to headphones and taking no notice of the world or wide awake and aware and ignoring Arthur anyway.

Arthur had arrived unannounced and expected a full reception. He had behaved as entitled as he had secretly scolded the taxi driver for treating him.

He left, embarrassed.

∞

It was him. Tobias was sure.

Arthur.

Walking away from Tobias's tent.

Did I open a can of something letting Arthur stay with me? I hope so.

He ignored the voice in his head that had told him just one night earlier that Arthur was troubled and likely better for Tobias away from his tent and on his way back to from wherever he had come.

Arthur made progress toward Temple Street. He was about to get away.

"Hi! Arthur!" Tobias called.

Arthur turned and revealed a smile that had a touch of gratitude and relief in it, which Tobias didn't understand but found charming.

Arthur headed toward Tobias. He was shaven and sober. He hadn't changed his clothes, but he looked refreshed.

"You're back," Tobias said. "How do you feel?"

"Fine. Much better than last night." Arthur smiled.

Tobias returned the smile. "Well, wherever you went after you left here this morning sure did you a world of good. You look better."

"Thanks." Arthur chuckled. "And thanks again for everything."

Tobias waved a hand to brush aside the thanks. "Nah." He chuckled, too. "Again, no worries. Glad you're feeling better."

They smiled at one another, and Tobias waited for Arthur to tell him why he was there, but Arthur only stared at him.

Tobias engaged in nervous chatter. "You moving in?" He said. He realized how that sounded. "To the area, I mean?" His face became hot with embarrassment.

"No, but I was walking past the courthouse earlier, and some fat-cat attorney must have won a big case or something. I asked for a little change, and he handed me a fifty."

"A *fifty*?"

"A fifty." Arthur laughed.

"Wow."

"You had dinner?"

"No. I just came from the library." Tobias tapped the bag that rested on his hip to give the impression he had worked on whatever was in it at the library. "Job hunting," he added, for realism. He didn't admit he surfed blogs for most of his hour on the library's computer.

"Join me, then? It's the least I can do after last night. Hell, bail would have been a hundred times this fifty."

Tobias was reluctant, but Arthur's smile said, "Nothing means more to me right now than your joining me for dinner."

Tobias wavered anyway. "I'm not really dressed for it. I didn't swing by anywhere today for a shower. I was hoping to do that tomorrow."

Tobias hadn't just skipped a shower. He hadn't eaten that day, either, yet he couldn't accept the offer of free food. He didn't feel clean enough. He had brushed his teeth and used his battery-operated razor after Arthur had left his tent, and he had combed his hair and used deodorant and changed into clean clothes, but that was all.

It had been one of those Los Angeles days when the air and sun were so hot, it felt like a giant hair dryer blew all over the city. Two days' layers of sweat were still on his body.

Arthur had spent the night in his tent one night earlier, and Tobias hadn't cared what he looked like or whether he snored or even how he smelled. One evening later, everything had changed. He thought he should decline the invitation—on an empty stomach.

"I took enough shower for both us," Arthur said. "Uh, I mean…."

Tobias laughed. "I know how you meant it."

Arthur grinned. "You look fine. You do. You have to let me do something to thank you." His face said, "Come, on."

Tobias felt himself give in. He wanted to go with Arthur.

"All right," he said. "Where to?"

"Chinatown's close." Arthur pointed toward Cesar Chavez Avenue and just beyond it, where the large twin dragons that floated over Broadway mounted on large posts—the gateway to Chinatown—were just visible.

"Chinese?" Arthur smiled.

"Chinese." Tobias smiled, too.

∞

"I'm gay," Arthur said. He closed his eyes and hung his head. "And dumb. I didn't mean to blurt it out like that."

He loaded his plate with vegetable chow mein to deflect. His cheeks were warm. He felt like a fool for coming out so indelicately and turning their casual excuse for a meal into what looked like a cheap attempt at a hookup.

Tobias, it had turned out, was even more appealing than Arthur had remembered from that morning, hungover, with sore ribs and a full bladder that distracted him. With sober vision, Arthur saw that Tobias's skin was smoother and his freckles were even subtler than Arthur had thought, and all of it covered a handsome face that seemed to belong to a kind person. The added allure caught Arthur off-guard and flustered him.

Tobias put him out of his misery. "I know," he said. "I am, too. Gay, I mean."

Arthur fumbled with the serving spoons. "I feel silly. All I meant by 'I'm gay' is 'I'm gay.' I'm such an idiot."

"No, you're not." Tobias smiled. "Telling our truth is always an adventure. If anyone understands, I do."

"Thanks. I appreciate that."

They grinned at each other.

Tobias used mini-tongs to select one of six potstickers Arthur had ordered as an hors-d'oeuvre. With a knife and fork, he gently cut off a small piece of the lone delicacy and ate it.

Arthur glanced at Tobias's plate.

Tobias took another bite. Other than the one bite left, his plate was empty.

I forced him to come. He doesn't want to be here with me.

"Uhhhm…" Arthur stopped himself from asking if there was a problem. He was afraid of the answer.

"Uhhhm?" Tobias said.

"Nothing." Arthur added broccoli beef to his own plate hoping to suggest to Tobias he was welcome to do the same.

"Okay, so I don't use chopsticks," Tobias said, with a shy smile. "I know it's weak, but I suck at them. Your fifty bucks are gonna end up on the floor if I don't use a knife and fork."

His voice was also more pleasant than Arthur recalled, and he had already found it had a mellow timbre with caring overtones that he admired.

I want this to go well, even if it seems like it's already over. Please don't let it be over.

"No, that's okay," Arthur said. "No rules." He focused on his food. His stomach knotted up a little.

Tobias finished the potsticker and looked at Arthur, who had just eaten a large piece of broccoli. Arthur watched Tobias watching him. His mouth suddenly felt like it was full of bricks. He swallowed his food mostly not chewed. The broccoli hurt the back of his throat on its way down. The evening was off to a bad start.

"I'm sorry," Tobias said. He leaned back in his seat.

"For what?" Arthur was full of dread.

"It's been…a long time…." He stared at his bare plate. "It's been a long time since I sat down to a normal meal in a normal place with a normal person. Restaurants used to be places I hid in to wait out the night and maybe nap with my head on the table before I was forced outside. Just sitting here like a regular customer? I'm rusty. And, I can't lie. The last food I had today wasn't food. It was that coffee this morning. I guess it's just a lot at once. I guess I suck at chopsticks and normalcy." He gave a little self-deprecating laugh.

Arthur had never met anyone with such an innocent charm he seemed not to even know he had. It was that unawareness that made Tobias so captivating.

Arthur took in the image of a hungry Tobias who sat before an empty plate, too unpracticed at helping himself to eat. Guilt washed over Arthur. He didn't know what to say. He had regularly left one-hundred-and-twenty-dollar tips after eating six-hundred-dollar meals with just one other person, maybe a client or Frank or a one-night stand he couldn't get through without a lot of pomp and circumstance to distract him from how much he didn't want to be there. Sometimes, it was just Arthur and a few thousand dollars in caviar and champagne, when he couldn't face his empty house. And he always had a several hundred dollars in his pocket. He never skipped a meal he didn't choose to skip. He had thought about Tobias's prospects for lunch earlier that day, but he had naively assumed no true threat to Tobias's eating existed. It was suddenly Arthur who felt embarrassed.

"Don't worry about it," Arthur said. "You're doing great at normalcy. For eating, the key is to ditch the chopsticks and go straight to the workaround."

He picked up Tobias's fork and put it in his hand. They both smiled.

Arthur loaded Tobias's plate with broccoli beef and fried rice and chow mein. He added two of the remaining five potstickers, which meant they each would have three. Arthur sensed Tobias would feel better about being his guest if the six appetizers were divided evenly and Tobias weren't charitably overloaded.

As a thank you, Tobias looked directly at Arthur and wore the same engaging smile Arthur had seen over coffee that morning.

It took Arthur a moment to gather himself and return the potsticker tongs to their place.

As they disengaged from each other to tend to their food, they stared at one another as though time moved a little slower.

Tobias lifted a fork full of chow mein and said, "Do you mind if I ask?" There, again, time slowed. Tobias gazed at Arthur for a moment before he asked the question. Arthur gazed back before he answered.

"Ask what?"

"You must be new at this." Tobias said with a renewed warm smile. "Usually, that only means one thing. It means do you mind if I ask how you ended up on the outside." He took his first real bite of food.

Arthur panicked. "No. I mean yes. I mean, I don't mind if you ask." He chuckled to stall for time. He hadn't rehearsed his story well enough, and he was nowhere near ready to tell the truth.

Tobias smiled and waited. Finally, he said, "Well?"

"Oh!" Arthur laughed again. "Simple," he started. "Was the boss at a construction site. Jammed up my rotator cuff. Lost my workers' comp claim. Disability ran out. Healed up okay," and, there, he paused to move his shoulder in several big circles to show he felt fine, a move he had practiced, more subtly, in the back seat of the taxi, "but the gap in time on my resume got harder to explain. And people get lawsuit-shy. They think I'll file a claim to use the bathroom." He wasn't sure where that layer of color had come from. "I temp. Better off right now without rent. Saving what I can this way." He dove into his fried rice.

"That's rough."

"Had to sell my car for cash. Lost some of it, though, when I broke my lease to save rent."

You'll never remember all these lies.

"Whoo, I can relate."

"I do okay, I guess. Sleep where I can. Shower where I can. It's easier on my hands, that's for sure, being away from construction, I mean."

That had popped out of nowhere, too, but explained his well-cared-for hands.

"If my temp agency sends me to a good office job, I live off the free coffee and hot chocolate packets and microwave popcorn." He stole that nuanced bit of story from his own office, which had a kitchen full of those same things. "Sometimes I get lucky and score some vanilla chai."

They both laughed.

"How about you?" Arthur asked. "Aren't there plenty of jobs for math teachers?"

"Not ones who were fired."

"Oh."

"And, before I came to California, I lived in Florida. Nothing really to return to there, not for years."

"I hear you. It's the same for me with Michigan. Forget it. Easier to figure out things here, you know?"

That part of his story was true. Arthur had fled his family in Michigan just after college. He was like a teenager who had been kicked out for coming out except he had been a tad older and had simply stayed away and visited seldom while he worked his way through the University of Michigan. After four fast years, he headed to California with a degree in finance in his back pocket and the excuse of distance to whittle down visits.

Contact with Michigan had been minimal since he had been in his late twenties. Right after college, his parents showed some fading interest in him. They had hoped that once he hit his mid-twenties, something about the real-world aspect of life would show him that he wasn't gay, that he wanted a life with a woman, that the delusions of a foggy-headed teenager wouldn't last with his more mature and wiser self. When they grasped that they were wrong—while blaming Arthur—they relegated him to the realm of the living dead, as though the man who called every couple of years were a gay impostor of their deceased heterosexual son.

He and Tobias ate in silence for a while. Arthur thought about Michigan.

"So, then, no wild flame out there anywhere waiting to come to your rescue?" Tobias said.

Arthur's fork stopped on its way to his mouth. The question shocked him. He looked up to see how serious Tobias was. Tobias's straight face and direct gaze told Arthur Tobias was dead earnest.

"No." Arthur set his fork down, and their eyes met. "No." He looked away a little and spoke to a place that was distant, in his mind. "No. There hasn't been for a long time." He picked up his fork and finished his bite.

"And, you?" Arthur asked his broccoli beef as much as he asked Tobias. For the second time that evening, he was afraid of an answer, afraid there was a geography or art or biology teacher somewhere, waiting for Tobias to get back on his feet so they could pick up their lives together.

After a long while, Tobias said, "No. There's no one."

Only then did Arthur look Tobias in the eye.

"This is nice," Tobias said. "Sitting here and eating…and talking with you."

Yes! Arthur smiled. "I'm glad you think so. I think it's nice, too."

"It's been a long time," Tobias said, "since I met someone who wanted to do more than just swap info about where there's free food or what the new shower hours are at the mission or whether the bicycle cops were in our tents while we were away."

"They do that? Search your tents without your permission?"

"Yeah. The Fourth Amendment is fluid when you're outside."

"Wow. I would think…"

Three hours later, they still smiled and talked and ate and drank, small glasses of house wine and tea.

And Arthur began to understand how Tobias had gone from homeowner to tent-owner. Bits of harsh luck and mismanaged money crises that Arthur could have solved with fifteen minutes of financial advice had wrecked Tobias.

From what Arthur could tell, Tobias was honest. Stringently so. He didn't pick pockets or shoplift or run scams. What he had, he scraped for on his own and combined it with the unemployment money he still received. He panhandled for luxuries and kept himself on an otherwise strict budget, knowing the unemployment money would soon stop. He had kicked aside his pride and learned to accept charity two years too late, a fact that frustrated Arthur.

Arthur didn't let himself tell Tobias he should have borrowed a couple of twenty-dollar bills from every friend he knew the minute he missed his first payment to anyone he owed and that a solution that simple could have kept him out of overdraft fee hell and from losing to the bank as empty currency paychecks that could have gone toward bills.

Other solutions occurred to Arthur as they ate water chestnut cake. Tobias could have sold some personal property, rented one of the rooms in his house, or even mowed lawns on weekends.

He could have made a drastic move sooner and moved into his car and rented out his condo for a limited time, to gather income while someone else paid his mortgage. He might have even made a profit on the rent.

He could have worked nights as a custodian in a fast-food restaurant or at the mall or in a twenty-four-hour gym and put one-hundred percent of those proceeds toward his mortgage or other bills. He could have driven for taxi service before his car became his home and made that impossible.

There were a million little pathways to finding a few hundred dollars' worth of cushion, but they were paved with pride, and Arthur realized Tobias hadn't been able to see his stepped on to get to salvation.

Tobias also hadn't seen devastation coming. He had placed his faith in traditions—working one, solid job, paying what bills he could, using downtime to worry and not act—and that faith had been misplaced. Arthur thought he should have invested in ingenuity, a second or third job, favors from anyone who'd give—especially since he ended up accepting favors, anyway, on the streets—and the actual financial markets. Arthur knew that growing money took a certain amount of boldness. Most people either didn't have it or were too polite to deploy it.

Arthur remembered that even some of his savviest clients had no idea how to invest, and he didn't dwell on Tobias's mistakes.

After the initial awkwardness, the night went well. They talked about more than their pasts and their problems. They discovered a shared love of books and film and opera and engaged in several hot debates about film directors, movie eras, and music influences. They learned that they both hated to wear sunglasses, that they each ranked baseball over football or basketball, that Arthur, a Michigander, had spent far more time on California beaches than Tobias, who had seen enough sand in Florida, and that they both had a deep affection for Los Angeles life.

And, so it went, through dessert and past the fortune cookies. Discoveries, delightful surprises, and divulgences filled the evening.

Arthur appreciated that Tobias never mentioned how bad Arthur had behaved the night before. Tobias allowed Arthur to forget that, twenty-four hours earlier, he had been drunk in public and had ventured to sleep on a storefront.

Multiple times, Arthur almost confessed that his story was a lie. But the farther in he got, the more Tobias revealed, and the clearer it became to Arthur that the conversation would not cooperate and guide Arthur to an easy admission.

And if Arthur were truthful with himself, he would admit he couldn't afford, emotionally, to reveal who he was. The balance would shift in a familiar way that he loathed.

People deferred to him the moment they knew he had money and subconsciously set him aside, *outside*. They asked him what he wanted, but they didn't care how he felt. If they were wealthy, they had master plans for connecting that were strange and seemed more about using dating—and mating—as a strategy and not as a way to find love or they lived in five different cities throughout the year and were elusive or they were as guarded as Arthur and hard to reach or they fit the stereotype of the selfish successful person.

If they had more standard means, like everyone Arthur grew up around, Arthur related easily to them, but they rarely invited him to do anything because they assumed he always had somewhere better to be. They didn't want to suffer the embarrassment of offering invitations and being foolish enough to think he would deign to spend an evening with them at a movie or a day with them on the beach only to be turned down, roundly and soundly, by the busy, busy rich man. And if he asked *them*, they thought he was being polite, or they assumed they wouldn't be able to afford any improvisations on the day that might spring up, as though he would

really turn a day at a museum into a trip to Paris on a private jet—
their jobs and obligations and money be damned—and they took
the safe way out and declined to join him.

Mostly, people wanted to know his cash and the world it
bought him but not him. They didn't mean to shunt him to the side.
It was just that his money loomed large and took all the attention,
even his, they assumed. Even honest people who didn't scheme
struggled to remember that his identity extended beyond how his
fortunes could define it. They thought *he* thought about his money
or himself constantly, so they thought about his money and talked
about him, his life, his next act, as a favor, to keep him happy, to
shield him from the burden of an unpleasant subject-change. They
didn't think he'd mind their approach. They thought it pleased him.

He did mind, though. It hurt his feelings. The shallow
exchanges isolated him and kept him chronically alone.

He hadn't realized how alone until he woke up in Tobias's
tent. That had been the beginning, anyway.

As the day had worn, and he talked to a string of wealthy
clients and pushed boulders up hills, the lonesomeness bore down
on him.

By the end of dinner, it was painful in a strange way. One day
with Tobias, someone who knew nothing about him, had levied
upon Arthur a profound loneliness.

It was somehow made worse by the realization that Tobias
liked Arthur as Arthur. He had observed Arthur at his worst, and yet
he went with the second impression he gathered the following
morning over a small Styrofoam cup of black coffee. He was the first
person in years to look at Arthur, in a broad sense, and in a micro
sense, in the park and in the tent and at the restaurant, and explore

what—and who—was there. Not since Arthur was in his twenties had anyone felt Arthur had more at risk than that person did. People assumed everything about his life was easy.

Tobias was different. He filtered Arthur through a basic human condition lens and had room in his perspective to see that Arthur could be at risk and could hurt and needed friendship and a little help.

After dinner, they walked back to Tobias's tent at a pace so slow, they almost traveled backward. Arthur wished he knew whether Tobias moseyed because he enjoyed Arthur's company or because there was less urgency in his life. A strange kind of jealousy came over Arthur. Tobias seemed to be out of reach in a way Arthur couldn't define. An odd longing set in, and Arthur saw no way to quell it.

They arrived at Tobias's tent.

"Thank you, Arthur. That was generous of you to share your sudden good fortune with me."

He didn't invite Arthur into the tent, a place in which Arthur had spent the night, just one night earlier, a space Arthur knew was tidy and presentable, a dwelling in which Arthur desired to spend more time, especially with the head of the household.

Their evening together had ended. The conversation and camaraderie had come to an abrupt halt.

"You're welcome, Tobias. It was the least I could do."

Before Tobias could step into the tent and leave him stranded on the sidewalk, Arthur shook his hand and walked away, out of survival and not pride.

He remembered he had no cell phone or way to get home. Pay phones no longer existed, and he knew of no formal taxi stands in downtown L.A. It wasn't that kind of big city.

In a replay of events of that morning, he cut through the park and walked to the Biltmore. The concierge knew him well and promptly ordered him a taxi.

He went home and spent the night alone in Beverly Hills. He was safer and soberer than he had been a night earlier in Grand Park and on Broadway.

And far more miserable.

∞ **5** ∞

MAKE BELIEVE

ARTHUR HAD NEVER SEEN KELLY flummoxed. Usually, while three steps ahead of him, she quietly disapproved of ideas she didn't like with a well-aimed facial expression. Silence helped make the point. Mostly, though, they got on so well, that conversation flowed without impediment.

Yet, she was confounded.

"I'm sorry. Wait. *What?* You're *homeless?*" She stared at Arthur as though she had missed three years of his life and not three days. It was Friday, and he was at work, as promised.

"No," he smiled. "I knew I was going to explain it wrong." He chuckled, although he wasn't necessarily in the good mood his laughter indicated. "No, I'm not homeless. But I'm going to behave as though I am, and, like I said, I don't want that fact to travel beyond the walls of this office, meaning my office, specifically, and not the firm. Frank and Charlie and Zara and the rest are not to know. I know you and Charlie are tight, but you can't share this with him."

"I won't, but I still don't get it."

"Well, I don't want to be a creepy boss. There's only so much I should tell you without it bordering on the very inappropriate. But we do need to map out some logistics with my schedule. I—"

"Try me. With just a little. Let the record show I asked. I'll stop you when it gets weird."

He contemplated her and thought hard. "Okay. I hope neither of us regrets it."

He gave her just enough details, about the mugging and the rescue, and embellished his genuine desire to learn more about homelessness to mask his specific interest in Tobias.

"Mm. That's a bad idea, Mr. Dewynter."

"Why?"

"Because you'll get caught, and it's going to blow up in your face."

"Don't hold back, or anything."

"I'm sorry, but it will."

She did seem sorry, or at least genuinely concerned. It hit the mark.

"Okay, something tells me I'd be stupid not to ask. What do you mean?"

"This new friend sounds like he's in a bad way. I don't think he'll appreciate your pretending you are too just to see what it's like."

"I want to fit in. The last thing I'll do is insult him if I can avoid it."

"You won't be able to. It's going to blow up in your face. And maybe his."

Arthur cleared his throat and shifted in his chair. "I think if I don't give it lip service, I can pull it off."

"And what about your business? Are you taking a leave of absence for this?"

"No. It'll be no different. I'll come here every day and handle the business and go home at night, except home will be downtown."

"Let me see if I understand."

He knew she already did, but it helped her illustrate to him how foolish his idea was if she feigned misunderstanding and made him listen while she explained the idea to herself.

"You expect to spend nights on the streets—"

"Or in a shelter, or maybe even a tent."

She raised her eyebrows with the same "oh…kay" doubt she had had the day before, when he had been nonchalant about losing his phone.

"—and then you expect to catch an Uber every morning back to Beverly Hills, maybe go for a run on the treadmill and then shower and change for work."

"Well, without getting into the details, maybe I'll hit a shelter instead. I don't know enough about how things work, but you've got the general idea."

She frowned in sympathy more than with disapproval.

"That's what I mean. You're not sure about things."

"But I know I can guess my way through it." But he wasn't so sure. He wanted to hear the rest of her theory on how he had no idea what he was doing. "Keep going, though. What else?"

"Well, you somehow shower, and then you plan to come here from Beverly Hills in your Maserati and oversee the financial destinies of your clients and meet them for fancy lunches full of rich foods and go home to Beverly Hills in your Maserati and change into something…"

"Comfortable."

"Comfortable. And maybe even dirty?"

"Which is easy. I'll just tell my staff to leave some laundry alone."

"*Maybe* it's easy. Then you'll Uber back downtown and go into homeless mode and wander around and look for dinner and somewhere to crash and say you're short on cash, even though you'll be carrying several hundred dollars, and you'll tell…"

"Tobias."

"Tobias that you've been working at some temp job all day where he can't call you. Or, you'll say you've been on the streets, scraping together an existence, which would also mean you can't be reached."

"Right. Yes, that's it." He tried to sound confident and resolute, as though she had caught up to his way of thinking instead of what she hoped for, which was that it would be the other way around. He wasn't sure it wasn't.

"Mm. I don't know."

He pushed on. "And I'll stop carrying the cash. And I'll order salad at lunch, which I usually do, anyway, and keep it simple if I'm not entertaining clients. Fruit, yogurt, soy tacos from the food truck. I'll do what I would do if I were homeless, on a constrained budget."

"Except you don't hear yourself, right now. I don't think soy tacos from the same food truck that offers lobster enchiladas are standard fare for someone without a job and a home. And it's more complicated than that. I mean, starting with the easy stuff, your hair's too neat, as though you get it trimmed every seven or eight days."

Damn. I do.

"You look rested all the time, even when you're stressed. You smell like…hundred-dollar musky shower gel."

Arthur smiled a little. He wasn't interested in what she thought of him as a female, even if he had been straight—she was too young—but he felt a little triumphant that someone her age, somebody perpetually bored with people his age, had revealed she paid that much attention to how he looked and smelled.

"If I really am sleeping outside, I don't think I'll look all that rested. And I won't smell like hundred-dollar musky shower gel. I'll buy bar soap and a two-dollar toothbrush and plastic razors at the drugstore and maybe a used backpack at the thrift store. And I'll pack the backpack with things an out-of-work construction boss would keep."

"That brings me to the harder stuff. You have the *Wall Street Journal* running around in your head. You'll have conversations about things you shouldn't be referring to. You'll hear something on this side of things that you'll let slip with him that will sound strange."

"I agree I'll have to be diligent about compartmentalizing, when necessary, but I don't think it'll come up that much. Every kind of person is homeless. Smart, well-educated, well-exposed and well-traveled, and on and on. I could be a construction guy and know those things. That's why I chose it."

"You lost me."

"Well, I could know those things, just because, but also, investments and large building acquisitions sometimes overlap. It felt normal and logical to claim I'm in some aspect of that business."

"Mm."

"And, he's a math genius. *He* knows things. I wouldn't be doing this if I thought I had to spend the day talking down to him. I can be me. I'll be lucky if he's willing to be himself around me. That would be a gift, and that's all I'll say about that."

"No worries. You haven't said anything weird."

"Thanks. And, you know," he looked away in thought and looked at her again, "I'm not supposedly temping on a deserted island. Office breakrooms have televisions, people leave papers lying around, and so forth. If I don't discuss bear markets and arbitrage and averaging down, I think I'll be okay."

"Will you be? Physically? You got assaulted." She looked at him hard, and for the first time he realized she was worried about *him* and not his plan and whether it would work.

Her open concern jolted him a little. She didn't usually show any sentimental emotions toward him. He felt touched and trepidatious. Her willingness to show alarm made him wonder if he should abort his idea.

He left that thought aside for the time being. His immediate goal was to reassure her. He had no desire to make her anxious about his safety for no reason or to make her feel uncertain about her future because he risked his.

"First off, I won't stumble around and act like a sitting duck."

She still stared at him. He wondered if she knew how vulnerable she looked. He realized the best tack was to show blunt confidence and dismiss her fears in a way that didn't insult her but that made her feel as though they were just unnecessary enough to let her be comfortable moving on from them.

"When I'm alert, I can handle myself."

She twisted her mouth and said, "Mm. I guess."

"It's true, and I'll stay alert. You said it yourself. I have access to everything. I exercise, rest, eat right. I dare someone to try anything when I'm drinking iced tea that's not the Long Island kind."

She laughed. "Okay. That's true. No one doubts you're in good shape." She chuckled. "*And I mean that clinically.*"

He smiled. "I know, I know. And you're right, if I do say so. And, besides, it's the new-and-improved downtown L.A., with bike lanes and baby strollers pushed by joggers and a bona fide park with mirrored buildings and a coffee house in it, for goodness sake. The worst I have to fear is getting mowed down by a latte-bearing skateboarder." He laughed.

She laughed, too. "Okay. It's definitely mellower down there, these days, with sidewalk eating and fancy pet food places and whatnot, but you were taking a pounding when this Tobias showed up."

"They got lucky once because I was a fool. Won't happen again." He held up his hands in surrender. "I promise. People are walking all over downtown right now, not getting mugged."

"Mm. All right, all right. I'm convinced. Sort of." Her mood eased.

He smiled. "All right."

"Convinced about *that*. What about your…affect?"

"I don't know what you mean."

"Your affect. Your vibe. Your aura. It's privileged and proper and more, well, financial advisor than construction site boss, building investments notwithstanding."

"But it's all work. If I come off as a hard worker, I think I'll be okay," he said.

He sensed a shift. She seemed to have moved on to practical matters and appeared to join his side of the debate about whether his idea would blow up in his face.

"What about your phone? I got you a new phone, you know. I was planning to unveil it with more ceremony than this."

She revealed a thousand-dollar phone she had hidden under her notepad and slid it over his desk.

"It has the same phone number, same apps, same everything."

"When did you do that?" The gesture touched him.

"After I left here yesterday."

He offered her a grateful smile. "I thought I told you to skip it. I feel bad. You've already covered me for three days."

"I know, but I couldn't leave you without a phone."

"You're the best."

"So is that," she pointed at the phone. "The very best. How are you going to explain it? He saw those muggers take your phone. How will you say you came up with a new one so fast?"

"I won't. I'll hide it. I'll keep it silent and tucked away."

"Mm. I'm back to smelling disaster, and it's playing with fire and wearing manicured nails and a nine-thousand-dollar Brioni suit with twenty-four karat gold thread weaved through it, no familiarity intended."

Too late, on that account. I'm not as marginal as you would like me to think. You know what kind of suit I'm wearing, down to the thread.

He grinned. He felt a little elevated, to WORTHY FIFTH PERIOD TEACHER. He used the levity to close the deal with her.

"For what it's worth," he said, "I very much appreciate your concern and your feedback. I don't even know that you're wrong. I hope I'm right and that, if you take my side, you'll be right, too. And, you know, it's only going to be for a few weeks. I just want to…I don't know."

"I do. You want to get to know…Tobias…without this," she gestured at the room and pointed to the magnificent view of downtown behind him, "getting in the way."

"Yes." He shrugged a little and left his shoulders hunched. "I'm sorry if this is awkward."

"It isn't." She stared out the window a moment, as though contemplating something, and looked at him again. "Is he cute?"

"You see right through my whole 'getting to know homelessness' angle." He chuckled. "Or, maybe you want to sue your way out of here, by goading me into a creepy conversation, is that it?" He grinned.

She smiled and gave him a *pfshh*. "Don't dodge the question, Mr. Dewynter. Is he cute?"

"Since you insist, very. Has the damnedest couple of freckles here and there…on his *face*…and a nice smile. Interesting voice. Kind of quiet. Math teacher-y. But it's not about that, truly. He's just an extremely nice person. And humble. Time flies with him. It usually drags, even with tickets to something. But I could have sat there with him and drunk free restaurant tap water all night and not noticed the hour."

"And you can't find that in the regular places?"

"You know, I don't think I can. Start taking notes for your lawsuit, but I've looked for a long time, and I keep coming up empty. And maybe I see what Charlie has with Bryce and feel hopeful the rest of us can end up that way."

"I don't know if *anybody* can be that happy. They may be the only couple on earth with something in the water at home."

Arthur had always quietly envied his numbers-cruncher Charlie's relationship with his significant other, Bryce. They were thirtysomethings who had been together since they had been in their twenties, and the relationship gods seemed to have declared that they, the gods, would be eternally unhappy if Charlie and Bryce weren't the most compatible pair in the world. Arthur was sure they went through things, maybe even bad things, but they never seemed as though they weren't together in all of it, even in that occasional separateness that comes with problems.

They had moved in with each other a week after they met, into a tiny apartment, Charlie had always said. They had graduated to a nice home in Santa Monica. They still dated each other like the relationship was new. They vacationed in Finland in the dead of winter and had a blast. Charlie had a fantastic singing voice that was trained well beyond "staying on key", and twice over the years

Arthur had walked by his office and caught him casually serenading Bryce over the telephone with a few lines from a song with overtones of love before shy laughter replaced the tune and the conversation turned to their dinner plans or suggestions for what movie they should see.

Arthur wanted that for himself. He wanted that playfulness, that good-natured respect between partners. He wanted to be with someone in a way that gave no quarter to power trips or envy of wealth or feigned interest designed to reach one meaningless end.

Over two days, he and Tobias had seen in one another raw pain, exposure, and social nakedness, but they had enjoyed, together, the pleasure of taking a humble meal, arriving at places on foot, smiling for no reason, coffee from a cheap cup, and spending the night in sleeping bags on air mattresses. Together, they had given Arthur the realest two days he had experienced in fifteen years. He could just see, over the horizon, that sensible utopia he envied of others waiting for him…and Tobias.

Arthur didn't know how to explain to Kelly that he thought the relationship gods may have avowed Arthur needed Tobias and Tobias needed Arthur. He only knew that he had to see it through.

"It felt like I lost my best friend," Arthur offered, "when I dropped him off at his tent and pretended to go back to wherever I was supposedly holed up. It's been a long time since—"

"—since a person wasn't pretending to watch *Wicked* or *The Book of Mormon* or *Hamilton* while mentally adding your money to their bank account."

"Right, again."

"It just feels weird hearing you say, 'When I dropped him off at his tent.' Not to beat a dead horse, but that's another thing I don't think you hear yourself saying. And you're taking a big chance that he won't hate you when he finds out the truth."

"I know. I'll make my way until I find an opening. And then I'll tell him. Hopefully, it won't matter. And, who knows? Maybe, once I get to know him, I'll see I made a mistake, and I'll backpedal out."

"I don't think so, and I guess you're gonna make me say it one more time. You really don't hear *a lot* of what you're saying this morning. You don't know it, but you're all the way gone."

"Does it show?"

"Yes. I just hope he doesn't turn out to be the same kind of person you're trying to avoid. I mean, he's kind of struggling. A year on the streets?"

"I hear you, but when I was coming up with my cover story, I realized it's possible to be unemployed for a long time and not be a loser. I just want him to know me before he knows my money, is all."

"Just make sure he has some ambition. You can't spend the rest of your life in a tent. I can't believe what *I'm* saying."

Kelly made such sense, Arthur had to remind himself that he was the one who was old enough to be *her* parent.

"I'll be careful."

"There's one more thing I don't think you've thought of."

Arthur braced for more truth. She had been right all morning. "Go ahead. Let me have it."

"What if somebody sees you? I mean a client. Downtown *is* swank, come to think of it. A lot of your clients work down there. What are they going to think if they see you coming and going from a tent on Spring Street? I don't mean that like it sounds. I mean it in a practical way, for the firm. I know image matters to you. And, as much as I hate to admit it, especially when I want to post videos of my besties and me acting up and can't, your approach to image is a good one."

"I appreciate that, and, *yes*, image matters, but I already thought of that." He was relieved it hadn't been something he hadn't thought of. "I'm going to tell our clients a strange truth. In my next issue of *Dewynter*, I'll mention in a sidebar—"

"Careful, there. Sidebar. Going a little nuts."

"Ha, *ha*." He smiled. "As I was *saying*, I'll mention in a sidebar that I'll be researching investment opportunities in downtown's expansion. I'll let everyone know they may see me around and that I hope to dig up some great opportunities for them, unique investments that no other firm has thought of."

"Keep going. I like this."

"I'll throw in a few other investment ideas and make it seem like it's just one of a bundle. If they see me, they'll say, 'Oh, he's doing his research.' They just need to have an acceptable context ready at the front of their minds to not give seeing me in casual clothes on downtown streets a second thought. And that's if anyone even sees me. And keep in mind, I'll still be driving my car around Beverly Hills. My neighbor clients will see me coming and going as usual."

"Well, I just learned something."

He braced again and waited.

"I learned that this really means a lot to you. You have put a ton of thought into it."

He smiled.

And she smiled. "So, then," she said. "We're going to have to be flawless."

He grinned wider. She was on his side.

"Quit grinning," she said. "And maybe take some notes."

"I'm listening."

"There'll be a bunch of places you'll have to watch it. Like, no casually dropping three dollars on a newspaper or wasting five bucks on a white mocha caramel latte or whipping out a twenty to pay for anything. No more fake fifty dollars. Don't buy anything that, on its face, seems expensive. Deliberate over every dime you spend."

"Agreed."

"You'll have to skip some days at work. I mean, the temp agency realistically might not have an assignment for you every day. We can arrange the on and off days around your client meetings."

He nodded his head. "We're on the same page. That's what I was going to say about my schedule." He was excited to begin the plan. "I'll talk to Frank and Charlie today and let them know I may work some days from home and not to worry. On those days, I'll find a way to call Frank, just to reassure him I'm not drunk. If I'm in the office consistently, I think he'll be okay."

"I'm starting to like Tobias. It sounds like you really *aren't* going to be drunk. Forgive the bluntness."

"Nothing to forgive. I brought it on myself. And, I'm done using drink as a toy. Not because of Tobias but because of me. I don't want that."

But he knew Tobias was partially the reason he wanted more than what using alcohol as entertainment would get him.

"And if it comes crashing down?"

"I still won't want it. At least, I hope I'll know what I almost had and realize that booze isn't gonna give it to me. My problem was beginning, by choice and not by need. I was almost trying to create a problem to make my life more visible to me. Drunk, I was doing something—something bad—that I could see. I mean, I'm not even sorry I got mugged, at least not as sorry as I should be."

"Hmm. That's telling."

"Before that Biltmore binge, nothing I did seemed worth noticing. It was the feeling of misbehaving that started it, and not the whiskey. I had to work at the whiskey part."

She stared at him a long while and finally nodded. "Okay," she said.

"Okay," he said. He suddenly thwacked his forehead. "Ugh," he said. "We're screwed."

"What? What?" she said.

"Something you just said. The temp agency. How are they calling me? If they're calling me, I must have a phone where he can reach me, too."

"Hmmm."

"Come, on. I know you can think of something."

"I got it. Use a prepaid phone."

"A burner phone. Perfect. In fact, duh, I own stock in two companies that manufacture those. Should have been a no-brainer for me."

"Wait. Why don't I own stock in either of those companies?" she said.

"Your portfolio's not ready for that kind of risk. I'll get you there. Don't worry." He smiled.

"Okay. Meanwhile, I think a burner phone'll work. You can tell Tobias you scrimped and scraped for it and that you've only added thirty dollars' worth of minutes you need to save for the temp agency. I'll add one to the shopping list."

"What shopping list?"

"Your drugstore list. I'm getting the stuff, the two-dollar soap and the cheap razors and whatnot. Charged to you, of course. It's gonna be fun to spend a bunch of money on props."

Arthur pushed aside the funny feeling he had at hearing the word "props". It made it all seem too much like playacting.

Like a lie, Arthur.

He focused on his goal and on the relief he felt that she would help him.

"You really are…the best, you know that?"

"I do." She smiled. "When do we start?"

"I'll use this weekend to get prepped. For all Tobias knows, I'm just wandering right now in places where he can't find me. I gotta do some more research. I'll connect with him on Sunday, with a two-day beard and wearing clothes I slept in."

"But don't forget Tannover on Monday. I rescheduled that. Don't make me look bad."

"I won't. I'll be here. I promise. And…you'll have to ring my burner phone, so I can have a temp-agency reason to head this way. Are you okay with that?"

"No problem. I call you all the time, anyway."

"I know. Just making sure." He tried to smile, but fear crept up on him. "I hope this works."

"We won't know until we try." She shrugged her shoulders. "And, you know, maybe it won't be so bad when he finds out, if you've made your lie as much a truth as possible."

Lie.

That word, again.

It startled Arthur a little, but he also felt excitement about what lay ahead.

"You know, you're awfully wise for someone who barely finished college a year ago."

"I work *here*, don't I?" She got up to leave. "In ten years, I'll decline college reunion invitations from the beaches of Australia. Don't tell me I'm not smart."

"I wouldn't dare." He grinned.

"I'll have those doo-dads in a couple of hours," she said on her way out of his office. "Fun with shopping!"

"Wait." He reached into his pocket and pulled out a key fob for his Maserati. "Take my car. Better if you use up my gas."

She smiled. "Agreed. I'll try to watch it, though. Won't go crazy, or anything."

He grinned.

She left his office and stopped at her desk to gather her things.

"Thanks, Kel. You're a peach," he called to her while she was still in earshot.

"I know," she shouted back.

He got up to head for Frank's office, but his stomach was suddenly in knots. Kelly's earlier words came back to him.

What if it crashes down? What if no matter how much I try to live Tobias's truth, he only sees my lie?

My lie.

Lie.

Whiskey.

He pushed those thoughts away and went to talk to Frank and Charlie.

∞ 6 ∞

THE HUNT

THE QUESTION SEEMED SIMPLE, SOFTBALL-ISH.

"Why do you want this job?" the woman had asked Tobias.

Because I'd like to eat, he had wanted to say. *I mean, why would anyone spend half their waking hours working for the dreams and wealth of others if food and shelter weren't part of the equation, math pun very much intended by this math teacher*, he wanted to say.

And what he really wanted to say was, *I had a date last night. I was a real person last night.*

He had wanted to say all that, even if it sounded overly cranky.

Instead, he gave an uninspired answer about "joining the team" and "making a difference".

The interviewer's expression told him he wasn't going to get the job. He fed himself a lie to assuage the disappointment—that at least he had tried, and on a Friday afternoon.

He hadn't tried, though. He had thought only about Arthur and, later, about *why* he thought about Arthur and what he hoped for.

His mind latched onto a strange future with vague notions of Arthur there somewhere farther out in the time continuum, but he couldn't discern what that future looked like. He didn't know Arthur well enough to shade in the outlines of him that he saw.

He hadn't even shared with Arthur that he had a job interview the day after their dinner together. He had learned that even though sometimes fifteen final candidates vied for the same job, people expected the person *they* knew to be the one who'd get it. They felt let down, by the employer, the job, and their person, if it didn't happen.

And he couldn't tell whether that formless vision of Arthur that lurked in his future cared about his job prospects. Yet, he cared what Arthur thought and didn't need the added pressure of not letting him down. So, when the fortune in his cookie read: THE MISSING PIECE IS BEFORE YOU, he hadn't confessed he wondered if the cookie intuited a new job for him. Instead, he joked about his last potsticker and popped it in one bite. Arthur had laughed.

But it turned out that whether the future looked clear or fuzzy and whether Arthur appeared as a life-sized portrait or a bad driver's license photo hadn't mattered. Two days had passed since Tobias's disastrous interview the previous Friday, three since his dinner with Arthur, four since Arthur had spent the night in Tobias's tent. Tobias hadn't seen Arthur since they had said goodnight in front of his tent after dinner at the Chinese restaurant. Tobias realized he would probably never again see Arthur.

The signs were there. People who lived on the streets tended to migrate toward anything resembling mainstream life. Sane company sat at the top of the list of desirable possibilities. Tobias was a normal, healthy man, down on his luck, for sure, but he colored inside society's lines, in spirit, if not in reality.

Yet, three hours with a math teacher who talked movies and books and politics like someone who waited in the first class lounge for his flight to Zimbabwe weren't enough to interest Arthur. He had seen Tobias's essential self and declined to explore the nuances, what few shades Tobias had left to show.

It wasn't as though Tobias was hard to find—Arthur knew the way to his tent—or that Arthur had other places to be, especially on a Sunday. At least, that was not how it seemed.

Tobias lay in his tent and wondered what had gone wrong. He wondered if he had blown it with the awkward way he ate one potsticker, even if dinner had gone well after that. The blunder may have made everything after that a moot point. Arthur may have just been being polite to get through the evening he started by extending the invitation.

A close second in Tobias's mind was that he offended Arthur when he hadn't invited him into the tent after dinner.

There hadn't been a choice. The tent had been tidy—Tobias kept a clean house—but Tobias hadn't been sure whether his lack of a shower showed. Bringing Arthur into his tight quarters was risky. At the restaurant, the delicious-food smells and the distance across the table had masked any odor there may have been. He had quit while he was even, at least.

He figured Arthur saw it differently and was offended Tobias hadn't offered him even an hour's refuge from the streets after Arthur had spent his surprise fortune on a stranger, even one who had rescued him from a mugging that was becoming a beating and maybe a night in County Jail.

You idiot, Tobias. Where are your manners? You continue to suck at normalcy. You blew it. The refrain ran through his head hundreds of times.

With sixty thousand homeless people in Los Angeles, in perpetual motion, even if they were planted on a sidewalk somewhere, ready to run from or be chased away by authorities, it was hard to track down one man who had no anchor to any one square foot in the city. Arthur held the advantages. He knew where Tobias was, but Tobias had no idea how to find Arthur. Tobias had to wait and hope Arthur gave him a second chance and came back to the tent.

It's not gonna happen. You blew it.

∞

"Are you sure you don't want to stay? We have two empty beds?" the woman at the shelter, Melinda, said to Arthur.

He was on the first floor of a 1940s ramshackle three-story building, east of the Toy District, where the top two floors had offices that hadn't been occupied for a few decades. The entire bottom floor had been converted to a small homeless shelter with eight beds, a kitchen, and a group bathroom.

"No, no thanks. Restroom was it. I'm good." Arthur had fourteen bedrooms to choose from in Beverly Hills in the main living area of the main house. He couldn't accept a bed knowing others could show up needing one. He planned to camp on the street.

Somewhere in his mind, he felt relief and then shame for that relief that no one he knew would see him in that part of town. His next issue of *Dewynter* was due out twelve days from then, and he had a strict policy of not bombarding his clients with "extras" in between the regular publishing dates. It meant his clients knew nothing about his Skid Row research. Still, he went through with his plan.

"At least take a cookie," Melinda said.

"Thank you." Arthur took a light brown cookie loaded with white chocolate chips. "And thanks for the use of the facilities."

"Sure thing."

He stepped onto the street and looked around. It was Sunday. He had stayed away from Spring Street and Tobias on Saturday and had roved around four, square blocks of abject homelessness and poverty closer to San Julian Street, the Pennsylvania Avenue of Skid Row.

He witnessed some of what he expected—a hovering loneliness, even in people who huddled together, some filth, vague shame, boredom, apathy, people who sat around as though waiting for an hour on the clock that would mean they should do something different even though Arthur could tell that for some, that hour would never come.

He glimpsed people who laughed with each other, walked with aim, carried bags filled with something they needed at their destination or filled with their entire life—but he also met unchecked insanity, uncared-for illness, hyper-cleanliness that compensated for deprivation, and exhibitionism—of body and shouted words, women who wore skimpy party clothes that were dirty and failed to cover their bodies and men in tattered shirts and pants that revealed sections of their private parts, the skin on which was also filthy. As with any society, it was all there, but more exaggerated. It shone brighter, smelled more pungent, exclaimed louder.

He had observed several tents, real ones from the sporting goods store, like the one Tobias lived in, and others made from tarp, plastic bags, retrofitted shopping carts, and blankets.

At random intervals, he saw people sleeping on the sidewalk, which was surprisingly clean in most places. He wondered about a city that regularly swept its streets and ignored the people living on them.

Where homelessness pervaded seemed undetermined by any pattern. Homelessness varied as much as the stories behind every person in it and was defined by them, and those variations, too.

That amorphous aspect—and that the people caused it by their assorted human natures—had been unexpected by Arthur and had chipped away the first layers in his walls of assumption and had broken through his simpleminded ideas about people on the streets as a homogenous group defined by one trait: destitution.

He had slept Saturday night in Beverly Hills in the clothes he wore that Sunday and wondered from his large bed, in the dark, how the panorama would look if people treated everyone he had seen on Saturday the way Arthur's taxi driver had treated him a few days earlier: as though they shouldn't be inconvenienced, even if they demanded it.

What if, he thought, instead of multiple people focusing so often on Arthur and others like him, leaving some, in perpetuity, with no one, each person looked out for just one other?

If we each carried one, nobody would be on the ground.

Tobias picked me up from the ground.

Tobias.

He stood near the door of the shelter and finished the cookie Melinda had given him. He reviewed in his mind the narrative he had rehearsed for Tobias—the *backstory* to the construction job, his landing with a temp agency, why he had a burner phone.

It all terrified him—the story, his bad delivery of it, and the chances of getting caught and getting called out and insulting Tobias and losing his access to him. If he failed, the reckoning would occur that afternoon. Arthur wasn't ready for his search for acceptance to be over so soon.

He dusted the last of the crumbs from his mouth and braced himself for whatever would come.

He began the long walk to Spring Street, and something caught his eye.

A few dozen feet away from the shelter, a fifty-something man with a matted beard, threadbare clothes, and jet-black fingernails, which Arthur could see even from a distance, argued with a bicycle policeman who poked at several items the man had gathered into a shopping cart and piled into a high, narrow tower. Some objects bulged out at random places.

The policeman said the man and his cart were a hazard that blocked the sidewalk. The man claimed he had a right against the illegal search of his property by the police.

The cop plucked arbitrary bits and pieces from the cart, examined them at his leisure, tossed them back into the cart, and said, "This is trash. This isn't property."

A couple of objects he was too careless with in his tossing teetered a moment in the cart and fell to the ground.

The owner protested.

The cop objected.

A half-dozen scattered observers who had watched from the same distance Arthur had moved closer by several paces. Still, they remained a safe distance from the conflict.

Arthur didn't move.

The man waved his finger a little too close to the policeman's face. The cop moved the finger with a gentle swat. The man pushed the cop's hand.

Ten seconds later, the man was under arrest, in handcuffs.

He said, "What the?" apparently too shocked by the sudden turn of circumstances to say more.

The policeman walked the man several feet down the sidewalk, away from his property, and Arthur watched realization come over his face. He understood what was happening.

The man shouted, "Bobby! Hey, Bobby! Get my stuff! Watch my stuff!"

One of the men who had inched a little closer, a man who appeared to be in his thirties, jogged over and took control of the man's possessions. He pushed the shopping cart farther down the sidewalk and spoke not a word to the arrested man or the police officer.

The cart was presumably still a hazard, but the policeman no longer cared. He spoke into a radio pinned to his shoulder and remained on the sidewalk with the handcuffed man. He appeared to wait for a back-up officer.

The man raised a continued ruckus, but he didn't fight the officer. He seemed too defeated to start a wrestling match that would end with him still in handcuffs. He stuck to verbal protests. He yelled, "My stuff!" and, "This is fucked up!"

A patrol car arrived, and the bicycle cop guided the man into the back seat. Before the car door shut, the man shouted one more time, "Bobby! Take care of my stuff!"

"I got you! Don't worry!" Bobby said. He seemed willing to speak once he saw the police made moves to leave.

The arrested man shouted more foul reflections. At the end, the invective devolved into a sad cry. "My stuff," was the last thing Arthur heard. He was sure the man sobbed.

The patrol car pulled away, and the first officer got on his bike to follow the vehicle. With traffic, the bike cop made quicker progress. Presently, though, the police car and the bike were out of sight.

The event startled Arthur. It also put him in a quandary. He wanted to help the arrested man, and Bobby, who waited with the cart, but other than his thousand-dollar phone stashed in a secret pocket of his backpack and his burner phone loaded with minimal minutes, he had nothing to offer. He carried twenty dollars in ones and quarters, for realism, and no credit cards or anything he could put into an ATM.

He planned to open a small checking account that would provide cover for where his supposed temp agency pay checks were directly deposited, an account with a small balance in case he ever used an ATM near Tobias and the transaction receipt came into view—his real bank account had an astronomical "available balance" and came with an ATM card that was a special shade of gold reserved for the highest end accounts and a dead giveaway—but he hadn't yet opened the cover account and therefore had no ATM card. After the twenty dollars, he was flat broke.

Even if he had wanted to step out of his self-imposed shadows, he didn't think anyone would take him seriously. He had traded his biometric wallet, outfitted with a carbon fiber case, a fingerprint censor, and a Bluetooth that linked to his phone, for a faux-leather one Kelly had found at the drugstore for twelve dollars. In the wallet, hidden behind a library card, was just his driver's license, the only evidence that he lived in Beverly Hills. He had thought it prudent to be able, in the end, to prove who he was. That was the only vestige of his real life that he carried with him. He didn't even have a business card.

He had nothing to offer Bobby to make it easier on him while he watched his friend's cart full of what seemed like his life. He had no food or money of an amount that would be of use and not viewed as a two-dollar insult. There was no way to know how long the arrested man would be detained or how long Bobby would be trapped keeping guard.

Two other bystanders joined Bobby, and their hands flailed as they appeared to recap what they had just witnessed. Arthur picked up the occasional F-bomb in their conversation.

He saw no solution, rare for him. But the words *Carry just one other* floated through his head. He was unable to walk away.

He headed down the sidewalk toward the small group. He figured as soon as he spoke either he would sound weird and maybe get his ass kicked, or Bobby would thank him.

He was bold. "Hi, Bobby is it? I'm Arthur." He didn't offer his hand. He thought it might look like an act of aggression. And then he wondered if that prejudgment was of the kind that made homeless people feel isolated. Bobby may have enjoyed the polite ritual, but Arthur withheld it, at least at first.

How do you expect to carry one other if you won't even reach out a hand?

He held out his hand. Bobby shook it without hesitation. His dry hand seemed unwashed, and the layer of grime felt like a rough, worn, suede glove, but the handshake was friendly.

One lesson learned already, Dewynter.

He looked at the others and offered his hand and introduced himself again. "Hi, I'm Arthur," he said.

They shook his hand and offered their names.

"Stanley."

"Darien."

"Nice to meet you." He looked at Bobby. "I can get your friend an attorney. What's his name?"

Bobby looked surprised and blurted out, "Terrence."

"Terrence what?"

"I don't know. Just Terrence. Do you guys know?" he asked Stanley and Darien.

"No," Darien said. "It's just Terrence."

"Yeah, I only know him as Terrance," Stanley said.

"Can you really get him a lawyer?" Bobby said. "I mean, how do you just stroll up and offer a stranger a lawyer?"

Go with the truth.

"I'm down here learning about life out here. On a coincidence, I just saw what happened. It's outrageous. I don't think that cop would have tried that in my neighborhood. And he damned sure wasn't expecting people not from here to see him. I'm sorry to say it that way."

"No, man. You're all right."

"Too bad for that cop I did see him. And I'm in a position to do something about it."

"Uh," Bobby chuckled and sounded surprised, "okay. Wow, man. That's cool." He nodded approval. He also stood a little taller, almost as though subconsciously he placed himself at Arthur's attention. Arthur was used to automatic respect and deference, but it bothered him, especially since he was clueless in that world, and they weren't. All if it was arbitrary, which was why Arthur hated it, but if he used those standards, he should have stood at their attention.

He had gathered the information he wanted and didn't know what to say next. His social skills in that environment lacked a natural flow. That bothered him, too.

What would you do in your own world? Provide information, instruct the client, facilitate conversation between married people who couldn't agree on how to invest, ask probing questions to help you craft solutions. This is no different, Dewynter.

"I don't know how long it'll take," he said. "You may be here with this stuff a while, but the guy I know, he's good. I think he can help. Do Terrence a favor and try to hang around if you can. I think my guy can get him out pretty quickly."

"I'm skeptical, man, I can't lie," Bobby said. "But Terrence is good people. I'll be here for a while."

Arthur offered his hand and said, "You're a real friend."

Bobby returned Arthur's handshake and said, "Well, we all saw what went down. This is complete crap." He pointed to the cart as if to indicate that everything surrounding his standing guard over Terrence's belongings was a travesty. "Whatever you can do. I got his stuff." He reached out his hand again.

Arthur took it and gave it an enthusiastic shake. "Hey, take it easy," he said.

"Okay. You too, Art. I hope you get Terrence out, man."

"Me, too. See you, fellas," he said to Stanley and Darien.

Arthur headed back up the sidewalk. He pulled out his real phone, scrolled through his contacts, and dialed Nathan Cresswell, his corporate attorney.

He glanced back while the phone rang and saw the group staring at him. He knew he must have looked like a federal agent and that they were still a little leery of him.

"Hi, Arthur," Nathan Cresswell said. He had Arthur identified in his phone by name and always greeted him first, ready to work. "What can I do for you on a Sunday?"

"I need a strange favor. Do you know a good criminal lawyer? I mean, you know what I mean."

Nathan didn't quite laugh, but he brightened at Arthur's inadvertent lawyer joke. "Yes, I know what you mean. Are you in trouble?"

"No, but a man named Terrence is. Needs a lawyer at whatever police station is closest to the Toy District downtown."

"What?"

"You heard right. I don't know his last name, and he doesn't know me, so it won't do any good to mention me to him, but you have to get him some legal help, asap."

"For a guy named Terrence. Under arrest. Downtown."

"That's right. Older-ish white guy. Thin. Likely hasn't bathed in a while."

Arthur knew the task was near impossible, but he still expected Nathan to deliver.

"Tell the attorney to bill me for their time at the station, if that's possible, and either of you can charge me for this conversation and for the legwork on the rest of it. I don't care how you work it out. If necessary, give the man enough money to retain, on his own, whoever you find. You can get in touch with Kelly, and she'll get you the money. Whatever. Bottom line, get the man out. Today."

"Does—"

"Hang on. Leave me a voice mail *on my office line only* when you get it sorted out to let me know what happened. Don't call my cell."

He had added several layers of mystery with that last directive. A harmless eeriness crept through the phone. Nathan's silence had grown heavier, deeper with the curiosity, as though he lay in wait to ambush the facts for the answers he wanted.

"And tell the attorney to assert the man's Fourth Amendment rights against illegal search."

"What?"

"It'll make sense to whoever you send."

"This may surprise you, but it makes a little sense to *me*. I *did* go to law school, but all right," Nathan said, in a tentative tone.

Arthur heard the desire in his voice to dig for information, but Nathan knew better than to pry. His relationship with Arthur was a lucrative one. Arthur had a pristine record, and he was a walking list of referrals. Any time anyone mentioned they thought they needed to see a lawyer about anything, Arthur gave them Nathan's name, and that was on top of the extensive work he did for Arthur at a premium cost. Nathan would happily ruin the Sunday of the best defense attorney in town to get "Terrence" out of jail.

"Make a big ruckus. Friends in high places and all of that," Arthur said.

"All right."

"Get back to me, soon."

"I will. Gotta get to it." He hung up.

Arthur texted Kelly to expect Nathan's call.

She texted back, *Put that phone away. You're breaking the rules.*

I know. Last time, I promise. Putting phone away starting right now.

He tucked the phone into his backpack, but he was unable to move, even as Bobby, Stanley, and Darien watched him through suspicious eyes.

What he had witnessed stunned him. The situation had so quickly gone sour for Terrence mostly because he was outdoors with no defense against police who pestered him. He had no front door he could close. There was no search warrant for him to demand to see. The police adjudged his property to be trash, and it became trash and treated as such. He was exposed, and it had landed him in jail.

Arthur was even more shaken, and grateful, to realize that Tobias likely *had* saved him from an unreasonable arrest for seemingly having nowhere indoors to sleep.

For many reasons, he suddenly keenly understood why Tobias had stopped what he was doing to take in a stranger and why he had bought such an elaborate tent. It kept him out of the line of sight of police and was private enough to give the police pause if they felt like searching it.

Arthur also felt guilty, though, and hypocritical for using the very status he shunned to achieve for Terrence what he claimed he hated that privileged people could attain anytime they wielded their position. Because of who Arthur was, he would probably get results, and yet, as he ran toward Tobias, he ran away from that very notion, for he knew there were umpteen Terrences who had no bystander savior.

But the decks were unfairly stacked against Terrence. He had pleaded his case to the officer and been ignored probably because he had black fingernails and dirty hair and maybe smelled bad.

Terrence had no one to carry him over that bad moment, no one standing behind him or lifting him up, as Tobias had lifted Arthur in that doorway on Broadway. The policeman knew it. Arthur felt justified breaking his own rules to swoop in and catch Terrence before he fell to the ground.

He gathered himself. To put Bobby and Stanley and Darien at ease, he called out, "I got Terrence some help. I think he'll be out soon. Hang in there."

Bobby, as the de facto leader of the group, nodded.

Arthur headed west, on foot, and forced himself to shift mental gears and focus on his next move.

It took a long while, but he eventually made it to Spring Street and turned north. He walked several more blocks, toward the business and government pulse of downtown, using City Hall as his beacon. He finally reached the Los Angeles Times building, on the south edge of Grand Park, and to his right was the tall tower of City Hall, close to where Tobias camped.

Arthur was nervous. With Tobias's tent coming up soon, his mind went blank on the speech he had rehearsed. He barely remembered what to say.

He arrived at Temple Street, just past City Hall and Grand Park. He was one block away.

What are you doing? This is crazy. You're crazy. You'll never get away with it, not for real, not beyond a dinner. Go back to Beverly Hills, where you belong.

Except you don't belong there, either. Not, really. You can afford it, is all, and you've taken a liking to some of its conveniences.

He arrived at the encampment.

He spotted Tobias's tent.

He resolved that the only thing for him to do was walk right into the situation. He took the final steps toward Tobias's tent.

Ten feet from the tent, he stopped.

A man got there ahead of him. He called out, "Hey, Tobe. It's me."

Me. Who's me?

The front door flap to the tent unzipped, and the man strolled in, as though he had been there many times.

A boyfriend.

Arthur turned to leave, crushed, but he remembered something.

Was that guy really a boyfriend? At dinner, Tobias said he didn't have one.

Maybe he lied.

You're lying, Arthur. Why wouldn't Tobias lie?

Because he's not like that. He didn't lie. I know he didn't.

Is that guy just a rival, maybe? Someone else who wants to know Tobias's vulnerable side and listen to his voice all evening? All night? A romantic interest who could be pushed aside?

Arthur moved toward the tent.

We'll see.

∞ **7** ∞

LONG NIGHT OVER THE 101 FREEWAY

ARTHUR STOOD IN FRONT OF Tobias's tent and listened. He strained to hear over the noise on Spring Street for the gist of the banter that went on inside between Tobias and the good-looking stranger with him. The Sunday traffic was sparse but steady. Every time he homed in on spoken words, a car drove by and muddled the overall conversation.

The voices were upbeat, jovial, easygoing.

They like each other well.

Arthur cocked his head in different directions until he found just the right position to pick up most of the words. He thought if he took a step closer to the door flap, he'd be able to hear everything with no distortion.

He moved in about eight inches and stood still. He hoped he didn't cast a shadow along the tent wall that Tobias and his friend could see.

One of Tobias's neighbors, three tents over, sat in a chair in front of his portable home and stared at Arthur. He was raggedy but alert. He watched Arthur eavesdrop.

Arthur considered stepping back from the tent, but it was too late. He got caught. By everybody.

The front flap of the tent came unzipped in such a short span of seconds, that Arthur suddenly found himself just six inches away from the two persons on the inside. With a closer look, he thought the fresh-looking, handsome man who carried a notepad and grinned wide was no older than thirty-two or thirty-three.

Young and attractive.

Dammit.

"Arthur!" Tobias said. It was half-exclamation, half-question.

"Hi." Arthur let out a nervous laugh.

"Hi," Tobias said. "Uh, Michael, this is Arthur. Arthur, Michael."

Michael.

Arthur shook Michael's hand and expected an extra squeeze, imperceptible by Tobias but felt plenty by Arthur, designed to mark Michael's territory and say, "Who the hell are you?"

But the handshake was friendly. "Very nice to meet you," Michael said. His smile was welcoming.

Michael turned to Tobias. They were still on the tent side of the door. "Hey, gotta rush," he said. "Let me know if Arthur has anything to add to the list."

What list?

Michael stepped out of the tent and around Arthur, who hadn't budged, and headed down the sidewalk. Tobias followed him out of the tent and stood on the sidewalk next to Arthur.

Michael turned back to Arthur but tilted his head toward Tobias and said, "He'll tell you about it." He walked backwards a few steps while he talked. "See you, Tobe. By Arthur. Good meeting you." He waved and turned around and continued down the street.

"You, too," Arthur said. He turned to Tobias. "I'm so sorry. I clearly have the worst manners in all downtown. Listen, I can leave."

"No, don't. He was just making his rounds."

"His rounds?" *What does that mean?*

"He's the head of an outreach group."

I'll bet he does reach out. "Oh?" he said aloud.

"They talk to people down here and find out what we're short on and go around handing stuff out. Band-Aids and ibuprofen and nail clippers and whatnot."

And whatnot. "Ah," he said and nodded understanding, even though he didn't understand.

"They'll help anyone in need with more than just the survival stuff, but gay people are their priority…you know…since it can be rough out here."

I'm sure the gay person I'm looking at is his priority. "I see," he said.

"Less control over your environment. No telling where homophobia might lurk."

"I didn't mean to intrude, especially if, you know…."

"Uh, no I don't know."

"You know, if, uh…"

"Oh! No, it's not like that. Not at all." Tobias smiled. "Michael's just a friend."

The friend zone. That'll work. Arthur returned the smile.

"In fact, my relationship with Michael is mostly professional. I mean, we're friends, but…"

Arthur's jealousy had dissipated, and he waited with no urgency for Tobias to gather his thoughts, a strange feeling for Arthur, who was always up, up for clients, up for co-workers, up for a date he could barely stand. In front of Tobias's tent, watching him struggle to find words, he showed a side of himself he rarely saw anymore. He was quiet. He felt at peace, untroubled. The atmosphere, the literal air between him and Tobias was serene. Somehow, it spilled out from the tent, sent on Tobias's vibe, and touched Arthur. The noise on Spring Street seemed to disappear.

"It's okay if you don't want to talk about it. I didn't mean to pry." Arthur finally said.

"No, you're fine. It's just that it's embarrassing. I used to volunteer for them."

"Oh." Arthur wished again that he had known Tobias in that precarious time when his life had blown up, when everything had fallen apart. He could have prevented it. He badly wanted to go back and undo it.

"And no one should get it twisted with Michael. He may be out here writing grocery lists, but he founded his organization and has been running it for ten years. He's a wicked-good fund-raiser. He hauls in crazy-large money from all over the city and the country. He folds more than ninety percent of it back into the foundation and still makes an easy six figures. I feel stupid in front of him, a little bit."

"You shouldn't feel stupid or embarrassed. You're probably a great asset to him."

"I doubt it." Tobias laughed the laugh of a cynic.

"I don't. He knows he can trust you. You know what he's trying to do and what's needed out here because, well, you live it firsthand." Arthur realized how he sounded, but he thought it best not to patronize Tobias. "And you probably have information about what goes on out here that's hard for him to get because people don't talk." Arthur had already figured that out after just two days on the streets.

Tobias offered a small shrug, but he watched Arthur intently.

"And you know who's really in dire straits, who needs what."

Tobias shrugged again. "I guess."

"You should be proud that you still have the spirit of a volunteer, and a teacher, helping him from *his* side of things. I'll bet the list you gave him had nothing on it for you."

Tobias looked again at Arthur, right in his eyes. Arthur didn't waver. Tobias smiled gratefully and a little shyly.

"It's true." Tobias laughed a little at himself.

"Have you thought about working for him, for real?"

"Yeah, and, knowing him, he probably wants to hire everybody out here, but he's fully staffed. The foundation is grand and small at the same time. He does big things with a modest staff that works in a small office in WeHo on a very specific budget, and he's got low turnover. Great place to work. No one leaves. No room for me."

"If I were doing the hiring, I'd find a way to make room for you." He smiled.

Tobias smiled, too. "You're kind. And, you know, you sound more like a businessman than a construction guy."

Arthur's laugh was nervous. "To run a site, you have to understand business. And people. I guess it shows."

"And you know what else shows?"

"What?" *Has he figured me out already?*

"It turns out, *I* have the worst manners downtown. Would you like to come in?"

Arthur grinned with relief. "I'd love to come in."

Arthur sat in the other camping chair and told an animated story about a man he'd seen arrested earlier that day. Tobias mulled over how to ask him to stay the rest of the day—and the night. He didn't want it to sound like an invitation for sex.

Tobias found Arthur desirable, but he wanted something different from sex. He just wanted Arthur to stay and talk and be there, to enjoy the seventy-three-degree weather and slower Sunday pace that turned downtown's Main Street into suburban America's Main Street. He thought they could spend the afternoon lounging in Grand Park and maybe splurge on a Sunday Times that they could share in the tent. He would even dip into his unemployment stash for a nice dinner somewhere with Arthur. He thought maybe after dinner they could relax in the lamplight of the tent and talk, and he would offer Arthur a free place to sleep for the night.

He listened to Arthur and appreciated his story. When Arthur got to the part where the man had been hauled away in a police car, at which point Arthur said he headed toward Spring Street, he found an opening and suggested a walk in Grand Park. Arthur said it sounded like a great idea. They walked and talked and found a bench and talked more.

Hunger took over, and they ate in a small diner on Hill Street half a block away from the park. Most of the tables were empty and there, they really *talked*, about life, about childhood, about tent realities, about downtown.

Around eight o'clock, they walked to a Starbucks that was just a few hundred yards from the tent, on the corner of Broadway and Cesar Chavez, and splurged on a Frappuccino each while the talk grew heavier and more intense, with an air of privacy threaded in it. At the table, each leaned in a little, and only they could hear their words.

Finally, it was ten o'clock and they were back at the tent. Tobias made sure not to repeat the mistake he made after they had eaten at the Chinese restaurant. He invited Arthur to come inside.

Arthur accepted.

In the tent, Tobias turned on the portable lamp. It looked like an old-fashioned oil lamp and had settings that mimicked low or high flickering flames. He set it to just below half-bright.

The mood was light but intimate. It was well beyond the time Arthur could find a bed in a shelter. He had a backpack, but it looked to Tobias like Arthur would be roofless for the night if he left the tent. Tobias had seen him leaf through a few one-dollar bills and count out quarters at the diner and Starbucks and knew he couldn't afford a night in a flop motel.

"I tell you, I was never so scared in my life," Arthur said. He laughed at himself. He had been telling Tobias about the time he had faked being a good skier to impress some high school friends and ended up tearing down a slope called "Devil's Tail". He had almost wiped out. The story was hilarious, but their laughter wasn't boisterous. The tone between them was mellow.

"I wish I'd have been there to see it."

At that, the tent atmosphere became serious. "Me, too."

They fell silent. The lamplight lit the area closest to them, but the tent was otherwise dim.

Arthur said, "Well, I guess it's way past time for me to go. Don't want to keep you too late. I'll head out."

Tobias touched Arthur's arm. "Don't."

The two men looked at each other by the soft lamplight and said nothing for a moment.

Arthur finally said, "Really. I should go."

"Don't. You can stay here."

Neither of them moved. Neither looked away from the other.

"Stay," Tobias said. "Not for…. I don't mean it like that. I just mean…."

Arthur waited.

"This is fun," Tobias said. "And, not trying to brag or flaunt this stupid tent, but I have plenty of room."

"This tent that saved me? Please brag about it." Arthur never looked away from Tobias. "I love this tent."

Tobias's hand was still on Arthur's forearm, gently cradling it from the underside, as though he were about to pull Arthur closer.

"You already know I have a spare bag. This place is warm and cool at the same time. At least my money got me that." His grin was shy. "Look, it's no different from the first time. You take one bag, I'll take the other."

Arthur didn't change his expression. He only stared at Tobias over the lamplight.

"Except, this time, you don't have to sleep in your clothes." Tobias felt a little awkward, but he talked through it. "The mattresses self-inflate fast. It won't take long to settle in."

"I guess I missed that the first time I was here," Arthur said. He spoke softly and smiled self-consciously.

Arthur's quiet honesty moved Tobias. He felt sympathy for that part of Arthur that had been driven to behave the way he had the night of the mugging.

"We'll roll out the bags," Tobias said, "and I'll turn off the light. I promise to keep the room pitch-dark while you change and get comfortable. You'll never find a place to crash this late at night." Tobias's heart beat into his ears. He was about to withdraw the offer, to avoid rejection.

"Are you sure? I can't keep asking you to rescue me."

"That's not the case. And, yes, I'm sure. It'll be like having a house guest. It's been a long time since I was able to have a friend over, just because." He gave Arthur's arm a light squeeze and said, "It's no trouble. Really." He took his hand away.

"All right. But this is the last time I forget to plan ahead and make it your problem."

Tobias smiled. "Maybe it's a problem I don't mind."

Arthur smiled. "Okay."

∞

Arthur was in trouble. He was in love with Tobias. He knew it, for sure. There was no question about it.

They had opened the nozzles on the self-inflating air mattresses, unrolled the sleeping bags, and doused the lamplight. In the dark, they had stripped down to T-shirts and underwear and crawled into their sacks. Arthur felt guilty that Tobias had tried not to brag about having a roof over his head when he thought Arthur didn't.

For a while, neither of them talked. Arthur listened to the occasional car drive by on Spring Street, and he picked up the stray sounds of other people up and down the encampment, coughing and talking. He relaxed to the hum of the cars below on the 101 Freeway, and he felt the presence of the man next to him and knew that he never wanted to experience another night when that man wasn't by his side because he loved that man, with everything he had in him, in the most painful way.

He sensed his love was unrequited, that there was no way the man could have felt as strongly about Arthur four days after their first encounter as Arthur felt about him, and that Arthur had fallen deeply because of who the man was, but that Arthur, a drunk, from the man's perspective, offered no similar reasons for the man to tumble hard into love with him. He was ill with heartache because he was sure he had only made his life worse. He dreaded sunrise and the light giving him a reason to leave and no way to come back.

Eventually, they talked more, and Arthur loved the man more, and the man said, "Good night," with a voice that reached across the tent and embraced Arthur and held him and for an unreal moment that fleeted told him, or so he dreamt and hoped, that the man loved him, too.

"Good night," Arthur said. He turned his back to Tobias and thought about how he would explain to Kelly the next day, after his meeting with Tannover, that she had been right and wrong.

Arthur's plan came crashing down, as she had warned him it might, but not because he had been caught in his lies. His idea failed because for the first time in his life, he was truly in love, in love with someone he didn't think could ever love him back, especially not after he found out what Arthur had done.

Arthur never slept. He lay awake and listened to the cars on the 101 and the even breathing of the man sleeping next to him, the man Arthur would love until the day Arthur died.

∞ 8 ∞

COLD CEREAL

"TANNOVER HAPPY?" KELLY SAID. SHE ducked into Arthur's office and closed the door ten seconds after Tannover walked out of the outer office.

"Very. We, or rather, you, with your well-played reschedule, made him about half a million dollars richer."

"I told you he needed you more than you needed him. But never mind that. I know I said I would only butt in for the big stuff, but I think your first night on the streets is buttinsky-worthy. And, besides. You look miserable."

"I am."

"Didn't go well?" She sat down.

Arthur got up and stared at downtown. The skyline looked perfect through his window.

The air was clear that day, and the temperature outside seemed as though it could exist only in a dream. It was the kind of weather that felt so wonderful while walking around in it, one thought it was a falsehood, as though it had been conjured up by witchcraft. It was typical for Los Angeles, but Arthur noticed it more and felt lonelier in it, in its beauty, without Tobias there to make it worthwhile.

Arthur imagined Tobias enjoyed his day, wherever he spent it, without a care about Arthur.

Maybe with Michael, volunteering and laughing and feeling reassured. Maybe with someone else.

Arthur had sneaked a glance through the window just as Tannover had arrived, and he had spent the entire meeting wondering about Tobias, behind him, through the glass and on the streets of downtown. He expected that, once alone, he would gaze at the city the rest of the day and wonder where Tobias was. And with whom.

He and Kelly had rolled out their first temp agency phone call early that morning, and Arthur had left the tent with far less ceremony than he had on the morning after the mugging, when circumstances almost demanded a meaningful conversation, when he had been special to Tobias, a rescue victim in whom he had a vested interest. Arthur had dressed at first light and made a move to leave early, out of politeness, and Tobias had let him go. Arthur had no idea what Tobias's plans were for the day or whether it was even within the realm of appropriate to ask or show up at the tent unannounced to find out.

His stomach hurt. He dreaded everything.

He had reassured Kelly and the others in the firm with his early morning arrival to meet with Tannover.

And he had received good news in a phone call from Nathan Cresswell. They had found Terrence soon after he had been arrested. An attorney from a law firm with four, prominent, named partners arrived at the police station, and the authorities released Terrence after the "misunderstanding", with no charges filed.

The attorney had applied so much pressure, a patrolman drove Terrence back to his cart full of stuff. The attorney had followed the patrol car and even taken a moment to speak with Bobby and Stanley and Darien, who had, it turned out, followed Arthur's advice to wait for Terrence to return. The attorney confirmed that Terrence had been reunited with his property with no trouble.

Nathan had guessed correctly that Arthur would want Terrence to receive a small gift of cash, and he instructed the attorney to give Terrence five hundred dollars that would ultimately come from Arthur. That had all been good news.

Otherwise, a gloominess hovered.

"Mr. Dewynter?"

"Mm?" Arthur didn't turn around.

"What happened?"

Arthur finally sat down at his desk. The beginning of the story spilled out, but he questioned the appropriateness of it.

"I'm not kidding when I say I'm not going to be that weird boss we read about. All I can say, or should say, is I'm in for real now, and I don't know that he is. And it won't matter anyway once the truth comes out." To himself, he sounded bleak, like a doomed prisoner.

"First, you and 'weird boss' are not in the same lexicon, so you need to stop saying that. Second, ugh. I'm reading between the lines."

"My only choice now is to back out while I can."

"Why?"

"Because…because of…how I feel about him, and I'll leave it there. And when he finds out how I've lied, he'll hate me. You called it."

"How do you know? Maybe I was wrong."

"Because it didn't go like I thought it would. I figured we'd keep on eating and talking and hanging, with no strings, and that, as new friends, I'd confess all. I hadn't expected…."

"To have…so much on the line by the time you spilled the goods."

"Right, again. It happened so fast. No details, although it's very G-rated. But I got walloped before I knew what hit me. Listen, I'm sorry for this weirdness."

"You're gonna make me quit in a second if you don't please stop with that. Believe me, you'll know when I've heard enough." She gave him a sympathetic and almost pitiful smile and leaned forward in her chair with her elbows on her knees.

They sat in silence, each finding a spot on the wall somewhere and contemplating it, deep in thought.

"There's only one thing to do," Arthur said.

"What's that?"

"What I already said. Get out now. I can't go back."

"You mean, just disappear on him?"

"What choice do I have?"

"Plenty. You could get back in there and fight."

"A losing battle? Right now, even as I sit here miserable beyond words, whiskey and vodka are still choices, not mandatory living. I'm fine—at least I think I'm fine—with ginger ale. I can't guarantee that will be the case if it really goes to hell."

"I don't think that's true. If it were, you'd already be there, based on how miserable you seem, and Tannover would be somewhere else."

He gave her a wan smile. "I really appreciate your saying that. I needed that. I did. But my temporary courage doesn't change anything. I can't win. I should get out while I can."

"So, that's it?"

"I guess it is."

"All that planning, and you're giving up."

"I'm not giving up on *it*. It's giving up on me."

"So, you say. And I was worried about *him* flaking on *you*."

"I'm not sure what else I can do."

"How about you give yourself a few days. Get some distance. Go back on Wednesday or Thursday, with the plan right back in place. And, you know…*spend the night on the street.* Be an impostor as little as possible. *Do what we said.* Give Tobias a chance to find his way to you."

Arthur felt like a coward in the face of her irritation.

"I don't know," he said.

"I do. You have to go back."

Arthur stared at her. "You're serious."

"I'm serious."

After a while, he said, "I'll think about it," but inside, he was past whatever thinking would bring, and he had moved on to the defeated stage.

His tired tone betrayed his inner thoughts. Kelly looked away and shook her head at nothing except maybe the disappointment that hung in the air.

"Okay," she said. "Okay." She got up to leave. "But you know, it couldn't have been easy when you started this firm with Client Zero and built it up."

"No, it wasn't."

"So, what are you afraid of?"

"Losing…everything."

She frowned in sympathy and tried to smile.

He felt the need to bring levity to the situation, for her sake. "You can't tell me this wasn't a little creepy." He gave her a sad smile.

"I'll say it was for your sake. And maybe I can sue my way out of here, like you suggested, and retire at twenty-five, once we get through all that nasty litigation." She mustered a small laugh.

"I'll settle out of court and fold on every one of your terms. You'll be out by twenty-three, after the lawyers have dragged it out some."

"Jokes aside, even though none of this is funny, I hope you get in there and win. Tobias, I mean." She left without letting him respond.

∞

Arthur stood over the sink in his overlarge bathroom and stared at the running water. He held a toothbrush full of toothpaste and did nothing with it. He watched the water run down the drain and thought about Tobias, who slept in his tent, as he had the night before, when Arthur had been there to see him, and listened to the cars below as they lulled him into sweet dreams that made Arthur jealous.

It was barely nine o'clock, and Arthur had avoided going to bed for as long as he could, but he hadn't slept the night before, in Tobias's tent, because he had listened to Tobias sleep, and exhaustion and stress and sadness caught up with him. Sleep finally beckoned him.

He hated his bed, hated his house, hated the high ceilings and empty air and ghostly and ghastly silence. He hoped to fall asleep and shut it all out the minute he climbed into bed.

He brushed his teeth with a little too much force. The toothpaste he spit out had red streaks in it. He rinsed it away, ran water over his toothbrush and placed it in its small stand, walked past the second sink that went perpetually unused, and waved his hand over the sensor to turn off the bathroom light.

He crawled into the half of the bed he used and thought about the downside to having housekeeping staff who made his bed so perfectly every morning. The half he never used remained flat and undisturbed permanently. Arthur was unable to muss it enough on his own, over a period of days, because his staff corrected it each morning with hospital-corners precision and reminded him each night when he saw it again that he was alone.

He turned off the bedroom light with a clap of his hands and lay on his back with his eyes closed and experienced a small burst of energy brought on by thoughts of Tobias. He tried to imagine the sound of cars on the 101. He wished he had memorized those hums better the night before since he thought he might never again hear them the way they sounded in Tobias's tent.

Go back, Arthur. Tell him the truth. Tell him you love him. How bad can it be?

He'll run from me, is how bad it can be.

That refrain stayed with Arthur. His business was back on track. Frank and Charlie and the rest seemed reassured that his three-day absence the week before had just been a much needed, unplanned vacation. Despite Kelly's urging him otherwise, he felt the wisest move he could make would be to return to work on Tuesday and forget he had ever known Tobias.

He fell asleep with the made-up sound of cars in his head.

∞

Arthur sat at his dinner table and read the cereal box in front of him.

His relaxed wardrobe wasn't his only dirty secret. His other one was that, despite the expensive meals and the flights to New

York on private jets to see the latest Broadway shows, he often ate Cheerios for dinner. He had loved them as a child and had never outgrown his taste for them. Mostly, they required little preparation and even less formality. He could eat them standing up or in his bed. If he chose to eat them at the table, he could finish quickly and escape his cavernous, overblown kitchen, which was what he hoped to do that night.

He examined the nutrition panel on the side of the cereal box and thought about Tobias.

And he thought about Kelly. Her disappointment that Arthur had let two nights pass and had not gone back to see Tobias, and that he planned to let a third night go by, that night, without even touching base with Tobias showed all day.

She had been the consummate professional. She kept her tone not only polite, but friendly and easygoing. There were no undertones or hidden tones. She executed every request without flaw and bade him a good night on her way out the door.

But it was that perfunctory attitude that told Arthur he had so disappointed her, she didn't even bother with a reproach. Arthur let Tobias go, so she let Arthur go and moved on to index funds. Or perhaps she didn't have the heart to pile on. He wasn't sure.

He drank the last of the milk from the bottom of his bowl and put away the cereal. The only sounds in the house were those he made as he rinsed his bowl and spoon and put them in the dishwasher. Even though they used his utility cars for errands during the day, his staff lived off-site and went home by four o'clock every afternoon. It meant that late at night, when the phone no longer rang and the occasional noise from the quiet road ceased, there were no movements by other people in the house, even people disconnected from him by a professional relationship, to make him feel less alone.

He left the kitchen and set the house alarm from the keypad in the foyer. He had no energy to trudge up the endless staircase and cheated and used the elevator at the end of the east hallway. The walk to the lift was long, but at least it was flat.

He rode to the third floor and entered the shadowy corridors. Recessed, elegant wall lighting adorned the walls at perfect intervals, but he rarely clapped on those lights. He found his way to his room using what he called the parking lights, very small lights spaced much farther apart lower down on the walls that served as guides, like those on the occasional aisle seats at a movie theater, and didn't shine brightly enough to make out another person's features, if anyone had been there. They were enough to get him to his room. He had walked that route, interchanged with the route from the top of the staircase, for over ten years and knew the way.

In his room, he brushed his teeth and got into the same side of the bed he always did, and the thought that would either change his life for the better or ruin it forever rushed into his head.

Fuck this.

PUNCHES

"WHY DO YOU WANT TO work with us?" the woman at the temp agency had asked Tobias.

Déjà vu.

"Because I need to eat."

Déjà vu, again.

That's redundant, Tobias.

Wait, no, it's not. I had déjà vu twice.

Either way he reconciled it, the answer had popped out of his mouth. He had skipped breakfast to use the saved money for bus fare. The low blood sugar had cost him his attitude filter. He also hadn't seen Arthur for three days, which made him wistful and cranky.

The temp agency declined his services. He lost his appetite, and his mood dipped even lower.

He was back at the library. He had bombed his interview by nine o'clock in the morning and had been lounging in chairs and reading at different tables in various sections since ten o'clock. He finished the day at one of the computers. He pretended to search in earnest for a job, but he couldn't concentrate. His head pounded, from hunger he had no desire to feed, and from loneliness.

He knew he had no right to be, but he was annoyed that Arthur had not stopped by to say hello since he had left three days earlier on Monday morning to go to *his* temp job.

Arthur owed him nothing. That was what made Tobias bad-tempered. He wished he had more rights where Arthur was concerned. He wanted more say-so in whether and when he saw Arthur. Instead, Arthur came and went on whims that took advantage of Tobias's stationary life. Tobias was jealous of Arthur's time away even if Arthur wasn't wrong to stay away.

Arthur had committed only one offense. He had made Tobias fall in love with him without warning. And he was unattainable.

Tobias didn't think Arthur played at being beyond reach. He was genuinely elusive, inaccessible, faraway. His lack of interest in Tobias mandated it. It was the natural result of the fact that Arthur felt nothing for Tobias other than gratitude and polite acquaintanceship that he used to kill boredom when convenient.

Tobias tried to behave rationally, but he wanted to know more about Arthur. At the library computer, he abandoned job hunting and googled ARTHUR DEWYNTER for the twentieth time that week. No matter how many times he received a slate of generic results for a bunch of men all over America with that name, he couldn't believe nothing came up for *his* Arthur, the one who had worked in construction.

"That makes no sense," he said aloud. He glanced at the librarian and hoped he wasn't in trouble for talking. The librarian hadn't even noticed.

He muttered more softly, "No Facebook page. Nothing on Twitter. No blog post from the early two-thousands. Makes no sense."

Then he remembered he had none of those things either. He googled himself and came up with a similar slate of generic people he had never heard of, except that they had his name, guys with LinkedIn pages, a man who had been famous in the eighteenth century, a garage band member. It was out of vogue for a teacher not to have social media accounts, but Tobias hadn't cared. One accidental friending of the wrong minor could cost him his job. The irony that it hadn't mattered because the district had fired him anyway crossed his mind, but his main thought was that the universe was telling him he should forget Arthur. It didn't seem to want them to know each other in a meaningful way.

The websites he searched weirded him out. Even as he sat there and googled Arthur, he thought it strange that so much information about people and their households was available, sometimes just two clicks deep. He spotted his condo mortgage and felt a little pang in his stomach and closed out the search.

The library computer flashed the three-minute warning, and Tobias shut it down. He gathered his things and stuffed his folder into his shoulder bag. He didn't care about the damage to his resumés. They were the copies he brought to interviews, but at that moment, he didn't think he'd ever again be invited anywhere to talk about his qualifications. He made his way downstairs and stormed out of the side door of the library, onto Fifth Street.

Outside, he received a shock.

Arthur stood on the sidewalk.

∞

The side door to the library let out onto a long walkway that led to a wide street sidewalk. The distance from the door to the curb was easily forty feet.

Arthur had remembered that Tobias mentioned he spent a lot of time at the library. Arthur took a meeting earlier that day, for Kelly's and Frank's and Charlie's sakes, and he dashed out of his office as soon as it was over. He sped home to drop off his car and take an Uber downtown. From the corner of Fifth and Grand, he walked fast to the library exit that had the most foot traffic and waited.

He had gambled that he could arrange an encounter with Tobias if he waited long enough.

He could have hung out in front of Tobias's tent, but he thought that would be strange and even invasive. He didn't want to intrude and overstep and alienate Tobias.

It had taken all day, and he had almost abandoned his plan, especially when he ran inside for four minutes to buy take-out from the food court off the corridor near the Flower Street entrance and wondered if he'd missed Tobias, but, finally, the doors opened, and his gamble had paid off. Tobias walked out of the building not long before the library closed for the evening.

Arthur stared at him across the distance.

Kelly's right. I want and need this fight.

He had spent three nights in Beverly Hills, sick of the distance circumstance put between him and Tobias. He had also worried about Tobias, about his wellbeing, a strange notion for Arthur. He hadn't ever wondered so much about another person's existence in a way that meant he depended on their being happy in order to feel content himself.

And he felt guilty and ashamed that Tobias slept in a tent over a freeway while he worried about his own problems in luxury in Beverly Hills and rode elevators to his bedroom if he was tired.

Still, a chasm existed between them, carved out by Arthur's money, with Arthur's prescribed life on one side and a place he felt he belonged—near Tobias—on the other side. He needed to find a way over the void and to the other side, where Tobias was.

He didn't know what would happen, but he knew when it ended, it would be after a contest between Arthur and Fate, and not because he had given up.

It wouldn't be perfect. It would be dangerous, for he still couldn't tell Tobias the truth about what he was. He would not allow money to derail and dupe Destiny. He would continue to pretend he was homeless and arrive where he believed Fate and hopefully Fortune had sent him.

Tobias was the other hurdle. Arthur had no idea how to make Tobias love him back or how to make Tobias see that Arthur had strung a tightrope over the abyss between them and begun the precarious walk toward him. Arthur needed support to keep from falling. He needed a sign from Tobias that Arthur should fight to make it to the other side.

At that moment, the hurdle felt higher, the tightrope thinner, than even five minutes earlier, when Tobias was inside the library and the unseen possibilities had no limits.

Tobias seemed angry. He walked with his head down and gripped like a vise the bright orange shoulder bag strap that lay diagonally across his chest. He looked up with a glower—about something he had been pondering, clearly; Arthur wondered what it was—and literally missed a step when he spotted Arthur waiting for him.

He stopped and stared. And almost scowled.

He's mad at me.

The fight began right there. Arthur could stand and wait for Tobias to approach him, or he could take the first steps across the veritable boxing ring, along the tightrope, over the abyss.

He started the long walk toward Tobias.

Tobias walked toward Arthur. He approached with no urgency. Then he walked right by Arthur as though he hadn't seen him, even though he had.

Arthur turned and followed him. He spoke first, threw the first punch in the fight, not at Tobias, but at the forces—confusion, jealousy, the love Tobias didn't return to Arthur—that might keep them apart.

"I don't come bearing fifty bucks or great conversation or any excuses for being such a flake."

"Then why are you here?" Tobias never broke his stride or looked up or took his hand off the shoulder strap he squeezed so hard his knuckles were white.

"Just to be here. Is that all right?"

Tobias didn't answer. He walked east on Fifth Street, toward home. He was several blocks west and south of his tent.

"It's not up to me." He sped up.

Arthur recognized what he saw.

Fury.

Tobias tried to stomp it off or maybe build it up with a hard walk right into it. Arthur wasn't sure.

What has you so angry, Tobias?

Arthur sped up, too. "I think it *is* up to you. It's all up to you, Tobias."

"Ha! That's a laugh."

"Nothing about this is funny."

"I'm glad you finally figured that out. Seems like it's a big joke to you. That's okay." He walked faster.

"What's okay?" Arthur stayed with him. He realized that between his home gym and Tobias's daily habit of walking all over the city, they were both in excellent shape. The race was on.

"All of it. You're in the clear. I'll see you later."

"I'm heading your way. We can walk together."

"How do you know where I'm going? Pretty presumptuous. And typical."

Shit.

"You told me you always go home after you leave the library. Are you going home?"

Tobias walked several more yards in silence. "Yes," he finally said.

"I'm going that way, too."

"If that's the way you want it. The streets are free."

"That's the way I want it."

They walked in silence, north on Grand, toward Grand Park.

They got stuck at every crosswalk. Some had a button that triggered the walk signal. Others turned green automatically, after a wait. At crosswalks where there was a button, Tobias banged it with the side of his fist.

No matter how long they waited for the light, Tobias never spoke. He never acknowledged Arthur standing next to him. At each green signal, he walked a little faster. Arthur didn't fall even half a step behind.

They arrived at the Music Center and were just a few feet from where Arthur had been mugged. It was also the top edge of Grand Park, which was high up enough to have an elevator that led to lower levels that let out into the park. Tobias cut through on foot, over the same large steps he had used to follow Arthur the night they had met.

He took the steps fast, coming down hard on each one. Arthur took them in lock-step, no longer oafish, as he had been on the night of the mugging. At Hill Street, Tobias dashed across the street against the red don't-walk signal.

Arthur dashed with him.

They continued downhill and through the park and hit Broadway, the street Arthur had tried to sleep on, and Tobias jaywalked there, too.

Arthur stayed with him.

The final stretch was a long walk over the lawn across from City Hall, to Spring Street. No crosswalks provided natural breaks. The trek across the grass, in silence, past people who tossed balls and walked their dogs and did yoga on mats and lay stretched under the sun felt interminable to Arthur, but he kept pace with Tobias every step of the way.

They exited the park onto Spring Street and turned north.

The crosswalk timer at Temple Street flashed twelve, eleven, ten seconds, and Tobias jogged to catch the light and scooted over Temple. Arthur jogged too and caught the light with Tobias.

They were almost to Tobias's tent.

The sun still shone, but twilight descended without warning, and it was gray everywhere but warm outside.

They arrived at Tobias's tent. They hadn't spoken since they had been just a few feet from the library. Twenty minutes had passed.

At the flap of his tent, Tobias turned and said, "I'm here. It's been a shitty day. I bombed my second job interview in just six days. I have a screaming headache. I haven't eaten since yesterday. And I really don't want to see you, right now, Arthur."

The forces had punched back.

Arthur got clipped, but he answered the blow.

"Why didn't you eat anything?"

"I told you. I'm on a tight budget. I used today's allowance for the buses."

For your second interview in six days. What happened, Tobias?

"What about the mission?" Arthur asked aloud.

"No time. I had to prepare for my interview. I grabbed a shower, but they hadn't started serving breakfast, and I had to leave. I wasn't about to beg for some early food before anyone else ate."

Arthur knew he had to remain undercover. Tobias had been lulled into embarrassing honesty by Arthur's dishonesty. If Tobias had known what was available to Arthur, what his life was like, how he hadn't taken out the trash in well over a decade or cleaned a toilet in that same time or washed even a T-shirt in the laundry, he would have been mortified to confess the truth of how dire and poverty-stricken and messy and disorganized and mentally unkempt his life was. None of it had mattered to Arthur, but Tobias wouldn't see that. His pride would cloud his ability to know that Arthur didn't judge him and that he had no need to feel shame.

Arthur's hole of lies got deeper, and he was sure that soon he would hit foul Sulphur. He dug on, though, metaphorically, and stayed in the fight, literally.

"You have to eat something."

"You're right. So, like I said, goodbye." He headed down the sidewalk to the gas station. Arthur followed him.

"Are you stalking me? You really *are* presumptuous."

"Not presumptuous and not stalking you. You said it yourself. The streets are free."

"Whatever."

They resumed their silence for the block-and-a-half walk to the gas station.

When they reached the gas station, and Arthur didn't continue down the street but instead followed Tobias inside the mini-market side of the lot, Tobias said, "Okay, now I know you're stalking me."

"Just seeing what's here. Maybe I'm hungry, too. Maybe this is where I was going. I told you I was headed your way."

Tobias shook his head and said, "Pfft. Okay. Sure." He selected an apple and a banana from a nearby basket. He moved to the refrigerated section and stood in front of the milk, but he didn't touch any of the cartons.

Arthur appeared at his shoulder.

Tobias shook his head, seemingly resigned to Arthur's unwillingness to go away.

Kelly had cautioned Arthur not to pull rescues out of thin air, but he ignored that warning. He grabbed a pint-sized carton of milk. He held it out for Tobias.

Tobias walked away with his apple and his banana. He set the items down at the cash register. Arthur added the milk.

"Excuse me, but I know what I came here to buy."

Arthur knew charity would cause Tobias to blow his top, so he did something that he felt was technically worse but likely more palatable to Tobias.

Arthur said to the cashier, "He wants that, too. Add that to his tab. And a bag."

"What the—?" Tobias said, but before he could protest, the milk and the ten-cent bag were added to his total, and he was forced to pay for them. He snatched the bag filled with his items off the counter and went out the door.

On the walk back, he never slowed. Almost with a vengeance, he pulled out the apple and ate it in five huge bites and threw the core into his bag. The banana was gone in three bites, and the peel also landed in the bag.

At the corner of Cesar Chavez and New High, which was just Spring Street with a different name on the other side of Cesar Chavez, he downed the pint of milk. He spotted a garbage can several feet away on the sidewalk and tossed the carton at it. It went in. He spun the bag a few times to make sure all the weight of the core and the peel settled near the bottom and flung it toward the garbage can. It dropped right in.

The light turned green, and he stepped into the crosswalk as though none of that had happened and still as though Arthur wasn't there.

They arrived at the tent. Arthur tried to find a way in, into Tobias more than inside the tent.

"Tobias, I'm sorry," he said. "About everything, especially that you went so long without eating. That *is* shitty, on top of the job situation. If there's anything I can do—"

Tobias's face became a contradiction of anger and astonishment. "I don't want your damned charity. Are you that clueless?" He exhaled. "Could you just please leave?"

"I wasn't offering charity. I was offering to help. I'm sorry. I just thought—"

"Look, what do you care? I've known you, what, a week? Friends come. Friends go, especially out here." He waved a hand to indicate all of outdoors. "Ignore me. I'm just in a rotten mood. And I'm not gonna stand here for everybody to watch," he said, and he swung his index finger back and forth at Arthur and himself, "whatever this is."

"I don't care who hears us."

"I *do*. I live here. Presumptuous, *once again*." He unzipped the tent and stepped through the flap. He tossed his shoulder bag in a corner so hard, the tent shook. "I don't mean to be rude, but I'm calling it a night."

"That's it?" Arthur stood on the outside of the tent, on the sidewalk.

"That's it." Tobias reached for the zipper to close the front flap.

Before he could succeed, Arthur did something that went against his grain. He walked into Tobias's tent uninvited.

"No, that's *not* it," Arthur said. Once he was inside, he turned around and zipped the tent shut.

Tobias looked up at the cloth ceiling on his home and said with mirthless laughter to the skies beyond it, "This is outrageous! I don't believe this, right now." He looked at Arthur. "I don't believe you, right now."

"Believe me, Tobias." Arthur felt a strange pang, a sense that irony watched him from somewhere and chuckled, as he stood in the middle of a larger lie and asked, in that moment, with the words "believe me", for blind faith.

An unanticipated uppercut, from the referee.

Tobias's pained, sarcastic laughter faded, and he said, "Arthur, please. I really need you to go right now."

Not a chance. The bell hasn't rung.

"I'm not leaving. Not until you tell me what's really going on."

Tobias sighed. "I. Just. Told. You." His hand moved up and down with each word, as though chopping something in mid-air, for emphasis.

"As bad as that is, I know there's more. Tell me all of it."

"You want all of it?"

Yes. I'm off the ropes and ready to go toe-to-toe with Fate.

"Here comes a bad pun," Tobias said, "but, do the math! I'm a fucking loser! I go to the library and pretend to have a life! I used to live in a house! I live on the sidewalk! And I'm starving, pretty much all the time!" He shook his head and laughed a little, seemingly at himself. "And I was waiting for you to come back. I don't know why. I'm an idiot, I guess. I had no right to expect anything. Especially since you come and go like I'm…a fucking convenience store." He spoke through tight teeth.

Ouch. Straight to the gut.

Tobias took a deep breath. "I'm furious with myself."

He looked at Arthur. Arthur saw it all, the pain, the loneliness, the despair. He recognized it. It had been inside of himself, and he had already known Tobias well enough to know it was the enemy that lurked within him.

Their loneliness stemmed from two different places, but each man's was identical to the other's in its magnitude and impact. Arthur empathized with Tobias, understood him, wanted terribly to unravel Tobias's pain and his own along with it.

He was sure people in nearby tents heard them. He didn't care. Nothing mattered at that moment but that Tobias should let somebody, anybody, have it, so he could release his rage.

"I don't think you're a…convenience store. I…have no…I can't say why I disappeared except that your convenience store theory is wrong. But maybe you can tell me why you're furious with yourself."

"Never mind. No reason." Tobias unclenched his teeth and spoke quietly. "It's nothing." He looked right at Arthur. "How long do you plan to go on being rude, staying where you're not wanted?"

The hardest punch, yet.

But not a knockout blow.

"As long as it takes."

"As long as what takes?"

"You tell me."

"I'll tell you. I would like you to please leave my home. I'm really very tired."

"No." Arthur took a few steps toward Tobias.

"Just leave." Tobias stared at the tent floor.

"No." Arthur stood close enough for their shirts to touch.

He lifted Tobias's chin and looked him right in the eye. "No," he said, very softly. "I'm not leaving. Ever." He leaned in and kissed Tobias.

Tobias returned the kiss without hesitation. They stood in the middle of the tent with their arms around each other and kissed as though it were prohibited by some evil, invisible force, and they had to take in as much as they could before they were stopped. Their kisses were measured and gentle, but also deliberate and desperate.

They kissed and kissed until darkness fell in the tent. It was barely light outside, but the tent received almost none of that light.

Arthur was afraid to say anything for fear that Tobias would stop their kissing and come to his senses and ask Arthur to leave.

Tobias finally pulled away, and Arthur thought his fear had come true, but Tobias only said, "What is this, Arthur? What's going on? I don't need pity."

"Is that all you think I have to offer? Charity? Favors? Pity?"

"No, I—"

"You know, you're beginning to hurt my feelings. I'm not here because I feel sorry for you." It was just light enough for them to make out each other's expressions. "I'm here because…."

"If you'd rather not say, maybe you shouldn't. I'm not sure I can take it."

"No, that's not it. I just don't know how to say it."

"Maybe just say it," he said.

"I'm here…to say…I'm sorry."

"For what?"

"For leaving and flaking and treating you like a convenience store and not telling you…."

"Are you sure I wanna hear this?"

"I don't know. You may be even angrier."

Tobias stared at him. "I don't have any energy left. It's okay. Just say it."

"I love you," Arthur said. He felt the outdoors moving in on them. The city was on the verge of settling down for the night, and it drew into itself. Arthur sensed it narrowing, quieting, becoming no bigger than the tent. He pulled Tobias closer and spoke softly. Nothing outside existed.

"I love you," Arthur said.

Tobias said nothing, but he kept his eyes on Arthur. He touched Arthur's face, and even the tent wasn't there for Arthur anymore.

"That is…," Tobias said in a soft voice.

"I know. I picked a helluva time to say it," Arthur whispered.

"No. No, you didn't." Tobias gave Arthur a long, uninterrupted kiss. He murmured right into Arthur's mouth, "I love you, too."

Arthur's head became lighter than the air around them.

"I realized today at the library that it was true, but I told myself to forget it, to forget you. And now you're telling me that you love me just as I realize that I love you. I love you, Arthur. I was going to say, 'That is a miracle.' "

Arthur almost floated out of the tent.

He hadn't kissed anyone with love in his soul in his whole life. He kissed Tobias deeply and savored the emotion, the touch, the love coming through, the warmth, the feeling of wanting to be connected, of wanting to get inside the other person, the relief that he had a chance, that his love was returned, *that Tobias loved him!* It was the happiest moment of his life.

"I can't believe we're here right now," Arthur said.

Tobias held Arthur's face in his hands and gently stroked his cheeks. "I can. I have thought of nothing else but you since you left here that first morning. I thought I was infatuated, but I couldn't understand why it all mattered so much, why I wanted to spend every moment with you, how I could forget my problems and talk to you for hours and tell you anything. I want you to know everything."

"It was the same for me, the minute you woke me up and told me what had happened to me without any judgment. I thought about you that whole day. I never really stopped."

They kissed again.

"You should have stayed that morning. I hated watching you walk away. Mentally, I followed you. I wondered where you went."

"I'm so used to living a certain way, I just left. I didn't realize what was happening."

They kissed deeply.

"Is it real?" Arthur said. "Are we fooling ourselves?" He didn't want to trust it too soon. He didn't want to risk the pain of it not being true. He feared the forces had a sucker punch up their sleeve, a cheap shot ready to blindside them.

Tobias talked with his mouth against Arthur's. "It's very real. That's why it feels like a fluke, like it isn't supposed to be. When it's real, when you've waited for it, for so long," he took a breath and let it out slowly, with his mouth still on Arthur's, "for *so* long, it's so good you can't believe it. But I believe it. I love you, Arthur. That's all there is. I love you."

"Tobias." Arthur dove into Tobias's mouth with his own.

They kissed for a long while. Arthur knew he should confess, everything, right then, while they were in a truth-telling moment, while they revealed earlier held secrets.

But he didn't confess.

He played with fire as he continued his ruse, especially as Tobias wanted to bare his soul.

But their bodies did a tell-tale dance, and Arthur knew he was about to make love for the first time in his life, really make love with a man who wanted and loved him for himself and whom he loved and wanted, and he could barely hang on long enough to wait for it. He refused to forfeit that with ill-timed truths that would ironically lead to an outcome that belied their destinies.

For he felt they should be together, and truth, at that moment, would probably tear them apart. And like Tobias, he wanted them to share everything. He wanted Tobias to know it all, but to achieve that, he had to know that as he gave himself, he was accepted for who he really was. He felt in that moment there was more honesty in *not* confessing, not then, not before they made genuine love, as the people they were meant to be.

"Let me make love to you, Tobias."

"That's all I want, right now. You love me. Show me."

"I'll show you."

They kissed as a final acknowledgment of the vows of love they had just exchanged.

Tobias moved to check that the tent was zipped tightly shut and quickly opened the self-filling nozzles on his air mattresses and unfurled his sleeping bags.

"I wish I had more to offer."

"It's everything. It's perfect." Arthur meant it.

They undressed swiftly.

Tobias turned the lamplight on, to the softest setting. The room had just enough glow for them to see each other in muted, golden tones. To Arthur, it made their first foray into lovemaking mysterious and sensual, full of touch and sound and taste.

They moved, on the mattresses, to the middle of the tent, to avoid casting shadows for their neighbors, and they became familiar with each other's naked bodies.

They touched each other everywhere and gloried in one another for a long while. It was darker outside, but it still wasn't late, and people occasionally walked by their tent but didn't know two nude people made love inside. The notion excited Arthur.

And then he remembered something he wished he had forgotten. "I don't…have any, you know…in my wallet," he said, just loud enough for Tobias to hear.

"Condoms?" Tobias whispered. Their hands and mouths were all over each other, but they made very little noise.

"I'm safe," Arthur said. "I've been checked. I promise, but…."

"So am I, but…you know what they say."

Arthur suddenly saw the most meaningful connection he would ever have slipping away. His body hadn't caught up, yet, and it was still ready to be with Tobias. He felt against his abdomen that Tobias was still primed to be with him. They rocked in a slow rhythm and did a kind of body-to-body mating dance on their sides. They were ready to take those movements, those demonstrations of desire, to the final phase, and they were foiled.

"Fortunately," Tobias whispered, "Michael doesn't just hand out vouchers for free HIV tests. He also gives everyone out here a box of condoms. He says you never know. Even gives us a tube of lube to make sure we have no excuses."

Arthur almost shouted with relief and joy. Instead, he laughed a happy, intimate laugh, with his face close to Tobias's. "God bless him," he murmured.

Tobias let go of Arthur long enough to go fish in the far corner of the tent for their ticket to paradise.

"I never used any of it," Tobias said, "but I think I remember where I put it all."

He shifted some things in the dark. Arthur heard him tearing at what sounded like thin cardboard.

"Voila," Tobias said. He reappeared near Arthur with a smile and held up in the soft light a squishy packet and a tube. He set them near where they lay. They resumed their body dance, in a close embrace, with their fronts touching each other.

"I got news," Arthur said, close to Tobias's ear. "I hope you paid attention to where you put that box. We're gonna need at least two of these." He reached for the packet and tore it open. He dressed himself in its contents and wasted no time adding what was in the tube.

He moved Tobias to a position where he could envelope him entirely from above. As Tobias lay back to accept Arthur, Arthur placed his hands in Tobias's and bent their arms at the elbows, with Arthur's palms facing down on Tobias's.

They hung on tight. Their faces were close. In the soft light, Arthur saw Tobias's freckles and let go of his hands to stroke his face and caress his ears and spoke soft words that made Tobias speak too, with the voice Arthur found so sexy, it made him pick up speed and give Tobias everything he had. They kissed and fell into a steady, back-and-forth rhythm that let them finally connect, as lovers and friends and exciting strangers.

They made no sounds that anyone but them could hear, and exalted, with hot breath and rocking hips and smiles and kisses and small bites and whispered groans. They cemented their newfound love without a care beyond the tent walls.

It turned out, they needed six squishy packets. They took turns, as they gave and received and whispered "I love you" to one another, smiling and laughing and talking, dirty talk and love talk, and kissing each other everywhere.

Arthur was the most contented he had been in his entire life.

Later, as they tumbled into slumber in each other's arms, he wondered something, first as a question, and finally as an answer: When it blew up, it would gut the world under his feet and leave his heart and soul scattered over a massive crater.

∞ **10** ∞

A Maserati on Fifth Street

ARTHUR WOKE UP TO THE sound of horn honks and cars that whizzed by on Spring Street.

He stretched and yawned and looked around and realized he lived the life. Tobias had asked him to move into the tent a month earlier, on the night they had made love for the first time.

At first, Arthur had demurred. He wanted Tobias to be sure he didn't mind having a second person in his tent. Tobias's response had been to unzip Arthur's backpack. He began to unpack it. Arthur stepped in and finished, to avoid Tobias finding his real phone stashed at the bottom of an inside pouch.

Other than that minor blip, they were comfortable from the beginning, not only physically—it was a four-man tent used by just two—but spiritually, emotionally, and conversationally. With no money to spend on distractions, they sat on benches in Grand Park, played Frisbee, found free events around downtown, toured museums that offered free entry, and talked.

They talked all the time, about everything. Nothing was off-limits. Other than Arthur's secret, it seemed to Arthur that neither of them held anything in reserve. If they thought it, they shared it. And they found they liked each other more each day.

Arthur didn't mind that he used the gas station's bathroom and took a shower some days several blocks away at the mission and lived without refrigeration and had no access to television and worked around so many privations that came with tent life. Those hardships only caused him and Tobias to need one another more as they came together to deal with them.

In his regular life, Arthur tended to be looked to for answers, authority, or determination of the tone or common goals, but on the street and "outside", as Tobias called it, he was the student, the follower. Tobias had been the one to show Arthur the way.

He had taught Arthur how to avoid problems with careful planning of big and small events. He had scolded Arthur good-naturedly to keep a water bottle handy, which let him brush his teeth after meals without needing a sink. He taught Arthur to eat light at night and take a sliver of an over-the-counter med after heavier meals, to keep things clean on the exit, and to make sure that that event happened in the morning, right before he showered.

He encouraged Arthur to make friends with others in the encampment and participate in an unofficial version of a Neighborhood Watch and share resources, where he could, which was the easiest for Arthur.

He showed Arthur how to interact with law enforcement and strike the right balance between confident eye contact with police officers and engaging too much, which would bring unwanted attention.

Along the way, a wonderful dynamic arose. They had begun to rely on each other, as partners in privation, as friends who sought each other's counsel, as confidants who shared their fears about the future.

Arthur was profoundly in love. The togetherness poverty forced on them, the reliance on each other, the emotional trust they fostered out of a need for that trust and for one another, the deep friendship they formed, gave Arthur a bottomless gratification he would have had to buy with his soul in his own world.

Instead, Tobias had given himself freely. Arthur took as much as Tobias would let him have and gave back all that resided in him, anything Tobias wanted. A freedom from the restraints of money and all its ceremony allowed Arthur to open himself to whatever Tobias wanted to explore within Arthur, and it let Arthur search inside of Tobias for salvation as an emptyhanded lover who brought only himself to their relationship.

Tobias had professed often that he, too, was deeply in love, with Arthur. It had happened quickly, but it had also happened completely.

They were as any other couple and yet not, in that Fate had handpicked first one, to get lost on a park's edge, and then the other, who found the lost one, and brought them together in the strangest of circumstances. They were destined in their accidental meeting. It was ethereal and surreal and somehow the most normal life had ever been for Arthur. He felt he and Tobias could withstand anything, except the one thing that had brought them together: Arthur's lie.

He watched Tobias sleep and tried not to let his deception destroy his warm feelings. He still felt he made the right decision in withholding the truth about what he really was. He was honest about *who* he was, and that would have to suffice.

His real phone rang. He gingerly exited their joined sleeping bags and then lunged for his backpack. He fumbled through a few useless items to get to the bottom of the sack, where the phone lay tucked away. He silenced it, but it was too late.

Tobias woke up. "What was that? Sounded like a cell phone, and not that cereal box one you use." He was still half asleep. "The one with the number I'm not allowed to know." He wasn't irritated. He sounded as though his biggest problem at that moment was whether he could get back into a good dream he was having.

"I told you. It's the easiest way to keep us from using my minutes."

Tobias covered his mouth and yawned. "I know. You're right. And I'm a hypocrite because I can't stand those things, anyway. I have such PTSD about my final few months with my cell phone company. I'm just glad all my job searches are online and that things are set up by e-mail. I won't need a phone till someone gives me a job." He closed his eyes and exhaled a sleepy breath. "Although, I should shut up since your last days with your fancy phone were a lot tougher."

"Don't remind me," Arthur said. He headed back to his side of the sleeping bags. "Although…," he said, "it *is* how we met, so there's that."

Tobias smiled, lazily, with his eyes still shut. "There *is* that," he said.

Arthur edged closer to Tobias and enjoyed the warmth. He felt Tobias's morning sexual awakenings nudging his own. He wanted Tobias, but he had no time. He had four meetings scheduled that day, and something about one of them had to have hit a wall, or his phone would not have rung that early. He had to leave the tent and pivot his focus to his firm.

"Go back to sleep," he whispered. His disobedient hand caressed Tobias's naked rear end.

"What about you?" Tobias said. His eyes were still closed.

More than a month into their knowing one another, Arthur remained taken with the sound of Tobias's voice. He let several moments pass as he watched his lover slip in and out of sleep. He gently stroked his warm, nude behind and lulled him into a more relaxed state. Tobias had never been sexier to Arthur.

"They told me yesterday I'm working today," Arthur finally said. "I'll leave soon." His hand settled and cradled Tobias's behind. He stole a string of kisses from Tobias's resting mouth.

Tobias smiled through the barrage of gentle busses from Arthur's attentive lips and rocked his hips a little.

"You know? You never told me the name of that place."

"Because who cares? They pay me. Speaking of which…."

"I know. I'll leave right after you and head to the library. I promise."

"All right." Arthur made a move to leave the sleeping bag.

"Stay," Tobias said. He was sleepy and intimate and irresistible.

Arthur mentally shortened the time on his morning routine, deducted, in his mind, a few minutes from his shower and visualized using an electric razor in his car, and convinced himself he had bought some time.

He rolled onto Tobias and nuzzled his nose and kissed him. His body got ahead of him and began an easy glide back and forth over Tobias, so that their male parts frotted with an arousing rhythm.

"Okay. For you I'll stay."

∞

A month later, it was Arthur's cheap phone that rang and woke him and Tobias.

Arthur answered it. It was Kelly. She had called Arthur several times over two months as his pretend temp agency, and she had her routine down. She easily switched from "Arthur" on the phone to "Mr. Dewynter" at work. She had told him that the first time she had said, "Arthur," she had had to stifle a giggle. It was the day he had met with Tannover, a day that was far in Arthur's mind, in time and in feeling. He had been miserable that day. He couldn't have anticipated then that bliss was a mere three days away, at the end of an angry walk home from the library and a borderline altercation at the gas station.

The phone was so cheap, there was little Arthur could do to control the volume of the person's voice on the other end. When Tobias was near, he heard every word Kelly said.

"Hi, Arthur? Kelly Donavan. How are you this morning?"

"Good, Kelly. Where am I going?"

To eliminate one element of faking it, Kelly always pre-selected the address of a real establishment that was unknown to the average person and far away by vehicle. In case Tobias had a sense of where it was, it validated the time Arthur needed to travel between multiple locations—his office, Beverly Hills, Spring Street—and explained why he didn't get home until after six.

Arthur wrote down the details and hung up the phone.

"She's perky," Tobias said.

Arthur adored Kelly and was protective of her. He gently deflected before Tobias descended into a litany of "temp agency girl" criticisms. He was protective of Tobias, too, and didn't want to hurt his feelings with even the gentlest rebuke.

"And she's the reason I keep getting good assignments," he said.

"Yes, she is. And, she's at her job right now, whereas I'm lying in a tent on Spring Street, so I'm in no position to criticize. I could take a lesson from the Kellys of the world, although, when I taught, I was an early riser. First bell was at seven-ten."

He became wistful. Arthur felt awful.

"And you will rise early again. Soon. In fact, now. Today. Library. We leave together."

∞

Arthur finished with his clients by one o'clock and came home to the tent early enough to see the police harass his neighbor, JoJo, the way Bobby's friend Terrence had been hassled. Arthur headed up the street to watch, just as Bobby had done for Terrence. Tobias wasn't home.

JoJo's camping situation was makeshift. He had attached a piece of painter's tarp to the overpass fence and draped it over the decrepit shell of what had once been a real but very small, one-man tent he had probably found somewhere. Because it barely housed JoJo, his things were in a collection of carts he kept in a semicircle around his tent. They functioned as storage space and as barriers to him when he slept. They were excellent alarm systems since they rattled if moved. But the police alleged his setup was a hazard. They demanded he vacate his spot.

JoJo made non-sequitur arguments in his own defense. He was in his sixties, and years on the street, an earlier drug habit, and no access to dental care meant his teeth were hit and miss. Many of them had fallen out. It made him sound somewhat like a child when he spoke. He had about him a pathetic air that saddened Arthur and made him furious with the cops.

"Let's go," the bike officer said.

Almost as if scripted, JoJo relied on the identical invective Terrence had. "This is crap, and you know it. What about my stuff?"

"You can take it with you. You can't expect to stay here forever," the policeman said.

No, but he has nowhere to go. If you ever push Tobias and me out, we're safe. Where's JoJo supposed to go?

Arthur took a few steps forward.

The policeman became assertive with Arthur. "I'll need you to stand back, sir."

"This is my friend," Arthur said. "At least let me help him with his carts."

"Thanks, Art," JoJo said. His voice shook.

Arthur thought he might cry. He was outraged. He kept himself under control. Not only could he and Tobias ill afford an arrest of either one of them, but JoJo wouldn't survive the eviction without help. Arthur let his arms dangle peacefully by his sides, in a show of non-aggression.

The policeman assessed Arthur from head to toe. "All right."

Arthur and JoJo downsized JoJo's existence into two carts. Arthur jogged several times to the corner to toss JoJo's most unnecessary possessions into the garbage can. The policeman never retreated, and JoJo had almost no time to decide what was essential and what he could let go.

He was shaken. It took everything in Arthur not to arrange another save, but he had to live the life he had claimed for himself. It was the only authenticity he had to offer Tobias.

He did have an honest idea, though. "Come on, JoJo," Arthur said. "I know a shelter that may be able to take you for tonight. If they can't take you, they can at least take your stuff."

"Is it far?" the old man asked.

"Very."

They began the long walk to Melinda's shelter in the Toy District, where Terrence had been arrested. By Arthur's estimation, he would be back at the tent by around his usual six o'clock.

The likelihood that one of his clients might see him at that hour in downtown was high, but he had begun shaping real investment options for them and updating them in *Dewynter* about proposals he soon hoped to make. He dropped into conversations during meetings that he volunteered with a few homeless shelters in his free time, to give back and dig deeper. Every client applauded him. If they saw him pushing JoJo's carts, they would assume he was mingling to get ideas.

As he and JoJo headed down Spring Street, with gratitude that it sloped a little downward for several blocks, Arthur replayed in his mind the conversation with the police. He tried to recall an impression he couldn't remember that nagged at him like a warning bell, except he didn't know why that bell rang.

Somebody had said something, or he had seen something, a moment, a mood, a body movement he thought he should have heeded, but he couldn't remember what it was. He failed to conjure whether it was word or action, even. By the time they were two blocks away from the freeway overpass, he gave up trying to summon what it was.

But an odd foreboding hovered like a portent. Calamity was in the air.

If only I knew why.

∞

Job hunting had taken on a different meaning for Tobias after Arthur had moved in with him. At the library, he surfed the Internet and ducked the librarian less. He searched for a job more and even explored options that had nothing to do with his math degree.

It wasn't just that he hated to depend financially on Arthur, although he didn't like that and was grateful for his unemployment money. He hadn't minded taking random one-off charity from strangers he'd never see again, but Arthur, and what he thought of Tobias, mattered.

Mostly, why Arthur's presence inspired Tobias to search in earnest for a job was that Tobias respected Arthur and hoped to achieve his level of executive functioning.

For three months, Tobias had watched Arthur. He set an excellent example for how to persevere in times of hardship and take what was offered, even if it wasn't what one preferred. There *had* been disagreements about Tobias's approach, one, especially, that had made for an awkward Wednesday in the tent.

It had begun as a benign conversation about Skid Row. Arthur had waxed nigh poetic about the conditions on the Row. He rattled off facts and numbers and didn't seem to hear himself pitch four, sound, tenable ideas for how to rehabilitate whole sections of the neighborhood.

"For somebody who hates math," Tobias had said, "you use numbers powerfully."

"And what about you?" Arthur had said. Tobias had sensed the conversation had headed over a cliff, but he went along, initially, and sailed through the air after it.

"We already know I like math."

"Yes, but are you doing everything you could with it? Are you really exploring all your options?"

"I think I am, but I guess you don't."

"I didn't say that. I only meant that there are lots of places that would be happy to have an ex-math teacher on staff. And until then, use your skills while biding your time. There are clinics down here. There's an organization that tutors homeless kids. You could volunteer at the Food Bank."

Arthur had simply been solving problems again, but the words stung, a fact that showed on Tobias's face. He tried to defend himself.

"I hear you, but, you know, you have to have a car to become a tutor at that place because you go where the homeless kids are, in their homeless shelter, and before I…landed in my situation, I used to volunteer at the Food Bank after Michael suggested it. That's how I knew to move down here. It's why I spent my last money on so much tent gear. I didn't know it then, but I was in training for homelessness. I've been stranded a long time. I know what's where."

"I didn't realize. I'm sor—"

"Technically, everybody's in training for homelessness, since there's no way to know if this'll happen to you. Who knew I would end up needing their food pantries? It's…embarrassing showing back up there out of work and living in a tent. Why do you think I starved half the time when we met? It was just like the situation with Michael, embarrassment-wise, but worse. Michael's at least a friend."

"Look, I'm sorry with my big mouth," Arthur had said. He had been full of remorse. "I'm in no position to criticize. I'm very sorry."

"It's all right. I know how you meant it." *Besides, it's true,* Tobias had thought. He could have gotten a job in a warehouse or an office. He had escaped into the tent to come down from the trauma, take cover from the barrage, and hide from the harshness of life, and, somewhere, while he didn't live comfortably, he had let himself get too comfortable on the fringes and then let the fringes turn him into somebody unemployable.

It had been a strange conversation. Arthur's reproach had felt kind of good to Tobias and made him feel worthy of what the rebuke implied—that he could achieve a better life. He hadn't felt worthy in a long time.

"I'm sorry," Arthur had said again. "Let me make it up to you. Please?"

"Funny, you should offer. I have just the right thing in mind."

And they had made love.

And Tobias had begun to rethink tent life. He dreamt about pooling his resources with Arthur's and moving into one of the hotels that charged by the night as a stopgap to something more permanent, like a very small apartment. Anything would be larger than the tent and more comfortable, with indoor plumbing and a kitchen. The only obstacle was that Tobias had suggested the idea to Arthur, and Arthur had shot it down.

"Granted, those places can be real dives," Tobias had said, "and Lord knows they can be filthy and full of bed bu—"

"And we have to leave every twenty-nine days, lest we claim our evil, evil renters' rights on Day Thirty—"

"You sound like Michael."

"He's right. The idea that people would try to prevent you from having something that keeps you protected…."

"Never mind about that. I'd rather come inside for basically a month and rough it one night than spend the whole month outside—"

"And one night in?" Arthur put his arms around Tobias's waist and flirted, but Tobias wouldn't let himself be distracted.

"We'd have our own bathroom and shower, and if we schmooze the landlord, I'll bet you we can get our same room back, every time."

"If we stay in the tent, we can guarantee where we'll be every night and save far more money."

"There you go again, sounding like a banker," Tobias had said.

"It's just common sense."

"All right."

Tobias had given in, as he always did, on that subject.

"If I didn't know better, though," he had said, "I'd swear you enjoy life in the tent better than anywhere else."

Arthur flirted again and leaned in for a kiss. "Maybe it's true."

"True, my ass." Tobias returned the kisses.

"Your cute ass."

"Oh, see, now you're gonna make me wanna—"

"That's the point." Arthur had smiled into a kiss. "Gimme that ass."

"What happened to 'cute' ass?"

"Oh, it's still cute. Give it here."

Tobias had happily surrendered.

But his main takeaway, besides the sexual distractions, was that the sooner he got a job, the easier it would be to decide what they should do next. He figured that while he brought home nothing but unemployment insurance, they had close to no options with Arthur's temp money as their only other support. Either way, he knew that he wanted his next move, and every move after that, to be one he made with Arthur.

It had to do with the kind of love he felt for Arthur, a love he didn't understand that he somehow, nevertheless, needed Arthur to understand. He had told Arthur, so often, about that love, hoping to explain it to himself along the way.

"It's strange and surprising and profound and unfathomable and of a magnitude I didn't know I had the capacity to feel," he would say, usually late at night, in a whisper, when the only sounds around them came from cars on the freeway and the occasional distant siren and the low, faraway roar of planes overhead.

He thought he sounded crazy and unreasonable, but Arthur only pulled him closer and whispered similar words.

Neither of them could define it truly the way it really existed. They both sounded a little crazy and unreasonable, and Tobias knew that, for him, it transcended and conquered his usual penchant for avoiding collaboration. He began to operate "in terms of Arthur" and conduct his ramshackle personal affairs in a way that would further his existence with Arthur.

That day, at the library, he tweaked his resumé to fit a few tutoring jobs he had found, expanded his "reason for leaving" response from a petulant TERMINATED to a frank but brief explanation about his situation, and saved his changes well before the clock ticked out on his Internet time at the library.

∞

Two hours later, at high noon, Tobias left the library through the Fifth Street exit and spotted something strange.

He thought he saw Arthur driving a Maserati on Fifth Street. The man behind the wheel looked just like him. The windows were tinted, though, so Tobias didn't see the man's face with clarity.

The car zoomed away from the curb lined with valet parking attendants across the street from the library, where restaurants and banks thrived, and stayed on Fifth Street through the last traffic light before Fifth transformed into an onramp for the 110 Freeway, which was within sight of where Tobias stood.

Tobias watched the car enter the 110 South, the Harbor Freeway. He knew the driver of that car couldn't be Arthur, his lover, his tent-dwelling partner who had, the night before, refused to spend an extra dollar on a lemonade, and who had mastered the art of making wild love with a quiet intensity, uttering sounds and words only Tobias could hear, and spanking and caressing with a soft, silent hand, so much was he of the world of downtown homelessness and tent life, but the resemblance had been uncanny.

Long after the car was on the freeway and out of sight, Tobias stared at the freeway onramp. He couldn't explain it, but he felt as though he had just been with Arthur, in his presence, talking to him. He almost thought he caught a whiff of his scent but knew that was his imagination injecting false senses.

He laughed out loud a little on his way back to the tent. He couldn't wait to tell Arthur he had a rich twin who drove a car that could have paid off most of Tobias's debts had it been his to sell for the cash.

He spent the walk home intermittently cracking up and mentally spending the fake Arthur's money. He mostly paid bills, in his mind, and stashed enough aside to avoid any disasters like the one that had already befallen him. He bought a few nice things for Arthur and moved them into a three-bedroom townhouse.

By the time he arrived at the tent, he had solved their problems with the imaginary money.

"He saw me!"

"What? *What?* He saw you?!"

"He saw me! In my car!" Arthur sat down hard in his throne-chair and banged his elbows on his glass desk on the way down.

Kelly was furious.

Arthur braced for impact.

"Mr. Dewynter. With *all due respect*," she said through a tight jaw, "*are you kidding me, right now?!* I told you not to drive down there in your car!" She let that sink in. "Right across from the library!"

"I know, I know. Who knew he'd be out there *right then*? Right when the valet brought my car? I once waited for him to come out of that door all day!"

"What happened? Don't leave out *one* detail."

"I saw him a few seconds before he saw me. The orange strap on his bag caught my eye. I tipped the valet guy a hundred and shoved him out of the way, trying to get out of there." His head was in his hands. "Thankfully, the motor was running."

"This is ridiculous. I told you not to take your car!"

"I thought it would be faster. I needed to get back *here* so that I could get back *there*! Tonight!" He moaned at the glass desktop.

"You could have Ubered from up on Hope Street! I don't know why you didn't Uber! Even if he had caught you in the backseat of a Toyota, who cares? You could have found an explanation, maybe told him your boss sent you on an errand on the company's Uber account. But no boss at a regular job gives a *temp* the keys to a Maserati! *I* only drive your car because I'm me! I mean, you know what I mean."

"I know, I know." His stomach hurt bad. "And I caught him in the rearview mirror staring until I got on the one-ten. *He saw me.*"

"Our whole plan is up in smoke, now." She let out a loud, wound up sigh, and sat hard in her chair on the opposite side of his desk. "If you don't mind me saying—and even if you do—this is a mess. A hot mess!"

"I know, I know." Arthur sounded to himself like a beached whale, groaning in misery.

Kelly sighed again. Her breath shook from irritation.

Arthur cradled his own head and saw his whole life disappear. He pictured Tobias throwing his things onto Spring Street. He was beside himself. He got up and paced.

He didn't care if Kelly sued for everything he owned. He was terrified. He had to share his fears.

"I can't lose him. He means everything to me. I was *this close*. Just another month, maybe two, and I could have made it make sense. I know he would have understood."

"Wait, let's think about this. Are you sure he saw you? Are you *sure*?" The last question came out in three bossy beats that ordered Arthur to answer.

"No, not entirely. I mean, like I said, I spotted him before he spotted me, but he watched me drive off. Why would he do that if he didn't see me?"

"Well, wait. Again, let's think about it. He only saw what looked like you, through a dark window, driving a car you couldn't possibly own. Maybe it was just weird for him, so he watched the car, but he didn't really think it was you."

Arthur looked at her. He blinked several times. "Yeah…" He stared at Kelly. "Yeah!"

"You gotta think that it was way out of context. By the time he figured out what he was looking at, your face was kind of hidden and then you were gone."

He stopped pacing. "Don't get my hopes up. Do you think I'm in the clear?"

"Maybe, maybe not. I'm dead fifty-fifty on this one. But go home like you *are* in the clear and convince him he was mistaken."

Arthur was down again. He plopped back into his chair. "You mean gaslight him? Like he's a child?"

"You've been lying this whole time."

"I know, but the lies I've told until now were about keeping the status quo until I could 'fess up. This will be hard for you to buy, I know, but I don't lie to him, otherwise. In that world, I'm transparent. I tell him how I feel, what I think. I give him my true impressions of things. We relate honestly, about who we are as people. I've just kept the details about *what* I am in the shadows. It would feel weird telling him he didn't see what he *did* see and that he doesn't know what he *does* know. He's not the enemy. I love him. I respect his intelligence. One time my real phone rang, and I deflected, but if he had said, 'Do you have a smartphone?' that would have been the end of it. I'd have 'fessed up."

"All right. All right. I'm actually glad to hear this."

"I'm glad to say it."

"Then there's only one thing you can do. Split the baby. Go home and act natural. If you're busted, you're busted. But if you're in the clear, ride with it and thank your stars."

"Okay." He was resolute. "Okay. I can live with that compromise."

She got up slowly, as though she'd been through a real fight, and headed for the door. From the doorway, she said, "I can't believe I'm asking this, with you under the gun, but you *have* to text me and let me know how it worked out."

"I will. I won't be able to hold it in until tomorrow, anyway, if we get away with it. You'll be the second person I think of, after me, and my hide on the line."

"Okay. Good luck."

"Thanks."

She left.

"You'll need it," he said to his reflection in the glass table.

∞

"So?" Tobias said, the second Arthur walked through the flap of the tent.

"So?" Arthur said. His heart was in his stomach. He had wanted to throw up the whole way home.

"When were you gonna tell me that you drive a Maserati and are actually filthy rich?"

That was it. Arthur was done. With the tent. With his life downtown. Maybe with any kind of life with Tobias. The only thing left to do was tell the truth and beg for mercy. "Tobias—"

Tobias laughed. "Okay, okay. So, you *don't* drive a Maserati, and you're *not* rich. But, damn, I saw a guy today, who could be your twin, driving a Maserati, likely because he *is* rich."

Arthur stood frozen. He was afraid to move in any direction lest it be the wrong one for his purposes. He managed a faux-pleasant smile and waited to follow Tobias's lead.

"You should have seen him. I was coming out of the library, and there you were, or there he was, behind the wheel of a fat ride that must have cost well into the six figures."

It did.

"I cracked up the whole way home, thinking about what we would do if you turned out to be rich and didn't know it."

Tobias skirted extremely close to Arthur needing to confess, even though he wasn't caught.

Arthur waited for Tobias's next words. They would either require that Arthur refuse to take Tobias for a fool, or they would let Arthur be in on the joke of the mistake, and he could let it go.

"It made me glad I found a few jobs to apply for today."

Arthur hadn't expected that. He showed genuine surprise.

"Really? What did you find?"

Arthur tried to act natural and do what he normally did when he came home. He stripped down to his T-shirt and threw on some sweats over no underwear, which he had also stripped away. His feet were bare like Tobias's, as though there was no way he was leaving anytime in the immediate future.

He relaxed a little. Tobias had tapped him on his naked rear-end before it disappeared under the sweats, and they were engaged in their usual, easygoing chatter. Tobias described some of the jobs he applied for and the changes he had made to his resume. They sat in their living room, which was just the far side of the tent, in Tobias's two low-to-the-ground, cloth camping chairs that were comfortable beyond expectation and let Arthur appear more relaxed than he was. His feet occasionally stroked Tobias's as they settled into their conversation.

Aside from praying he remained in the safe zone, where he barely held onto his territory, and feeling encouraged by Tobias's shift in his job-search strategy, Arthur was extremely interested in how his wealth, even his fake wealth, affected Tobias.

"And how would a rich me make you want to look for a job? You never said."

"Oh, yeah. It just made me think about the day we finally get to a place where we're a little more stable. I really want to be a healthy part of that equation. Even though I *did* pay a bunch of fake bills in my mind with Rich Arthur's money." He chuckled. "I had us driving a couple of Audis and living in a three-plus-two. Otherwise, I paid my way. Your fake money made me fake successful, so I could keep up and contribute for real."

"You already do contribute for real. But, hey, I couldn't be your sugar daddy?" He chuckled nervously.

"No. Okay, I wouldn't mind the occasional over-the-top meal."

"Your food wish would be my command." Arthur smiled.

"But it got me thinking about life with a regular income. Paying bills regularly, owning a small home. I guess that's really what I mean. I want that back."

Arthur had wanted to hear words that kept him from having to confess, but instead, he heard words that wouldn't allow him to confess. Tobias felt spurred on by what he didn't have and by what he could have. For the first time since Arthur had met him, where it had to do with earning a living and working within society's norms, he had sounded like the man he must have been before the financial trauma had stun-gunned him. He had seen what was possible, what it looked like on Arthur, and by extension, on him, and the recent increased drive Arthur had noticed seemed to be boosted.

For Tobias's sake—something he hadn't expected to be the case—the best thing Arthur could do was keep his mouth shut.

He was relieved beyond words. His life wasn't over. His relationship was intact. Later that night, he would turn off the lamplight and sleep next to the love of his life. He never felt better.

Five hours later, Tobias stepped out of the tent to empty his bladder and water a corner of the courthouse's expansive, manicured lawn with the iced tea he had drunk at dinner. Arthur reached into his backpack for his phone but kept the device in the bag. Since the morning it had rung and almost busted him, he had begun turning it off overnight instead of merely silencing it.

He turned it on. It booted up with a high-pitched *"bling!"* that Arthur hated at that moment because it could have given him away. The phone lit up in the dark bag. Arthur entered his unlock code, pulled up his messaging app, and typed fast. He sent Kelly a two-word text: *We're good.*

He thought Kelly must have cancelled her life to sit by her phone, *with it in her hand*, because he wasn't able to move to power down his phone before she texted back a GIF of five hip-hop dancers, lined up and dancing in synchronized fashion. They smiled and appreciated themselves sporting perfect moves. It was a three-second loop. The message was clear, even if the actual words were absent: *We got away with it.*

He smiled at her creativity and sent back a happy-face-with-sunglasses emoji, but he also felt a sense of dread as he shut off the phone, suffered through a *"blang!"* as it said goodbye, and tucked the device into its secret pouch in his backpack. He wasn't sure why he was uneasy, especially since he had survived the Maserati mishap.

Tobias returned and smiled at him as though he hadn't seen Arthur in days and was glad he was there. He was honest and innocent, and he trusted Arthur.

Then Arthur understood what he felt.

Guilt.

And fear.

He couldn't shake the feeling he was doomed.

11

NIGHT IN THE TUNNELS

ARTHUR PACED THE TENT FLOOR. He debated with himself whether to pull out his real phone and call the police and his lawyer, Nathan Cresswell, or whether to wait ten more minutes. Already, he had waited ten more minutes eighteen times.

Three hours.

He didn't want to wait again. Every time he went for his phone, though, he thought he heard Tobias approaching the tent, which would make it a moot point. He didn't want to get caught for no reason.

Either way, they were in for a row once Tobias got home, if he got home. That last question was why Arthur paced and expected an argument once he saw Tobias.

Tobias was way overdue from his usual time to get home. Arthur had last seen him that morning in a shower stall at the mission. Arthur had dressed in a hurry and left the mission, for work, ahead of Tobias. He presumed Tobias made his rounds—the library, outreach with Michael's group, shopping for certain supplies—and, somewhere along the way, had been sidetracked.

Or worse, Arthur feared.

They had lived together four months. Summer had waned, and the darker nights of autumn reigned. In those four months, summer or autumn, light or dark, unless Tobias put in a marathon at the library, he came home a few times in the day, to check on the tent and make sure the battery-operated rat-repellent devices hadn't died out.

Some days, he hung around for much longer, to keep anyone from catching on to a pattern of absence that might encourage them to break in. Sometimes, he was tired and stayed home most of the day.

When Arthur's work schedule was light, and he could skip days in Century City, they stayed in together and made intermittent trips out of the tent for food and sunshine or a cultural outing, or they lounged all day and lay naked and napped and read and talked and made love and lived off of earlier procured food or maybe a shared meal in a diner after sunset if they had willed themselves to get up and go out.

No matter how Tobias's day went, on days Arthur worked, Tobias returned for good around six, but that night, it looked like he hadn't been home during the day, and he still wasn't home.

It was after nine o'clock. The library was closed, and Michael's group tended not to do outreach too long after dark.

Tobias could have been in jail or dead. He had no fear of any aspect of Skid Row, and the teacher in him sometimes reached out to people who had no capacity to respond the right way.

Michael didn't help, Arthur thought, taking Tobias on volunteer expeditions constantly. As Tobias's mood had improved over the recent weeks, he spent more time on outreach, even as his struggles to find employment had meant others could have reached out to *him* to offer help. He didn't see himself as being as disadvantaged as his street neighbors.

Arthur liked it that Tobias had an outlet to feel productive and that it wasn't a game. He *helped* when he volunteered. But Michael relied on him too much, as far as Arthur saw it, and Arthur's imagination overtook him. He feared Tobias had encountered some bad element of downtown, right around twilight, when an indefinable "edge" descended on the city, and was dead in a gutter somewhere.

At nine-thirty, he gave in. He got down on his knees and dug in his backpack for his phone. He didn't care about the consequences. His hand found the device in its hiding place at the bottom of the bag.

Just then, Tobias came through the tent flap with two take-out containers full of what smelled like enchiladas.

"Greetings, lover," he said. He wore a huge a grin. He offered one of the containers to Arthur.

Arthur let go of the phone at the bottom of the backpack and stood up. He stared at the container. He looked at Tobias.

"Didn't anyone ever tell you it's not nice to leave food hanging in mid-air?" Tobias said. He still smiled.

He was handsome and charming and exuded good temper, with eyes that flirted with Arthur and had gleam that reflected love, and Arthur fought to resist how emotionally and physically appealing he was. Irritation helped him stay focused.

"Seriously, Tobias? Are you kidding me, right now?" He heard Kelly in his own voice.

"Uh, yes and no. I was kidding, but you're not being very nice." He set the food down on their makeshift fold-up camping table, which was so small, the two containers each had one end precariously hanging over the table's edge.

"Do you have any idea how late it is?"

"No. I sold my watch three months ago, remember?"

The atmosphere became prickly with the gargantuan mistake Arthur was about to make. He felt it, but its electricity wasn't powerful enough to run a current through his panicked frustration and jolt him to his senses. Somewhere in his mind he thought he should have heeded Tobias's remark about his watch and heard the polite reminder Tobias tried to send about how one more thing had gone wrong for him and slowed down, but he barreled past logic and fell through the trap door on the other side.

"I'll tell you. It's nine-thirty. Where have you been?"

"Nowhere you need to know about until you check your tone."

"What?" Arthur was annoyed.

"I think it's pretty clear. Please don't talk to me like I'm your child."

"How about you not make a person worry for no reason?"

"What do you mean, no reason? Are you implying I'm out there wasting time? That I don't have the right to come and go as I see fit?"

Arthur's antenna went up, sending him a vague signal that trouble lay ahead, but, once again, he ignored the warning.

"I'm saying I can't believe I've been pacing this tent for over three hours, waiting for you to come home, and you stroll in with food like that didn't happen."

"How would I know what happens when I'm not here? And how else should I come home late on days I get home late?"

"How about you not come home late? How about you tell Michael you can't always traipse around town passing out nail clippers?"

"Okay, A, how do you know I was even with him, as though I have nothing else to do, and, B, what's wrong if I was? And you may not care about nail clippers, since you have a pair, but the people who need them do care."

Tobias's anger matched Arthur's, but his tone was reasonable and polite.

Arthur envied his comportment but took no lesson from it. He was disaster-bound.

"Because, A, it seems like I see him three times a week, *so*," he shrugged his shoulders in an overly dramatic way and turned his hands into scales he balanced one way, then the other, "I'm feeling like that's a good guess, and, B, you don't see what's wrong with that? When I'm out during the day and have nothing to go on when you're gone till all hours, even if, yes, I get it that people need that stuff?"

"All hours?" Tobias laughed incredulously. "Nine-thirty is all hours? Okay. I see what's really going on. You earn the money, so I have no rights. You're my father? Is that it? What's next? I ask for your permission to have friends? To have a life? To go outside?"

Arthur began to read the signals a little clearer.

"No. No, I'm not saying that," he said.

"You know I'm looking for a job. You don't need to throw up in my face that I don't work and you pay for everything I can't scrounge up. I get it."

"What? That's not what I meant, at all. I never said that, and how could you even think I'd think that?"

"Because of how you sound, right now."

Arthur took a deep breath. "No. All I meant is that I'm out all day. If I come home and you're not here, I have no idea what's going on."

"What do you think is going on? I'm outside living my life, tiny as it is."

"Your life is tiny? I'm sorry you feel that your life is tiny with me in it."

"My *outside* life is tiny. I didn't realize you wanted me to confine it to this stupid tent."

"Stupid? This is our home."

"And I'd like to have the same schedule you have, which is I'm outside of it for most of my day, if I choose."

"I get that. But I thought you were dead, or in jail."

"Because I was outside after dark? Please. Just say that you thought I was with Michael, and not in a good way."

"You're dead wrong." Arthur was offended and very hurt. He took another deep breath. "I'm not jealous of Michael like that. Okay, maybe I'm a little envious that he's known you longer, but I trust you."

Tobias exhaled a long breath. He looked terribly displeased, but Arthur was hurt, too. He wanted that tinge of ugliness that had crept into the conversation to go away.

"We fell in love fast," Arthur said, "but you know me well enough by now, literally better than anybody on earth, to know that I would never think you'd do that to me or *us*. I wouldn't *be* here if I could think that. If only you knew how much I wouldn't need to bother if that were in the realm of possibility. And I know I wouldn't be here if you thought *I'd* be capable of that."

"Okay, yes. You're right about that. No way I share a space this small with anybody I don't have a thousand percent faith in. And I know you trust me. I'm sorry. I'm sorry. And, sorry, too, for thinking you'd throw the money in my face. I know you wouldn't do that, even if maybe you have a right to."

Arthur shook his head. "Would you stop?" He took another deep breath and spoke slower. "None of this is what I meant to say."

"Then what?" Tobias still looked upset and put out.

"I only mentioned Michael because I think he leans on you too much when you're trying to achieve your own goals."

"And tonight, I was out doing that. If you had *asked* me when I came home instead of grilling me like I was a naughty teenager, you would have found that out. I know I'm an exponential loser, but I would still like *some* credit for knowing how to manage priorities in my life."

"*Please*, would you stop that? Please. You're not a loser, exponential, or otherwise. Far from it. I've learned…so much, about a lot." Arthur was flummoxed and starting to get a little scared. He couldn't make his point, and he wasn't getting through to Tobias on any front. He came close to telling the truth about it all to make Tobias see how much he wanted to be there, with Tobias, because he respected him and thought their relationship was worth the effort, and because, together, they meant everything to Arthur.

He knew it was hasty and total folly to confess, but even if he had wanted to take the leap and do it, he didn't get the chance.

"Then you'll understand," Tobias said. "I need to take a walk. I'm going to the Third Street tunnel, or Second Street."

"Seriously? You're going to the tunnels?" *At this hour?* "With the rats and the noise and one car-jump up the curb standing between you and disaster hitting your head and…without me? That's not necessary." He reached for one of the food containers. "I'm over it. I'll eat."

"Don't do me any favors. And I'm not hungry anymore. And it's not just about you and how you feel. Just pretend we live in a mansion and that I'm going to the other side of it for some solitude."

Arthur cringed inside at Tobias's use of the word "mansion". "The tunnels are a lot farther away than the other side of a…mansion," he said.

"Speaking from experience, and all," Tobias said. "The tunnels are it out here. And contrary to what you think, I can actually figure out how to be out at night."

"I don't think you can't be out at night. Tobias, please."

Tobias grabbed one of the sleeping bags, which was still rolled tightly.

"You're taking a sleeping bag? Aren't you coming home? You said you were taking a walk."

"To sit down somewhere and get my head together. It's cold out there. I don't actually own a jacket."

Shit. "Stay here. Please."

"I can't." Tobias headed for the front door flap. At the flap, he turned and said, "And this isn't a tantrum, or a tizzy fit. I just need some space." He left the tent.

Arthur stepped onto the sidewalk, too, the food container he had grabbed still in his hand. It was eerily quiet outside. The cold seemed to have frozen everything into place. The street was empty and the 101 below them carried light traffic. It looked to Arthur as though everyone who had a home of any kind was inside of it. It made watching Tobias walk away from theirs that much harder.

"You don't have to do this," he said. "It's not safe. Let me come with you." Arthur was sure the entire encampment heard them. He didn't care.

"What would be the point in that?" Tobias called over his shoulder. He continued down Spring Street, toward the tunnels.

∞

At five the next morning, Tobias returned to the tent. Arthur knew because he was awake, with the light faintly glowing.

He hadn't slept. He had wanted to walk to the tunnels and find Tobias, but he was afraid to leave their tent unguarded in the middle of the night, so he lay there and waited and hoped he hadn't created the situation he had dreaded in the first place. Every siren terrified him. Every distant cry was analyzed for whether he recognized the voice at the base of it.

All he had wanted was to hear the tent unzip and for Tobias to walk through their makeshift front door. When it happened, he felt immeasurable relief and gratitude.

He resolved to get it right that time. He had had more than seven hours to replay in his mind what a condescending boor he had been the night before, and he had obsessed throughout the early morning hours about making it right. Every minute that ticked by felt like an hour and as though Tobias moved exponentially farther away from Arthur.

Exponentially. Tobias's favorite word.

A small battery-operated space heater kept the tent warm. Tobias opened his sleeping bag, stripped down to this T-shirt and underwear, and climbed into the sack.

Arthur got up and unzipped both bags. Tobias lay exposed. He didn't seem to care what happened around him. He waited for Arthur to do what he wanted with the sleeping bags.

To Arthur, it was as though Tobias's thoughts were still outside, in the tunnels maybe, or comingled in his head with his anger, with no room for Arthur, or perhaps wherever he had been earlier in the evening, before their fight.

Someplace nice, Arthur figured. He detected a faint whiff of men's cologne coming from Tobias in the sleeping bag. He had smelled it earlier, during their argument. As he had lain, waiting for Tobias, and replayed their fight, he realized from his flashback images that Tobias had been dressed well. He noticed it again when Tobias had returned from the tunnels.

Cologne.

Nice clothes.

Good mood.

Food.

It ties together, but you don't know how.

He wondered what else he missed with his overreaction. Facial expressions, nuances of tone, hurt feelings.

He reached for the sleeping bag zippers, and his hand grazed Tobias's foot. He was alarmed. "Your feet are freezing," Arthur said.

"I didn't want my shoes to get scuffed in the tunnel. I took them off. And, it's a long story, but I wasn't in the sleeping bag. I guess my feet caught a chill."

Arthur began a slow massage of Tobias's left foot and then of his right foot. He kept at it for several minutes, until both feet were warm to the touch. Tobias didn't resist Arthur's hands on his feet.

Arthur zipped his bag to Tobias's. Once he had created one, big bag, he turned off the light and climbed in next to Tobias.

The morning light was on the horizon, and the tent was not completely dark. Arthur admired Tobias's quiet, sensual countenance just visible in the snug tent.

He lay on his left side, facing Tobias. Without hesitation, he put his right arm as far around him as possible and pulled him close.

Tobias didn't fight him. There was a small space between their faces, but their bodies were touching from chests to feet. Arthur gently worked to intertwine their knees and lower legs, and Tobias again gave no resistance. The cologne hovered pleasantly between them. Tobias had selected something expensive. Arthur wondered whether he had saved for a bottle he kept on reserve or had owned it long before they foreclosed on his condo and held onto it, hoping for his life to change enough to use it. Apparently, it had changed the day before, but Arthur had no idea in what way.

What he realized he *didn't* wonder was whether it had come from another man. He knew that couldn't be the case. He trusted Tobias. He drew strength from that faith and the way it made him feel—bolstered, loved—and began the awkward journey of explaining himself.

"I thought you were dead," he said. "Or in jail. I don't care if you're out at night, alone, with me, with Michael, with friends, whatever. But if I'm used to seeing you here, and we met because you saved me from a mugging and maybe kept me from going to jail, forgive me if I worry you may have been mugged to death or were locked up in County Jail. I'm sorry I was such an insulting oaf about it."

"Apology accepted. I'm sorry for storming off. I know you were worried. Once I got to the tunnel and calmed down, I realized that's what it was."

"How come you didn't come home?"

"I was tired." He closed his eyes. His scent and mien intoxicated Arthur. "I've been up for almost twenty-four hours." His speech slowed. The exhaustion combined with the warmth of the tent, the sleeping bags, and Arthur's body, and the ease of the tension between them seemed to have lulled him into an almost-sleep. If he weren't talking, Arthur would have thought he *was* asleep.

"I walked a lot yesterday. Had to go to the library twice. I came back here in between. Tidied up. Then to the showers. Then the bus stop." His speech crawled to a halt almost. He barely got his words out. He spoke clearly but in spurts, a sentence at a time with a pause to rest in between them.

"Three buses," he dragged on. "Job interview. Tense energy. I really wanted it. One of those afterschool tutoring places. Pays twenty-six an hour. Thirty hours a week. That's where the food came from." He fell asleep. Arthur shook him a little. He wanted to hear the rest of the story.

Tobias woke up. He had only been out for three or four seconds. He picked up where he had left off.

"They were having a reception for the parents, now that the school year's really going. Asked me to stay. Tons of leftovers. Anyway, by the time I got to the tunnel, I was exhausted. I couldn't find anywhere clean to put the sleeping bag, so I just sat down with it in my lap." He sighed, worn out by the longer sentences. "I'm lucky I don't have to be at work until next Tuesday." He drifted off again.

"Work next Tuesday?" Arthur shook him. "Tobias."

"Mm?"

"Work next Tuesday?"

"Yeah. I got the job." He opened his eyes but sounded drowsy. "Met a lot of the parents. Felt like old times." He woke up a little more. "They complained about theorems and sin and co-sin and the same things I heard when I taught. I have the late shift, as the newbie, but it should be fun. I'll get the after-marching-band-practice kids. They're always a hoot." He uttered a sleepy giggle. "A hoot. Get it?" His speech slurred. He was almost asleep again.

Arthur was ecstatic. "You got the job!" he whispered as loudly as he could. He shook Tobias again with the rush of excitement. "You got the job! You got the job! That's fantastic!"

Tobias opened his eyes, more awake after the gentle shaking and Arthur's exuberant reaction.

"And if you had just eaten your enchiladas, I could have told you that seven hours ago." He smiled and seemed to wake up for real.

Arthur hugged him hard and kissed him. "I'm so proud of you," he said softly. "I'm so happy for you. You're on your way." They kissed again. "Twenty-six an hour at thirty hours a week is thirty-one-twenty a month!"

"Okay, you're good at math. Just own it."

"Never mind that. And, I'm so sorry I ruined your good news. I gave away the food. I didn't want it to spoil."

"Don't worry, Babe. It's been a rough overnight for both of us. I'm glad someone was able to eat it."

"You called me 'Babe'. I love that. I love you. You know how much I love you, right?"

"I do. I love you, too."

"You know, there's an easy solution to this silliness."

"A second burner phone, so we can stay in touch like normal people? If I'm working, we can afford to use our minutes."

Arthur tried not to stiffen at the idea, especially since he had to admit he would prefer they be able to call each other. He'd still be able to keep calls to a minimum, the way a temp would have to, and they would both want their phones available for emergencies. With Tobias working, the likelihood that he would call Arthur during a meeting with a client or wonder why Arthur never answered and always waited until he could find the right time to call back decreased dramatically.

Ultimately, he agreed. "A second phone," he said. "Okay. This weekend?"

Tobias closed his eyes again, awake but sleepy-looking. "Okay," he said. "And I know how much you love e-mail," he said with a lazy giggle, since they both knew Arthur had professed that he hated the way e-communicating had replaced real conversation, "but tomorrow, let me have your job-hunting e-mail. I'll send you an e-mail from mine. I'd give it to you now, but it's complicated and nerdy, and I'm too tired. And I won't remember yours." He sighed a deep, sleepy sigh. "Tomorrow."

"Okay, tomorrow," Arthur said. That would work great for him. Tobias was exhausted. Later, he would fall into a deep sleep. Arthur would step away from the tent and open a generic e-mail account using the browser on his real phone and be ready with it when Tobias woke up.

Tobias stirred. With his eyes still closed, he stretched a sleepy, lazy arm over Arthur and stroked Arthur's back.

Arthur snuggled into the affection. He said softly, "I'm very much in love with you, Tobias. I need you."

Tobias opened his eyes. "I love you and need you, too. So much. I'm sorry you were worried. And glad."

"Glad? Wait a minute. Glad?"

"Yes, glad." He kissed Arthur. "This. What we have. I'm blown away by it. I sometimes think I've stepped into a false universe. It hasn't been long, but it's as if it had been. This is good. What we have is *good*. It's solid. It can last. I think it will last. It's hard for me to believe you're here, and so real, and so right. For me. And, I may be wrong, but I think I'm right for you."

"You're not wrong. I've waited a lifetime for you. Longer, even, because the wait made time drag. And it *is* right and solid. And real. I wish I could tell you why I haven't settled down until now."

"You can tell me. You can tell me anything, Babe."

That's almost true. How I wish it were simply true. We're almost there, Babe.

Babe.

"I know, but I'm not sure how to say it in a way that will make sense. When I was young, I was selfish and on a mission. By the time I matured, I was hard to get to know, for a lot of reasons. Life put me in a box, and no one would let me out." *Just tell him.* "Hell, I could have lived in that mansion you talked about, and I would have felt like I had nothing." That was as close as he could get.

Tobias stroked Arthur's face. "I get it. As a young teacher, I wasn't closeted, but I kept to myself. I didn't want to deal with what we deal with when we're teachers. Later, I was all about upward mobility, buying a house, going for tenure, which never happened, and wanting a light load for that. No strings, no*body*. Then, the downward journey started, and I was just trying to keep my head above water. I can't wait to tell you about the job, though. It felt great standing there, among the employed, belonging, being introduced as a staff member." He put his arm around Arthur again and drew light circles on his back. "The guy who interviewed me was totally sympathetic to my story. We got on well. I think I'm going to like it there."

"Ha! Yes! Tonight, it's you and me and dinner, no matter the cost. You can tell me about the job and how you found it and how you knocked 'em dead."

"And how the parents loved me. That's always key for a teacher." His chuckle said he was kidding about the bragging.

"Just stay away from the handsome dads, especially if you're gonna smell this good."

Tobias smiled. "You like that?"

"I like that. I'm glad you've never worn it before. I don't think I would have ever left this tent."

"Hmmm. I've been sitting on a secret weapon this whole time and didn't know it. I got it from a rep handing out samples in a swank hotel I stepped into one time to use the bathroom. It's been stashed, but I may have to dip into it a little more often."

"Tonight, with me. And not Tuesday, with those dads." He chuckled.

"What dads? No dads. For you, I only smell good for moms."

Arthur kissed him. "Just what I like to hear. Tonight, we celebrate in style."

Outside, Spring Street livened. A few heavy buses rumbled past, and the occasional horn honked.

"Have you been keeping secret money?" Tobias teased.

Arthur kept his tone natural. "Enough to have a good time. I've been waiting for this, even expecting it. I've had nothing but faith."

"I haven't. It's been so hard to get inspired by anything."

"I know, but you're not a loser. I hated hearing you say that. Even if you didn't get the job, you're not a loser. Like I said, I've learned a lot out here about how people, how we…end up on the edge. It can be for a lot of reasons, and not just financial ones. It hurts to hear you put yourself down when you're working to lift yourself up."

"I appreciate that you notice, and I can't lie. I wasn't as motivated until I met you. But I don't want you to think that's all this is about. Us, I mean, like I'm just so happy to have somebody here encouraging me that it doesn't matter who it is or that I only want to be with you for that. That's not it. I've been alone a long time, in a house, in a car, in a tent. I could have kept doing that. But you came along and changed everything. I want to be your boyfriend because I love you."

Arthur kissed him deeply. *God, I love you.*

"I'm glad I have you," Tobias said, "*you*, and that we're going through this weird trip together. When they told me I had the job, all I thought was that we can have more and not that I needed you less. Please know that. And, I don't know…."

"Go ahead and say it, whatever it is." He kissed Tobias. "You can tell me anything, too." *Anything, Babe. Anything.*

"Well, the day we make it out of this tent will be cause for…."

"Wait. I take it back. Don't say it. Don't jinx it. I know what you were going to say," Arthur said.

"They say you have to imagine where you want to be to get there." Tobias said.

I know. I tell my clients that, but I don't want to jinx this, Babe.

Early, autumn sunlight broke through, densely, and not in rays, and made Tobias appear peaceful and angelically innocent and righteous and right. Arthur's heart swelled to capacity. He thought it would burst through his chest. His mind danced and skipped with a light dizziness that came from feeling tremendous love, for he really did know what Tobias wanted to say.

"And is that where you want to be?" Arthur said. He wouldn't risk saying more and cursing them.

"Yes. And why shouldn't we say it?" Tobias kissed Arthur as punctuation to the question.

"Because…Babe…I'm scared that if either one of us says… okay, I'll say it, 'marriage,' what we have will go poof." Arthur kissed Tobias back, and lingered a little longer, as subconscious reassurance that he hadn't jinxed them, that they were still there, together.

"You just said it, and we didn't go anywhere. And, wow, you *did* know what I was thinking."

"Have you really imagined it? Because I know I have," Arthur said.

"I've imagined it more than you know. I'm crazy about you, Babe. I want to be with you, always."

Arthur fell from the dizzying heights of love in a spectacular swoon.

They French kissed for a long while and hugged each other tighter and rocked a little together, as a cradling comfort, their knees and legs still intertwined.

"Does it scare you?" Arthur finally said. "I mean, are we moving too fast?"

"No," Tobias said. "It took us far too long to find each other and get here. We're catching up to ourselves, making up for lost time. Does it scare you?"

"Not one bit. It feels right."

They kissed deeply.

"Don't look now," Arthur said, "but I think we just got engaged. That is, if you'll have me."

"Yes, I'll have you, Arthur Dewynter. I'll have you."

"He said, 'yes.' "

"And he said, 'yes.' "

They made love, that half-sleepy, half-dizzy, euphoric, otherworldly love, and said many more times that they were sorry for the earlier strife and that they loved each other and couldn't wait for the day their lives settled enough for them to get married. They fell asleep nuzzled closer than usual.

At seven o'clock, Arthur's eyes popped open as more deliberate sunshine found its way into the tent. He woke Tobias and reminded him that he, Arthur, had to work that day.

Tobias couldn't force his eyes open. "Did you get any sleep?" he said. He slurred his speech.

"Enough to get by," Arthur said. He would take a little extra time in Beverly Hills and catch a few hours' sleep there, before going into the office.

"Mm." Tobias nodded off and woke himself again but kept his eyes closed. "Let's do the e-mail swap tonight," he said.

"Okay." That worked better for Arthur. Kelly could help him come up with a good e-mail address, one that sounded like it fit the Arthur Tobias knew.

"Have a good day, future hubby," Tobias said. As soon as he finished the sentence, he fell asleep.

A little later, Arthur packed his backpack with what he needed if he were really going to the mission for a shower, got dressed, and kissed Tobias's sleeping mouth goodbye. Tobias's lips formed no response and were soft and warm and sexy. Arthur was tantalized and tempted to stay home and make love to his fiancé all day. He had too many meetings in the afternoon, though, so he stole a few more kisses and stepped outside.

The three bicycle cops who usually patrolled their section of Spring Street were joined by two others. It looked a little strange to see five police officers convened on the corner on bicycles, but the temperature was low, and Arthur figured they formed a small kaffeeklatsch until the day warmed a little.

He had no idea that a bomb was about to blow up his life and that it was those police officers who had brought with them the detonator.

12

LOST

ARTHUR SWUNG THROUGH BEVERLY HILLS after work and ditched his suit and car. Normally, he would have gone through his mail and quickly ordered an Uber to head downtown. He barely cared about his house other than that it held some meaningful personal possessions. He paid his staff, who mostly just kept up the place—a full-time job for a small group of people—but he, himself, caused them very little work.

Except for the nap he had taken earlier that morning, he hadn't slept in his own bed in four months. He hadn't turned on the television, not even for the news as he got ready for work the mornings he was there. He hadn't eaten one meal in that house or dirtied one dish there in months. He hadn't given catered parties for a long list of guests who were more like strangers than friends or popped popcorn for a movie in his home theater or required even that the billiard balls on his pool table be racked up. He hadn't swum in the pool and used the overlarge spa towels or run the water in the faucet on the second sink in his bathroom. His home was in the tent, with Tobias.

That evening, though, since he and Tobias planned to celebrate Tobias's new job, he cheated a little on his routine and took another shower.

He grabbed some cash from his safe. He thought the most he could get away with having claimed he had stashed away over the four months was one hundred and twenty-five dollars. That would buy them a very nice dinner, compared to what they were used to, and a glass of wine, each, at several mid-range establishments downtown. Just in case, he took ten twenty-dollar bills and Ubered downtown.

As usual, the driver dropped him a few blocks away from the encampment, on the Chinatown side, which was in the opposite direction of Skid Row and the library and minimized the chances that Tobias would see him exit the car.

A staggering blow awaited him at the cut-through that led from Cesar Chavez onto Spring Street. It was as though he had been struck dead.

Their tent was gone.

Their neighbors were gone.

Tobias was gone.

The City had razed the encampment. Every tent had vanished. A chain-link barricade ran down the middle of the sidewalk where their tent had been just that morning. It barred all foot traffic.

Arthur spotted a cop mounting his bicycle. He broke into a sprint. "Excuse me! Excuse me!"

The officer rode away.

Arthur slowed to a stop. He turned himself about, in a circle, scanning everywhere with panic as he worked his way around the three hundred and sixty degrees and didn't see Tobias. Out of nowhere, he screamed, "Tobias!" A few people stared at him, but Tobias never appeared.

"Can I help you?" It was a bystander. He carried a leather man-purse across his shoulder and held his phone like a tape recorder as though he talked into the end of it. He looked semi-official.

Arthur ran to him. "Yes. I'm trying to find someone who had a tent here. There were tents here. What happened?"

"Raid. They cleared everyone out."

"I can see that. Why? Without warning?" Arthur almost reached out and shook the man for answers.

"That's why I'm here. I work down the street at the Times. Got word there was a ruckus around nine-thirty this morning. I caught the tail end of it, but, really, it was over almost before it began, from what I've gathered from witnesses. Lots of screaming in the streets about 'this is effed up' and you can imagine what else. More profanity than I can print."

Arthur was dumbfounded. *Where is Tobias?*

"Next thing," the reporter said, "they rolled out dumpsters. Told people to toss what they couldn't carry. Warned 'em about not setting up in the park. Truck pulled up with the fencing, and that was the end of it. I was gonna file a quick story, but there's more here. The City has *not* used money voters dedicated for homelessness. Stuck around till now to gather reactions, including from the guys who laid the fence, to see how they felt about their role in this. You're not the first person I've talked to today who's shaken. Can I get your name and ask how this affects you?"

Arthur couldn't think about the question. He thought of only one thing. "Was anyone arrested?"

"A few who lipped off and got edgy and a little physical, yeah. They got carted away and their stuff was tossed."

Oh, no.

"Did you see the man who had the big tent that would have been right there?" Arthur pointed to the spot where their tent had been. "Tobias Pelletier?"

"The tents were down by the time I got here, and, again, most people were gone. Even my cell phone footage is of people describing what they saw. I didn't get to film any of the initial raid and roundup, first-hand. Hard to say who in the crowd belonged where. The name doesn't ring a bell, though." He pulled out a tiny notepad. "Even though I do most of my reporting into the recorder on this," he held up his cell phone, "for clear records, I write down the names of everyone I talked to." He thumbed through the small pages.

"Did you talk to him?" Arthur's tone bordered on belligerent. He had asked a question, but it sounded more like a directive, as though he expected the man to answer the question simply because he had asked it in a tone that said he wanted an answer.

"Hang on, sir. I'm looking." He searched through more pages. "Pelletier…Pelletier…"

"I'm sorry. I didn't mean to be rude."

The man smiled and continued to look for Tobias's name. "It's okay. I understand. Mm. I don't see the name. I didn't talk to him." He looked up from the notepad. "Sorry. He's not here." His expression was sympathetic. "If you can tell me your—"

"Thanks," Arthur said. "Sorry, again." He walked away.

"Can I get your name?"

"Arthur…."

"What's your last name?" the man called after him.

Arthur never answered. He walked in a daze to the place where his and Tobias's tent had been. He stood on the spot and hoped to gain understanding. He leaned against the chain-link fence.

Then something from the day the police evicted JoJo came back to him. One of the officers had said *You can't expect to live here forever.* That was what he had tried to remember as they walked to Melinda's shelter with JoJo's carts. At the time, Arthur had mentally answered the threat of harassment and displacement with a "not Tobias and me; we have somewhere to go" and dismissed the idea that he and Tobias could be intimidated the way JoJo had been. It didn't apply to him, so he disregarded wholesale anything about being moved out. It never occurred to him, not consciously, that it could happen while he was away in Century City or Beverly Hills, when all the power he ever had would be meaningless.

And, yet, it *had* nagged him, almost from the minute he and JoJo walked away with JoJo's carts. He *did* know there was a threat.

And just the night before, he had known it a little more when he hadn't been able to reach Tobias and had no way to figure out where he was. But he had focused on Tobias's safety—and on a petty scolding of Tobias's so-called misbehavior—and failed to see that waiting even a day to exchange contact information could cost them everything. *We're well-intentioned and not really from here, so we'll be fine,* he had thought, even as he had learned over the months that no one was "really from there". Homelessness was unnatural. Nobody belonged in it.

He was furious with himself. He walked around like a seasoned downtown dweller, but years of privilege were hard to shake. It never struck him that he wouldn't be able to do what he wanted for as long as he wanted and "revert back" if he and Tobias ever faced the trouble JoJo had.

The raid that happened to them that day could have happened any day. Every day that he went to work, he thoroughly separated himself from Tobias. Anything that immobilized either one of them—a car accident, a more brutal mugging, a trip-and-fall with a brain injury, an arrest, appendicitis—could have produced an insurmountable separation if there was also just the slightest tectonic shift in the other person's existence, so that it would be impossible to get word back to him.

Yet, Arthur had headed to Century City every day with not a care about those outcomes—they didn't even occur to him—because the aura surrounding his life had given him so much cover, he couldn't fathom an instance when that aura wouldn't be there for him, and not because he bowed to its power and talked with it and worked with it and shaped it and brokered a deal with it that guaranteed it would show up for him and have his back, but because subconsciously his aura seemed more special, more organized, better funded, more respected, automatic, *subservient*, with no massaging needed. Things would have to work out, were destined and ordained to go his way, to submit to his stature and status, he assumed. He didn't even think he'd have to demand it. It was far more innocent. He simply thought it would all work out because "it" was equipped for that result since it stemmed from him, would be working out *for him*, someone who was special and unique and separate from the real targets of calamity—everyone out there but him. And Tobias.

He felt stupid in his smugness, hoisted on his own petard of ignorance caused by an ingrained sense of exclusivity that was caused by yet another sense, one of entitlement that he thought carved out a separate world for him, and by extension, Tobias.

The paradox wherein he lived, in which his truest self existed in his life with Tobias while his routines consisted of elitist access to everywhere, had tricked him. His efforts to appreciate one carrying the other had fooled him into thinking he understood his new world and had become an expert in it such that he couldn't be tripped up by misconceptions. He didn't think he misconceived anything. He thought he saw it all correctly, even righteously, and Fate wouldn't bother the righteous, he figured.

He had been wrong. And he had been a hypocrite, shunning a world he expected to rely on if pressed, and he had tripped up Tobias in the bargain.

He feared he would pay dearly for his mistakes, with the permanent loss of Tobias, who might have eventually become furious with Arthur once he found out that the latest upheaval could have been avoided by a grain of honesty from Arthur that would have freed them from the tent long before. Tobias lost everything a third time, and if Arthur had come clean a day earlier, Tobias could have been spared that misery.

And all those outcomes and sad endings to their story presumed Arthur could locate Tobias.

He leaned harder on the fence. His skin turned hot and prickly everywhere as immense panic settled in.

He drew quick, accurate conclusions: Tobias may have struggled in his recent life, but craftiness didn't fail him. Since high school and his break with his family, he had looked for innovative ways to survive, and most of them—college, his move to L.A., finding a reliable profession—had worked. He wouldn't give up, toss the tent, and sit in the park and wait for Arthur. He would try to keep everything, and barring that, to keep a little less, then a little less, and still a little less, until he had pared it down to what he could manage. He would scramble to install himself somewhere else as quickly as possible and get back to Spring Street to meet Arthur.

Somewhere along the way, that had gone awry. It had to have. If Tobias had succeeded, he would have met Arthur at six o'clock.

On the one hand, he couldn't get far very fast, but on the other, he had had several hours, and there were dozens of encampments throughout downtown. He could be anywhere, including on his way back there to meet Arthur.

That was, unless he landed somewhere he couldn't easily leave if he wanted to stake a semi-permanent claim, which he would have tried to do, with a new job and the welfare of a fiancé with a tenuous temp job to consider. As he saw it, *he* was the one who worked steady. He may have had to squat for several days to establish his territory. Arthur could wait on Spring Street, but there was no guarantee Tobias would be back that night or at any predictable time.

Autumn darkness hovered. Arthur cursed aloud as he realized for dozenth time they had planned to exchange e-mails that evening and buy a second burner phone that weekend, and after four months of living together in perfect synch, their plan was scheduled for a time that was nine hours too late.

Arthur tried to argue, to a Fate he felt was asking him to step up and serve penance for his arrogance, that it was because none of it had mattered. They had no cause to e-mail each other. They were together every free moment, on Arthur's faux days off and in every free moment besides that. They met at the tent around six o'clock every evening and remained together until they woke up the next morning. With Arthur's supposed unpredictable work assignments where Internet access for the temp wasn't guaranteed, and Tobias's spotty hours at the library, by the time they saw each other's e-mails, it might have been days after they had seen each other in person. The idea that either would e-mail a person who stood next to him or feel the need to share something in writing when they would see each other a few hours later and talk about it in person was preposterous. Tobias had never even asked Arthur for his e-mail address, especially not after Arthur had professed a dislike for e-mail communication with loved ones. The subject simply never came up.

And when they didn't venture out to explore a free festival or get food from the gas station or relax in the park, they hung out in the tent, where no communication devices were needed. It was their home. It was where they enjoyed the breeze and slept late on weekends and read books from the library or the Sunday Times they splurged on and played chess on a tiny set Michael had gifted them and chatted in the dark, with freeway noise and sounds from around the enclave adding flavor, and made love until they were so tired, they slept deep, contented sleep. Other than the previous night, when Tobias had gone to the tunnels, they had spent many, many days, every evening, and every overnight together for four months.

And they weren't the only ones in their community to use little or no electronics. No one in the encampment had a cell phone. Phones, laptops, MP3 players, and the like weren't part of the culture of their small society. They were luxuries that no one would spend money on, when that same amount could buy food and other necessities. Arthur and Tobias had fallen right in with that thinking. Tent life made them like someone's married grandparents. They related only in person and were entertained by what they could sense in real life.

Still, Arthur leaned harder on the fence and thought, in the darkness of night that had fully arrived without his noticing the transition, about how he could use the Internet to solve the problem, and he hit the same dead end. Neither of them used any form of social media. Google would turn up nothing on either of them, other than those sites that listed people's addresses based on mortgages and maybe a blog comment or an old roster from a local sports league, but Tobias's last known address no longer belonged to him, the other references would be obsolete since Tobias had disengaged from his former life, and Arthur had had his name stripped from the Internet. Even if he found a link to Tobias's family's address in Florida, the chances that Tobias would contact people he shunned almost twenty years earlier, thinking that Arthur would use them, of all people, to find Tobias were nil. It was much farther in the distance than a longshot, and the same was true of Arthur's folks in Michigan.

Meanwhile, Arthur had no steady work address as far as Tobias knew. Tobias had no idea where Arthur was each day or how to find him. It purportedly changed so often, Tobias had officially decided he didn't care about the specifics. He asked, generally, what Arthur "did that day," but he hadn't cared about whether it was for an accounting firm or a law office or a graphic design firm. It wasn't construction, so it was exactly what it sounded like—a temporary job not worth emotionally investing in.

Even more frustrating for Arthur was that he had been planning to find out at dinner that night which one of the hundreds of tutoring companies in Los Angeles and its vast environs had hired Tobias. All Arthur knew was it took three buses to get there. It could have been three long rides, two long rides and a short one, two short rides and a long one, or three short rides. That Tobias had returned late the night he was hired provided no answers since there had been a party after the interview. Arthur had no idea how much of the time up to nine-thirty was party time and how much was bus time. He would not be able to narrow down, using the three bus rides, where in the city Tobias worked.

Those thoughts caused Arthur to think more broadly about Tobias's job and panic even more. Would Tobias lose his job? Or would he go there every day and possibly have no home because he wouldn't have time to plant his tent somewhere? Would his new employer do to him what his last one had done and fire him for living disorganized?

Would he resort to the same measures he had before and stay close to his new job and leave downtown, if his job was not near downtown? Or would he bounce from shelter to shelter downtown for the sake of having a place to shower and take the bus to work? Arthur prayed that since he was much more familiar with downtown that time around, he wouldn't feel the need to do anything drastic or leave the area for good.

Arthur, you have fourteen fucking bedrooms, and the man you love is wandering around downtown Los Angeles with a tent.

Arthur was desperate.

He could stake out the places they showered, but if Tobias was stuck with the tent, he may not head to the showers until he had to go to work. He had said he would start his new job the following Tuesday, but on that first day of work, Arthur had no idea whether the upheaval would let Tobias get to the showers, and if it did, which one. He had probably been hoping to map out a game plan that factored in Arthur, and after what happened, Arthur wouldn't be there.

Arthur lost his composure. He broke down with frustration and fear. He clung to the chain link fence and tried to gather himself. He realized they didn't even have photographs of each other because Arthur didn't use a phone with a camera, and Tobias had no phone, period.

Tobias would have been skittish about photographs, anyway. He felt that homelessness had beaten him up. One of the things he looked most forward to about finally getting off the street was seeing some of the stress leave his own face. Other than Arthur sometimes wishing he had a picture of Tobias to show Kelly, it would never occur to either of them to arrange to take a picture of themselves or each other. They were together all the time. And if Arthur had sneaked a photo on his real phone while Tobias was asleep, it would have resulted in a picture too intimate to show Kelly, so he never took a photo like that, but he wished he had done it for himself. He had never wanted to risk having the phone out, though, so his mind didn't go there.

Fucking lies. They've ruined you, Arthur.

Arthur was close to tears. The back of his throat was tight with the pain of holding them in. He thought and thought and thought and came up empty. He and Tobias had no way to find each other. As far as one was concerned, the other was lost, maybe forever.

∞ 13 ∞

WANDERING

TOBIAS COULDN'T TAKE ONE MORE syllable of bad news. He had already ruined his life and Arthur's. He didn't need to be told, as the policeman had just told him, that if he pitched his tent where he stood, he'd be arrested.

It had started that morning with a loud shout through the tent by police officers. He had been in the middle of that deep, exhausted slumber that was a couple of hours old and that left one feeling as though one had been hit over the head with a sledgehammer if awakened before it came to a natural end.

They gave him sixty minutes to vacate the sidewalk or lose his belongings. He was staggered.

It was then that he knew his life was over. He moved to turn to Arthur, to reach out in some way, for guidance and fellowship, and realized he wasn't just alone in the tent. It was far worse. Tobias had no way to find Arthur, no way to be found by him.

For Tobias, the math was easy. There were multiple ways human beings stayed in touch, and he and Arthur had only practiced one of them: in person, offline. Every other means of communication was foreclosed to them somewhat by odd choice but mostly by how they lived.

In the early stages of their relationship, they had given each other space and didn't push for other ways to bother one another, with e-mails and texts and phone calls in places they shouldn't be talking, like at a temp job or in the library, if Tobias had had a phone. His disjointed life was one of the reasons he didn't bother with one.

That system had made it easy for them to fall into a pattern of using togetherness to stay in touch. They spent almost every hour Arthur was not at work with each other. Occasionally, they split their errands, but it was always with a casual, "Gonna hit the store and drop off a library book. See you in a couple of hours," which worked fine.

Homelessness was complicated, logistically, but their lives together were simple. There was between them predictability and even reliability and patterns they could count on, day in and out. They were happy to let their relationship flow and add layers and offshoots as they naturally came about, as their lives blossomed and required them.

And the night before the raid, they had reached the point of needing to add an element to their relationship. They needed each other's contact information. If Tobias hadn't left for the tunnels, at the end of his argument with Arthur, they would have come to the same conclusions they did when he returned from the tunnels and exchanged information then. Tobias probably would have jotted down Arthur's phone number, too. They had been so close to being just eight seconds away from each other. If Tobias hadn't been impulsive and stormed out, they wouldn't be lost to one another.

But they *were* lost to one another. It meant they would either run into each other and recover their life together, or they would never see each other again.

With the police rousting him that morning, he had aimed for the first scenario, for naturally finding Arthur at six o'clock that evening where their tent had been and continuing life with him, and he hoped to orchestrate its eventuality with quick and clever action.

Until six-o'clock, they were technically still connected. No matter how chaotic their days, they had a standing date every evening on Spring Street. He tried with everything in him, with all his wits, to make that meeting.

He had failed. And he had failed Arthur and left him without anywhere to sleep that night and maybe many nights. Arthur earned money but wouldn't want to waste any of it on a flop motel, and he wouldn't buy a new tent in the short run. He was stranded between the rock of spending money he didn't have and the hard ground he'd have to sleep on without a sleeping bag or air mattress or tent over his head.

Tobias felt like even more of a fool and, somewhere in the back of his mind, embarrassed in front of Arthur that he had blundered so badly and left him without cover. He had thought he could fold up the tent and hoist it on his back and carry their belongings, in a duffel bag in one hand and in a shoulder bag in the other, to the park, where he would wait for Arthur, but he learned that the park was in the arrest zone, and two people had more things than one, more clothes, more mementos of places they had been together, more scavenged items each thought the other might need, more books. Their lives were heavy.

The books turned out to be the wickedest joke, for Tobias had checked them out at the library, and they had been his and Arthur's savior, the guardian of their sanity, and yet, if he threw them away and didn't return them, he would rack up a large and ever-growing library fine and end up banned from borrowing more books until he paid it. He would have bad credit with the last bastion of decency in his two-year hellhole, the one place that expected nothing for its charity of loaning books and gave peace of mind to those who had nothing left. He had found his job and what he thought was salvation because of the library. He held onto every book.

Thus, with bitter remorse, he tossed into a dumpster his entire makeshift kitchen—the camping table, chairs, dishes, and lamp—as well as every item not essential for safety or survival, except for one memento from his first date with Arthur, and packed in the duffel bag the books, as many clothes as would fit, the deflated mattresses and pillows, the floor heater, and the rat-repellent devices.

He wanted to punch the officer who stood by and weighed in and agreed with choices for what to abandon and repeated at nauseating intervals, "Yep," and, "Mm-mm. That's right. Into the dumpster. Let's go! Yep. That can't stay here, sir." And, to those who lingered with an item, debating what to do with it, some of them crying, others holding their tempers to avoid arrest, "Toss it in. Less to carry. Let's go!" And, pointing, "You'll need to get that," then pointing more fiercely, "that, right there, that. Yes," like parking lot attendants who stood in the spot a person aimed for and guided them to it, more in the way than a help and forcing the driver to maneuver to avoid hitting the attendant, as though pulling into a parking space were some difficult, two-person feat. Tobias needed no instructions for how to *throw away things.*

As he watched friends get arrested and caught sight of neighbors with small pets they had no way to transport along with their belongings standing on the sidewalk looking lost and heard loud, foul cries of outrage that lifted up into the air and over the freeway to nowhere, the outer corners of his eyes had burned with salty tears as his world became miniscule, no larger than the spot on which he stood. He was back in the school parking lot, alone against the repo man who drove away with his Honda, except he lost something far more valuable. He lost Arthur.

He had hoped Michael had somehow gotten word of the raid and would arrive and help him and even volunteer to wait for Arthur to come home and give him a message about when and where they could meet after Tobias got settled, but Michael had been occupied somewhere else in the city, and Tobias never saw him.

He realized that while what happened to him was colossal, to the rest of the world, the raid concerned thirty people on a short block in a megalopolis, people no one got in touch with, people no one would miss.

He tossed into a dumpster the last of the items he couldn't keep and slipped his bag over his shoulder, hooked the sleeping bags onto either side of the folded tent, hoisted the tent by its straps onto his back, picked up the duffel bag, and walked away from Spring Street.

That was when the second wave of destruction had arrived.

Sleep deprivation, fear, urgency, and morning hunger caused him to miscalculate how long it would take to find a place to pitch his tent. He walked miles in different directions, but everywhere, he encountered disqualifiers that only made themselves known once he considered settling in a place. A nearby business who called the police or an unwelcoming encampment or a space too desolate to be secure thwarted him at every turn.

He lost so much time coming up empty on a new place to set up that even if he left everything right where he stood and walked away from it and went back to Spring Street, he would be too late. He had waited too long. Arthur would have already arrived and seen that he was gone and begun his own search, angry the whole time with Tobias for leaving and not thinking and facing within a few hours the mean reality, created by Tobias, that he would have to scurry for a safe place to sleep.

Desperate at that thought, Tobias forgot what he had just realized about the impossibility of meeting Arthur and told the cop who had said he couldn't pitch his tent, or he would be arrested, that he no longer cared about the tent. He would capitulate and not pitch it. He would drop everything where he stood and find Arthur. The officer threatened to arrest him if he didn't vacate the area with his possessions. Pitched or not, the tent had to go with Tobias.

Tobias considered letting himself be arrested. He remembered how worried Arthur had been that he had landed in jail the night before. He thought jail might be the first place Arthur would check. But it dawned on him that if he were arrested, Arthur would have to come up with bail money, which would be impossible. And, aside from not wanting to go to jail, he'd lose his job, which would be disastrous. He also knew that two of them searching was better than one. Tobias would take his chances on the street and avoid arrest.

It was after six and dark. He walked to the nearest bus stop and sat down and fought tears. The magnitude of his blunder crashed down on him. He wondered why he hadn't simply left Spring Street for the day, waited out the police, and returned with his bundles to meet Arthur, or why he hadn't thrown everything but his shoulder bag away, found a bench in the park like any other member of the community, and, by that evening, hunkered down with Arthur and their two jobs as they figured out a plan to rebuild.

He knew the answer.

More than two years of having to hustle to avoid the next bad moment as he ran from the last bad one meant he acted more than he waited. If he remained stationary, he'd be caught, trapped, lose more, fail worse.

The endless cycle of privation caused him to bolt, to pivot, if a threat loomed. His car had saved him from his lost house. His last good money had saved him with a comfortable tent from his lost car. In the heat of what had become the third hard foreclosure in his life in less than the same numbers of years, he assumed a new place to settle would save him from the Spring Street eviction. He rushed to find it, to get to his solution and past the problem, and he had blundered in his estimations.

He sat at the bus stop and gave into the tears and cried because he had been wrong at every turn. Nothing he adjudged to have been able to rescue him had helped. His system of using one thing to compensate for the other had been a disaster that day as much as it had always been. Overdrafts at the bank hadn't gotten him back on his feet. Using the money for one bill to pay another hadn't kept him in his house. Living in a car hadn't kept the rain off his head in any permanent way.

Until he met Arthur, he had been failing at life because of his approach to crises and unable to see it. He had landed on his feet just enough times—a full ride at college, teaching jobs, the condo he bought—to cloud his vision. He had thought life with Arthur had helped clear away the fog, but he knew, sitting at that filthy bus stop with everything he owned in the world, that he had many lessons to learn.

The hardest for Tobias to take was how that returned insistence on doing things a certain way had caused him to disregard Arthur's presence in his life during the scramble. They loved each other and were caring and loving partners. It was why they wanted to marry each other, but in crisis, Tobias forgot, not because he didn't care enough to remember but because that was how his mind worked in his post-trauma existence and in crises, in general. He had reverted to his typical chaos instead of leaning on the man he loved and getting through whatever the next phase would have looked like if he had pitched everything into the dumpsters and waited for Arthur. In the process, he had left Arthur unprotected.

He felt guilt and shame, and he wanted to see Arthur more than anything, to apologize for fouling up their lives and losing faith and endangering Arthur's well-being and possibly causing them to be separated forever.

He stood up and strapped the tent onto his back, gathered his bags, and left the bus stop.

He walked nowhere.

He cried the whole way.

∞ 14 ∞

MILES TO GO BEFORE I WEEP

ARTHUR SEARCHED FOR TOBIAS EVERY moment he was awake. The police had refused to file a missing-persons report on one adult who had lost touch with another, so Arthur walked the streets himself, looking for Tobias.

He went to every mission and shelter where they showered. He scoured the library, the park, Skid Row. He slept nights on the last street he searched before he dropped. He regularly went back to Spring Street, in vain. Every note he had tied to the fence that stood where their tent was had been snatched down, by police or meddling pedestrians. He thought about finding Tobias through Michael, but Arthur wasn't sure where Michael worked or what his volunteer route was. Michael was just another person Arthur couldn't find.

Arthur surmised that Tobias was out there looking for him too and that they chased each other in a big circle around the city. Their behaviors were unguaranteed, formed no patterns. It was impossible to leave word somewhere and be sure the other would ever again arrive at that place to retrieve it or that the people they left word with would know who the other one was to pass along the message.

Desperation gave Arthur a strange idea. He hired an investigator to plaster around the city flyers with a message that said TOBIAS, I'LL BE AT THE OLD LOCATION EVERY DAY AT 10:00 A.M. — ARTHUR. The "old location" had been code for their space on Spring Street. Arthur's investigator had told him that every crazy person in the city would call a phone number, if listed, or show up at the location, if stated, so Arthur had been forced to be cryptic. The problem was, it had taken Arthur two days to come up with the idea, with an additional day needed to prepare and one more day needed to post the flyers.

His investigator warned him that people had a penchant for tearing down or defacing flyers, which Arthur already knew. The man predicted that people at indoor locations would throw away the flyers if they rested on counters or library tables. And Arthur knew that there was a strong likelihood Tobias would be immobile in those initial days as he tried to get stationed, which meant he wouldn't see the flyers, or that he would be steps ahead of or behind the persons posting the flyers, as they began to fan out.

In his overall prognosis, the investigator had been dour. He had said that in his experience, the longer people were separated, the harder it became for them to find each other. If Tobias stayed at one job long enough, they could eventually get a hit on his Social Security number, but that required that Tobias not quit or be fired from his new job. In a moment of weird cognitive dissonance, Arthur wanted to talk to Tobias to tell him, "Don't quit your job. I'll be able to find you that way," not thinking that if they could have that conversation, they wouldn't need that conversation.

The investigator recommended that Arthur stick to his local routines and pray that Tobias didn't do something radical like leave town to find a way to survive.

After four days of searching, Arthur was beside himself. He became intoxicated with sleeplessness and fear. It made him histrionic.

On the night of the separation, he had instructed Nathan Cresswell to hire a criminal law Dream Team of lawyers for Tobias. One of the members of the team confirmed that Tobias was not in Los Angeles County Jail's system and that he had not been arrested. By day four, Arthur then dramatically assumed Tobias was either dead or injured. He wondered if he had missed some earlier unspoken message between them that would tell him where Tobias was.

In a moment of awful déjà vu, he checked into the Biltmore, to be closer to the search, even though he rarely used the room. He knew that if he was going to find Tobias, it would be on the streets.

Kelly had been great through it all. She offered to drive Arthur up and down streets, in search of the tent. He had thanked her, full of emotion and gratitude, and told her he needed her in the office. He reminded her that he was sober and not missing, as he had been the week he was mugged. He could dash back to the Biltmore if he needed a quiet place to take client calls, and he was otherwise reachable by phone if she needed him.

He directed his investigator to find the name of the last place Tobias had taught, a school that had obviously removed Tobias from its online presence since Arthur couldn't find the information anywhere. He hoped the investigator could obtain a yearbook with a photo of Tobias in it. He desperately wanted a photo of Tobias that wasn't a mugshot-looking driver's license photo, and finding an old yearbook was the only way he could think of to get one.

It was ten o'clock. He waited on Spring Street. Tobias never showed.

∞

The lone thing that kept Tobias from giving up his search for Arthur was Arthur. If it had been a quest for anything else—money or the key to life—he would have capitulated to failure in the search and moved on to other pursuits. With finding Arthur at stake, and with Arthur exposed, he intended to search forever.

His feet were numb below the ankles from walking dozens of downtown blocks again and again and again. His eyes ached with scanning every human being on the streets to be sure he didn't miss Arthur. His head ached from sleeplessness and living in a state of constant hyper-alertness. His heart ached from the dreaded truth that lurked around every corner where Arthur wasn't waiting. After four days of searching every mission, tent, shelter, diner, alley, tunnel, and grassy patch, and sometimes just standing on the corner of a street with a row of gathered people and makeshift structures and tents and yelling Arthur's name, he reached a crossroads.

The following day, he was due to start his new job. If he hoped to show up as expected, he would have to halt his search right then.

He couldn't imagine taking a bus to a Los Angeles suburb to unlock theorems for high school sophomores while his life caved in so completely. The law of averages required that he and Arthur keep searching for each other if they were to find each other. Taking himself out of the equation meant the problem literally could not be solved. He hadn't even taken a bus to West Hollywood, where Michael's office was, to ask Michael to tell Arthur where he could find Tobias if Michael ran into Arthur. He didn't want to risk removing his face from the crowds of downtown and ruining any chance Arthur had of spotting him.

Not going to work, however, also made no sense. Arthur would tell him he was crazy for giving up the one job he wanted and had managed to land. Arthur thought always in terms of possibilities and diversification and encouraged a multilateral approach to everything. Where Tobias found that one needed to fill in X, in his case, finding Arthur, if one wanted to solve problems, Arthur believed having a hand in everywhere was bound to bear fruit somewhere. He loved the unknown of the Y factor. He would tell Tobias to go to work and look for Arthur in the off periods.

Tobias listened to phantom Arthur. Desperation and exposure were what had put him in the position he was in in the first place. He dreaded landing there again. He was determined to repudiate a lifelong behavior and did not, for once in his life, assume the most immediate course of action would save him just because it looked different from the problem.

He hadn't found a patch of land where he could pitch his tent that was as well-situated and well-suited as his space on Spring Street, but he hadn't thrown away the tent, either. He located a temporary place that required him to tear down his tent every morning. It was a nightmare, but he had been desperate and had had no choice. He stored his tent during the day with a man who guarded artists' lofts in an old building in the Arts District. The man had said that if he was there every morning by ten o'clock to drop off his tent and back by four o'clock to pick it up, he could stash it in a room adjacent to the ramshackle lobby of the building.

Tobias had agreed but realized that if he went to his job as scheduled, working the evening shift, he wouldn't be home in time to retrieve the tent, which would put him on the street overnight and make his second day on the job more difficult.

Yet, for once, he refused to panic and compound his mistakes. He would move in forward motion. He wouldn't jerk from side to side to cover too many eventualities. He wouldn't come up with multiple schemes.

He would go to his new job and force the tent to conform to that plan.

He retrieved his tent from the Arts District and searched desperately for a place where he could settle more permanently. As on the first day, he expected to find nowhere to set down stakes.

The difference, four days later, was that he was prepared to chuck everything. He needed his job and would remove anything that got in his way, including the tent. Still, having the tent was better than not having it if he wanted stability in the longer term.

It meant he lost his final full day to look for Arthur. He fought tears for hours as he walked first in one direction and then another. He hoped to find a space to set up and establish with any new neighbors what penalty they would face if they bothered him.

Four days in, he had wrath on his side. He felt sure he would kick the ass of anyone who gave him problems. As hard as the earlier two years had made him, the previous four days had turned him into granite about his boundaries. He dared anybody to tangle with him.

His mind raced with what he had to accomplish in the ensuing sixteen hours. He had to pitch his tent, find a laundromat, and determine his bus route to work from his new location, wherever that would be. He skipped lunch and chose instead to invest the saved money in a healthy breakfast the next morning, and his low blood sugar worsened his mood beyond the darkness that already hovered.

Around four o'clock, he approached Seventh and Wall Streets. The foot traffic was sparse, and the sidewalk was wide. He was just a block or two away from Skid Row. His tent wouldn't appear out of place, yet he was far enough away from the crowds to avoid being troubled by too many criminal elements. The advantage to a larger tent was that no one knew for sure who was in it. Anyone who entered in Tobias's absence risked finding him—and maybe five friends—on the other side of the flap with weapons. He didn't think anyone would bother his tent, even if just for the first few days, until they figured out his pattern of coming and going.

There were a few other tents already in place, which meant the police had ignored that area. Most appealing, though, was that, with the tent permanently set up, it could be a beacon for Arthur.

For the first time in more than two years, he had taken the longer way around. He had insisted on a better place for his tent, and he had benefitted.

With a head that throbbed nonstop, he pitched his tent, laundered his clothes at a laundromat seven blocks away, figured out his buses, and settled in for the night.

His air mattress was full. He was undressed and in his sleeping bag with it pulled over his head. He had lost his lamp in the raid, and he lay in the dark, guilty for the cover and the warmth he had stolen from Arthur when he walked away with their home and abandoned him.

He shed the tears he had held in or cried intermittently for days, at full strength.

He wanted Arthur with him. He missed Arthur terribly. He had a strong feeling he would never again set eyes on Arthur and that maybe Arthur wasn't even looking for him because he was glad to be done with someone who had caused so much damage to him and cost him everything he owned with one lamebrained action.

He would go to work the next day and begin the cycle of staying employed, and that would be the end of it.

He wept for a long time, with his cries muffled by the sleeping bag, and fell asleep with the harsh realization that Arthur would be lost to him forever.

$$\infty$$

Arthur threw away most of a taco he bought at a food truck and headed from Spring Street back to San Julian Street, Ground Zero for downtown homelessness, for the eighteenth or nineteenth time.

It had been five days since he had seen Tobias. It was Tuesday, Tobias's first day at his new job. The import of the moment, one Tobias had worked so hard for and that Arthur would miss, brought down on Arthur a tremendous sadness. Arthur hoped that, wherever Tobias was, he had not been foolish enough to walk away from his first good job opportunity just because they were separated.

He couldn't lie to himself and say it wouldn't be the height of romance to have Tobias shun his dreams in search of Arthur, but he knew better and wanted better for Tobias, and with that knowing and wanting, a dark insight came over him. If Tobias went to work that day, Arthur's own search would be fruitless, unless he happened onto the tent. It also meant Tobias was probably far away from the area and any flyers Arthur's team had posted.

Arthur added an element to his search, but, once again, he had come up with the idea later than he wished, and he was unsure it would work. Through his investigator, he would hire people to stand in front of the places Tobias was most likely to frequent with a sign, akin to the kind limousine drivers used for people they picked up at the airport, bearing Tobias's name. If Tobias spotted the sign, the person carrying it would inform him where to find Arthur.

It would take the investigator roughly a week to hire enough people to cover the places Tobias might be during the time he was not at work or asleep, with the library, every place they showered, Spring Street, a few places where they regularly ate, the spot in the park where Arthur was mugged, and "their" gas station at the top of the list. It was a longshot, though, because by the time Arthur rolled out that plan, Tobias may have given up searching any or all those places figuring it would never pan out.

It was three o'clock on Tobias's first day at work. He was probably there, waiting to tutor kids after band practice.

Arthur returned to the Biltmore and came to terms with the truth: If he didn't find Tobias that day, he was probably not going to find Tobias in the short term, and if he found him much later and confessed that he could have prevented the nightmare with honesty, Tobias might no longer care that he had been found.

∞ **15** ∞

SPRING STREET

ARTHUR SAT BOLT UPRIGHT IN bed in his room at the Biltmore. His phone pinged and woke him from the fitful slumber he had finally fallen into just an hour earlier.

He welcomed the interruption, for, with it, he received his first bit of good news. His investigator had found a photo of Tobias in the yearbook of the school where he had last taught. He texted it to Arthur with the message *Photo found.*

Arthur stared at the picture a long while. The sprinkling of freckles was there. The studious mystery was there. Even the gentle voice was there, somehow, coming to Arthur through Tobias's image. He stared at Tobias's mouth. It had been ten days since he had kissed Tobias's soft, sleeping lips on his way to work, the morning of the raid.

His eyes became wet. Tobias's best smile for the yearbook during a time when life had been easier tore Arthur to pieces. Arthur had seen flashes of that Tobias often, in the tent, during a long walk, even on the morning after the mugging, and most surely in the early hours after Tobias had returned from the tunnels, as they proposed marriage to one another, and always when they made love. They were close to having a life that brought back *that* Tobias for good, for life, Arthur had hoped, and their future had dissipated.

Arthur had thought about posting Tobias's face on a new set of flyers, with an appeal to anybody who saw the man on the flyer to tell him to meet Arthur at the old location, but he had no idea where Tobias worked and how much job-threatening embarrassment he might cause him and opted to keep the photo to himself. The last thing he wanted was to cost Tobias the first thread of stability he had had in two years.

Arthur's investigator had hired the team who would stand in front of establishments and wait for Tobias with a sign. They would train on Monday and be given their location and deploy on Tuesday. Until then, all Arthur had were his own feet and his flyers. He had little hope.

Still, he jumped out of bed. If even one of his flyers worked, that would be all they needed. He had to be on time.

∞

Tobias was relieved to have the day off. It was Sunday. It had been ten days since he had laid eyes on Arthur, and he planned to spend the whole day looking for him. If he didn't find him, he also had all of Monday to search since his thirty work hours were spread over Tuesdays through Saturdays.

As the days had gone by, he began to believe Arthur had written them off and moved on. He wanted to find him to tell him he was sorry and say goodbye.

In his new location, he was much closer to the mission and a shower. He could get there on foot in just a few minutes.

He was headed back to his tent after his shower to deposit his dirty clothes and gather what he needed to walk the streets for the day, and he spotted something strange.

He thought he was crazy, but he looked closer and saw that he wasn't.

It was his and Arthur's names on a flyer on a street light pole.

He approached the pole. He had passed it on his way to the mission, but he had not seen the flyer because it was on the opposite side of the street light and was only visible on his return trip.

The flyer said, TOBIAS, I'LL BE AT THE OLD LOCATION EVERY DAY AT 10:00 A.M. —ARTHUR

Arthur!

Arthur!

Arthur!

Arthur had been standing near the fence on Spring Street since quarter to ten that morning. He paced up and down a tight space that was four feet long and looked for Tobias in the distance, whether he paced in one direction, or the other. Occasionally, he kicked the fence with a light tap, seemingly to kill time, but subconsciously, to lash out at it.

The streets were almost empty. The weekday foot traffic generated by City Hall and the courthouses was absent. Arthur had always enjoyed the tent most on Sunday mornings for that reason. Just past their encampment, one might have strolled several blocks before seeing even one other pedestrian, right in the heart of one of the world's largest cities. Some of his most romantic walks in the park with Tobias, when they had dreamed big and imagined much, had been on Sunday mornings, when they had had the park to themselves.

It was ten o'clock. He paced and scrutinized the horizon for one man.

And then he spotted something.

He stopped in his tracks and stared hard, and he was sure.

It was the fluorescent orange strap of Tobias's bag.

Tobias.

Walking up Spring Street, crossing Temple, and heading toward me.

Tobias.

Tobias.

It had worked. He had received the message.

They had found each other.

Still several hundred feet apart, their eyes locked, and they each broke into a half-jog.

And then it was over.

The misery, the loneliness, the fear of never seeing each other again, the loss, the terror, the trauma.

They came together and stepped into a hard embrace.

They each muttered words akin to, "Oh, god."

Arthur had thought when he saw Tobias again, he would kiss him forever, but it turned out that what he needed was to feel Tobias, to squeeze him and know that he was truly there. He never wanted to let go.

They held one another for several moments. They gripped each other as tightly as two grown men could, each with his face buried in the other man's shoulder.

They murmured in the crooks of each other's necks words such as, "I was so scared," and, "I thought you were gone forever," and "I love you, I love you," and "I'm so sorry."

Finally, with their arms still around each other they pulled away enough to share more frantic words of love and relief and, with moist happy eyes, short kisses peppered with laughter tinged with disbelief that their nightmare really had ended.

Arthur didn't care how melodramatic they may have looked to the few people who were out, near the park. He didn't care if they were arrested. He didn't even care, for the moment, where Tobias had been. He only cared that they were together.

He couldn't hold back any longer. He moved in and kissed Tobias deeply. It wasn't a passionate kiss, full of gyrations and sexual innuendo. It was a steady connection of their lips with more tender words spoken as their mouths touched.

To Arthur's delight and relief, they gloried in each other and picked up where they had left off ten mornings earlier. They kissed and laughed and hugged and exclaimed how hard and long they had searched for each other and swore that what happened would never happen again.

"I love you," Arthur said. "If you ever have any doubts about me, about us, just know that I was prepared to bring an army out here to find you."

"I didn't doubt the man you are," Tobias said, "but I started to doubt me and whether I was any good for you. I wondered if you thought the same thing. I screwed up bad," he took in a shaky breath, "and I felt so guilty that I left with the tent and left you stranded." He was full of remorse. "I've been imagining you on sidewalks all over the city and feeling horrible, miserable. I'm so sorry I screwed up. Where have you been this whole time? I'm sorry I left you out here with nothing." His eyes became wetter. "I'm sorry. I've been wanting to tell you that for ten days. I'm really sorry."

It was Arthur who felt awful. He kissed Tobias and talked right into his eyes. "No. No. Stop." He gave steady, reassuring kisses as he talked. "I was fine. I was fine, Babe. I promise. I dug into my money and stayed at a hotel. I only spent nights on the street when I was out looking for you, but I still had my room. I was okay. I promise."

Tobias almost dropped with relief. "Thank goodness." He closed his eyes and let out a little laugh that almost sounded like a cry. "Oh my god, thank goodness. You have no idea. I was so worried you thought I left you on purpose or just that I was so dumb you were glad to be done with me. These have been the worst ten days of my life. I thought you were gone forever."

"Never." They kissed. "Never. I knew it wasn't your fault, and there was also a reporter from the Times hanging around who told me how it went down. I knew you didn't have a lot of time to come up with solutions. I'm the one who's felt like an asshole this whole time for never giving you my phone number or asking you for your e-mail address. I had a phone. *I have a fucking phone*, and because I was such an idiot about the number, you couldn't call me. So stupid! This is literally all my fault."

"No, it made sense at the time. It's not your fault, and maybe it's not even mine. They kicked us out without warning!"

"The Times guy gave me some details, but what really happened that day? I saw extra cops that morning, but they gave no sign they were about to destroy everyone."

"It's about like you've probably figured. You went to work, and they showed up a couple of hours later. I was sound asleep. It was scary. And total bullshit. I don't even want to tell you what we lost. They gave us just an hour to pack everything or throw it away. I'm sorry. I panicked and went into survival mode, thinking I could save our stuff and get back on time, and it was a nightmare. Cops at every turn. Nowhere to set up. I moved around the first four days. I screwed up. I'm sorry."

"Stop saying that." He cradled Tobias's face in his hands. "Look at me, Babe. Officially stop saying that. It's not your fault. It's

theirs, those assholes. I'm gonna sue the shit out of all of them."
Arthur stroked Tobias's cheeks. "All I care about now is did they hurt you? Are you hurt? Were you cuffed or roughed up or anything?"

"No, no. I'm fine. In fact, I went to work."

Arthur closed his eyes. "Oh, thank god. You have no idea how much I worried about that."

"I felt super guilty giving up the search, but I figured you'd think it was smarter to go to work."

"It was! It was. Thank god. I'm relieved. I didn't want that to get screwed up, too."

They took deep breaths.

"I finally found a place for the tent. It was hell figuring it out, but I'm way over on Seventh and Wall."

"Dammit. I was there a few times, right after the raid."

"I didn't get there until the fourth day, late in the afternoon, but it's okay. It's over."

Arthur heard the words, but Tobias seemed sad.

"I found you," Tobias said. "You found me." He smiled wistfully. "I mean, I can't lie. I had no clue what you might do, where you might go."

Arthur couldn't explain it, but he was suddenly nervous. Something about Tobias's countenance worried him.

"You know, me screwing up. The way my life's gone, you know?"

"Babe, I told you—"

"I thought you might leave L.A." With that, Tobias lost his composure. He broke down.

And Arthur was scared. "It's okay," he said. "It's gonna be all right. We're all right."

"It's just been such a shitty couple of years," Tobias said.

He was a contradiction. His face expressed fear and relief and a strange dread of what lay ahead. He gazed into a nothingness and talked to an undefined nowhere.

And Arthur was terrified.

"I thought I must be cursed, I must not be worthy. I must be doing *something* wrong."

"Shhh," Arthur said. He wiped Tobias's tears and fought his own. "Shhh."

"I thought you might be so angry with me, you'd leave forever."

"Oh, Babe. Never. Never. I told you, I could never leave here without you, ever."

"Every time I threw something into the dumpster, I flashed back to packing up my house, moving my stuff into storage, my car being dragged away, my stuff being sold. I don't….I don't know. It was too much. I couldn't think."

"Shhh."

And it hit Arthur. He finally understood that life had terrorized Tobias for a long, long while. Strangely, at least to his mind, he hadn't seen it till then. They had lived together, in a tent on the sidewalk, but their happiness in each other's company had masked something dreadful from Arthur. It had hidden that life had threatened and intimidated Tobias for years. It took their being separated and Arthur being away from his utopian feelings about the tent to realize the way Tobias had lived had traumatized him greatly.

They had both been made distraught by recent events, but Tobias had experienced two years of extreme distress, on big and small fronts. He worried about his safety and if he would ever work again, or be worthy again, and he worried about the next meal and whether he smelled okay and how to not get mugged or arrested and whether his coworkers and students would discover his secret and whether the black coffee at the gas station was, out of nowhere, twenty cents more expensive on some given day and whether there was a bus that would get him to a job interview and whether he had enough money to take it and how he could still contribute as a volunteer, to feel worthy, and maybe even to save face from feeling like he only took, in poverty, and gave nothing. Everything in his world had to be negotiated. Nothing was a given. He could take nothing for granted, not privacy or protection from shame and violence and the loss of freedom.

He could only count on Arthur's love, and he had almost lost that, through external forces that, once again, controlled him and proved he had no say in his destiny, except in the ways that he had made mistakes and derailed his own life.

Arthur knew what he had to do.

He never thought the moment would arrive that way, but it had done so. And he would do what he had to do.

Even if Tobias never forgave him for his lies, even if he suffered one more raging disappointment with the loss of trust and faith and love, Arthur would not let Tobias spend one more night on the street, worried about his safety and whether he would lose everything again, with his identity, self-esteem, and sense of worth tied to his ability to watch over his few belongings and stay alive.

He had a final conversation with himself, to gain the courage to take the next step, for he was petrified of what would happen once he took it, and in that conversation, he made himself understand that he had one thing on the line. It was the most important thing in his life, but it was just one thing. Tobias had everything at risk, his entire existence, constantly, with no respite. Every aspect of his life was in peril. Arthur couldn't watch it anymore. He couldn't aid and abet it with his own lies.

With that, Arthur accepted his fate.

The reunion wouldn't go as planned.

He had thought they would bring a feast back to the tent, share the awful details about their time apart, comfort each other, and settle in and make love until Monday.

Instead, it was over before it started. For a few more moments, only Arthur would know it. He'd take in a few more kisses and get one final look at Tobias while his face still reflected full faith and trust in Arthur and a deep love for him. And that would be it. For Tobias's sake, it had to be.

It was confess-and-die time.

∞ **16** ∞

THE BILTMORE

ARTHUR HAD WEPT HAPPILY WITH Tobias in their first
moments together again, but the tears he stifled soon thereafter came
from a different place.

He and Tobias had moved from the sidewalk to a favorite
corner in Grand Park. Sounds of water flowing and drops of mist
coming from the fountain seemed to put Tobias at ease. Arthur was
the one who struggled to get hold of himself.

"Tobias, I want you to come with me, and when we get where
we're going, I'm going to tell you the rest of why I've been alone my
whole life."

Tobias regarded him for a moment with a kind expression. He
stroked Arthur's cheek and stole a kiss. "You look scared. And
you're scaring me. We found each other. I know I kind of lost it
there for a minute, earlier, but I'm okay. I feel great here. This is the
happiest moment possible, but you don't seem happy." He kissed
Arthur again. "I love you. We love each other. I have today off, and
it's just us today—"

"Tobias, please. I need you to listen."

"I'm listening, Babe. I'm listening. I'm sorry. Tell me."

Babe.

"I'm afraid. Of losing you. I'm terrified of it, actually." Arthur
added a scared laugh and shook his head as if acknowledging the
inevitable.

"After we just found each other? No chance. No chance of
that, at all, Babe. No way that happens. *Today,* we buy me a phone.
Before we even go back to the tent and have our fun, if you want. We
swap e-mails right now—"

"That's not what I mean."

"You know, I think you're as wiped out as I am. You seem tired and way strained." He gently rubbed Arthur's back. "Let's swing through Target to see if they have phones, and then we can grab some food and go back to the tent," he glided his hand easily over Arthur's back, "or maybe that fancy hotel of yours, and eat and make out and, you know, do dirty things." He smiled and leaned over and kissed Arthur.

Arthur returned the kiss but immediately said, "No, Tobias, we can't."

"Why not?"

Arthur waited a long while. He was scared to speak his next words, for then it would be over.

He exhaled and looked Tobias in the eyes.

Finally, he said, "I'm getting you off the streets."

"That's what I said. Let's get some foo—."

"That's not what I mean."

"You keep saying that."

Arthur pulled out his real phone.

"Whoa. That's fancy." Tobias laughed. "Where did you get it?"

"It's mine." He didn't have the courage to add, "I've had it all along." What he did say didn't help much, either. "I'm getting us an Uber."

"You're getting us an Uber? On that phone." Tobias sounded half-whimsical and half-skeptical.

Arthur figured he had about twenty seconds left in his happy relationship before it began its rapid slide down a steep grade that ended in a deep ravine full of piles of dung.

Tobias stared at the phone. He pondered it as though it were a strange object he hoped to identify after further scrutiny.

It clicked. Arthur watched it happen in real time.

"Have you had that a while? That doesn't look new."

"Yes, and I promise I'll explain."

The Uber app told Arthur their driver was four minutes away. They would need to exit the park on the Grand Avenue side, almost exactly where Arthur had been mugged several months earlier. Arthur subconsciously shook his head at the irony, as if to try to make it go away.

He stood up and looked down at Tobias. "Ready?"

Tobias stood up, too. "You look like you're being led to the guillotine."

I am.

Arthur started the dreadful walk toward Grand Avenue, and Tobias naturally walked with him. Tobias was mostly still jovial. His questions didn't yet carry the bite of anger or suspicion. He was simply curious as to how Arthur had acquired a phone and signed up for Uber.

"Can I ask a favor?" Arthur said.

"Of course."

Tobias was thoroughly agreeable. The onslaught hadn't yet arrived.

They made it to Grand Avenue and waited on the wide, pristine sidewalk across the street from the Music Center.

"Can we just be here together and not say anything until our car gets here?"

Tobias reached for Arthur's left hand with his right. He spoke in a gentle tone as they faced each other. "Babe, it's going to be fine. For better or for worse." He leaned in for another kiss.

Arthur accepted it with gratitude to Fate that it had let him have one more kiss from Tobias.

"I hope you're right."

Their car arrived. Arthur and the driver quickly acknowledged each other as Arthur opened the back door.

Tobias hesitated. Just a moment earlier, he had said, "For better or for worse." But the reality of climbing into a hired car with Arthur seemed to have given him pause.

Arthur's insides were water. His voice shook when he spoke. "Tobias, please get in."

Tobias slid into the back seat of the car, and Arthur climbed in behind him and, while they settled in and figured out legroom and seatbelts, sent a quick text to Kelly that said *Found him. More later. Let Parkerson know.* Phil Parkerson was his investigator. She sent back a GIF that he barely noticed. He was too nervous.

All three occupants were silent as the car pulled away and made a wide, illegal U-turn over an empty Grand Avenue. The Biltmore was five long blocks away, where Grand met Fifth Street.

They drove down a street that was familiar to Tobias and Arthur. It was the street Tobias used to walk home from the library, as he had the afternoon Arthur had waited for him, and Tobias had stormed home in a silent rage, and, later they had made love the first time.

The streets they crossed on the way to the Biltmore were home, their backyard and front yard, their playground and prison, yet Tobias looked up at the tall and short buildings as though he had never seen them.

Suddenly, he turned to Arthur. He took Arthur's hand and whispered, "Okay, so you spent some money on a phone and used your bank card to sign up for Uber. I wouldn't have minded knowing, but it's not a crime." He smiled. "You were getting back on your feet and you used your money how you saw fit. I know you. You're thoughtful. You didn't want to rub it in that you upgraded your life a little while I was still looking for a job. And, as we now know, you and I weren't phone people, anyway. It's okay."

Arthur's stomach rumbled.

Tobias squeezed Arthur's hand. "It's going to be fine," he said. "It'll be nice to roll up to the tent in a car." He told the driver, "Whatever the GPS says, you can go straight to Seventh and make a left."

Before the driver could say anything about the conflicting information as to their destination, Arthur said to the driver, "No, it's okay. We're going to the address you have. That's fine."

"Oh, a surprise," Tobias said with a mischievous grin on his face.

A moment later, he said, "This is the first time I've been inside a regular car in more than half a year. The last car I was in was mine. It feels strange. Much quieter and smoother than the bus."

For the first time since he'd known Tobias, Arthur wished he'd stop talking.

Their car approached the Biltmore, which was across the street from the Grand Avenue side of the library. Arthur had noticed the irony when he'd checked in after the raid.

"The library? You want to go to the library?" Tobias chuckled and lightened a little more, as though normalcy had returned and the most mainstream thing he and Arthur had in their lives was still the library, and the Uber ride ordered up on a fancy phone had no significance.

"No."

Their driver pulled into the Biltmore's long, covered driveway, and two hotel greeters opened the doors for Arthur and Tobias. One of the staff members at the valet station recognized Arthur.

"Good morning, Mr. Dewynter."

Arthur watched Tobias, who exited the car slowly and stayed a few steps behind Arthur.

"When you said hotel, you meant *this* hotel? Not a motel but this hotel?"

"Yes."

They entered the lobby and Arthur led them to the elevators. They passed marble fountains, extravagant tapestries, boutiques, quiet restaurants, and wrought iron gates that led to lushly carpeted alcoves and walked under elaborate and intricate crystal chandeliers.

At the elevators, Arthur didn't hesitate to select the UP button. He didn't look around as though he wondered where he was. He was comfortable with the wait because he had waited there many times before. He knew that every move he made pushed him farther down the hill and caused him to pick up speed toward the ditch at the bottom.

On the elevator ride, Tobias said, "You really have a room here?"

Arthur noticed the "you", which was very different from the "we" who had a tent and pooled coins and rode the bus to take a shower.

"Yes."

"Well, I don't get it," Tobias whispered. They were alone in the elevator, but it had a public feel to it. "Where's your flop motel? I know you didn't stay here the last ten days, but I can't figure out how you booked this from the park bench and how everybody knows you, especially when you couldn't have known we'd find each other and be together again specifically today. I don't get the timing. And isn't this kind of expensive? You're usually super cautious with money."

"I can afford it." He stared straight ahead.

The elevator stopped on the seventh floor. Without hesitation, Arthur exited and turned toward his room.

Tobias followed, still a few paces behind.

They reached the door of Arthur's room. Arthur said, "I love you, Tobias."

"I love you, too," Tobias said, but his tone bore a hint of dread.

Arthur wore a guilty look as he pulled out his room key and inserted it into the door. A green light flashed. They entered the room, which had been tidied to perfection while Arthur was on the streets that morning, searching for Tobias.

Tobias took a long look at everything around him. Arthur knew what he thought. The room looked like a home away from home for someone whose home looked like the marble and crystal Tobias had seen downstairs, complete with two laptops and an old *Wall Street Journal* waiting on a table for the occupant to return to his room and relax with Friday's financial news while he browsed the Internet.

"What's going on, Arthur?"

Tobias's tone was foreign to Arthur.

They had become strangers.

SUNSET, WEST, TO BEVERLY HILLS

TOBIAS LISTENED TO ARTHUR WITH a dull expression.

He terrified Arthur.

Neither sadness nor fear nor dread nor disappointment nor hurt alone rose to the surface and dominated Tobias's face. Rather, all those emotions and feelings shone through, together, most centrally in Tobias's eyes, which were full of pain.

Arthur knew he was doomed. Dread hung over his head and stood on his shoulders and compressed his heart and made it hard for him to breathe. The only thing to do was to tell more truth, as he had done for ten, straight, rambling, horrible, sick-making minutes, during which Tobias stared at him through his hurt-filled eyes.

Arthur rounded out his confession at the place where he had started. "I never needed the tent. My shoulder was never injured. I don't work in construction." He took in a heavy, shaky breath and sounded his own death knell. "I've never been homeless a day in my life. My…home can comfortably house thirty people, not including the staff's quarters or the guest house. If I let people crash in the pool house and on couches in side rooms I never use, the number probably goes up to fifty. Add the floor space and sleeping bags, and we're into the hundreds." Arthur could at least say that once he had been honest, he had bared it all.

Tobias watched him from a chair near the hotel room window, in front of brocade drapes, barely blinking. He seemed to be trying to decipher who stood before him and spoke strange words about fourteen rooms in Beverly Hills and a fake temp job.

He still wore his shoulder bag with the orange strap. The incongruence he presented, sitting there in discount clothing with an all-purpose satchel that offered "an orange strap" as the thing that set it apart from other bags, reinforced for Arthur not that Tobias didn't belong in his world, but that Arthur had no interest in his own world. He wanted to be back in the tent with Tobias, at that very moment, making love and reading books they carried home from the library in that bag. That was his world.

Arthur hadn't been dramatic as he tried to explain. He never paced. He stood, homed in on Tobias as though he were a light who would guide Arthur to eternal happiness, and spoke to one place, one countenance, one being.

Tobias.

Arthur couldn't tell what Tobias saw when he looked at Arthur. He longed to know and understand how bad it was.

What am I to you, Tobias? Beast? Demon? Liar? Lover? Please tell me.

Tobias didn't utter a word.

Arthur couldn't bear the stillness anymore. He knelt before Tobias and placed his arms beside Tobias's thighs, as if to embrace him from a kneeling position. "I'm sorry," he said.

Tobias allowed Arthur's hands to remain where they were, but he offered no safe quarter or reassuring touch or return embrace.

"You lied about everything."

He had finally spoken.

He didn't shout. It was the same, quiet, perfect, mathematician's voice that Arthur could have listened to for an eternity, into infinity, as Tobias would say.

"I lied about almost nothing. If you'll let me tell you everything, let me make it make sense…."

"I've heard all I need to hear. I can see it, too. You've been laughing at me for months."

"No, I've been laughing at me, at myself, for years."

"What an *idiot* I am." Arthur felt Tobias's warm breath on his face as he spoke the word "idiot". Tobias's statement was as much a realization about himself as it was an accusation aimed at Arthur. He really meant, "You made a fool of me."

"I can't believe I didn't see it the whole time," Tobias said. "The fifty dollars out of nowhere. Not really caring when I told you they stole your phone. The strange absences, early on, when I was baffled as to where you could be spending your days. And nights. Always acting a little like a tourist no matter how hard it got. I'm so dumb!"

Tobias sounded to Arthur as though he were complaining to a friend about an enemy, recounting an awful deed done to him, only he told his woes to the enemy who had perpetrated the pain and done the deed. He seemed confused and alone, as he lamented about Arthur, his best friend, *to* Arthur, his newfound foe.

Tobias stood up and stepped around Arthur and headed across the vast room toward the door.

Arthur got up fast and took three big strides to catch Tobias and touch him gently on the arm to keep him from getting to the door and leaving for good.

Tobias stopped for a moment.

Arthur talked to Tobias's back. "You're not an idiot, and you're not dumb. Just please listen. You promised me you would listen."

Tobias never turned around. "That was a different you I made that promise to. I don't know who this Arthur is." He took the final steps for the door.

Arthur chased him. He overtook Tobias and slid in between Tobias and the door. "Wait. You said you would listen. Please. Please. Let me explain."

"Who are you? *What* are you? What is this?" Tobias's eyes were wet.

"I love you. I'm the man who's going to marry you, if you'll just let—"

"We're not getting married." It was an announcement that foreclosed all discussion. "We're not doing anything. We did jinx it, talking about it."

Arthur was dumbstruck.

"You're getting out of my way, and I'm going back to my tent. *My* tent and *my* things."

"Please, Tobias, please. If you ever loved me, you'll let me explain."

"That's just it. Did I love you? *You?* Get out of my way."

"No. I need you to listen. Please."

Tobias refused to look at Arthur but didn't move him aside and walk out, either. He spoke to a blank space on the door, behind Arthur, which was nowhere, really. He appeared lost. "What good will it do? You'll still be somebody who made a fool of me in the end."

"No, I'll be the person who loves you, who needs you. I need you. And I think you need me, or else what have the last ten days been about?"

"I was out there searching for someone who doesn't exist."

"The me you love *does* exist. He's the only one who's here. And he wants to be there, for you and with you, in everything. Please hear him out. Hear me out, Tobias."

Tobias exhaled and stared at more space to the left of Arthur. He gathered the strength to look Arthur in the eye.

They watched each other. Between them, they were angry and scared and tearful, but neither of them moved or spoke or fully cried.

Arthur resolved not to look away, not for anything.

Tobias let out another long breath. "I will listen. And then I will leave."

Arthur closed his eyes for a long moment then opened them and said, "Thank you. Thank you."

"Make it quick."

"Not here."

"Not here? You want me to go somewhere with you?"

"Yes. Yes. I know I'm pushing it, but yes."

"Fine. Where are we going?" Tobias seemed resigned to doing whatever Arthur asked so he could quickly get away from him for good. Arthur settled for it.

"My house."

∞

The drive in Arthur's Maserati west on Sunset Boulevard toward Beverly Hills was the longest ride, anywhere, of Arthur's life. He could have taken the freeway, but taking Sunset gave him more time to plead his case. He hadn't factored in utter silence from

Tobias that made Arthur feel as though they drove toward eternity, a place they'd never reach.

The valet had brought Arthur's car to him at the Biltmore. Tobias had said, more as an answer than a question, "So, that *was* you I saw that day." His tone commanded there be no dialogue. He didn't want Arthur to waste his time with a perfunctory, "Yes."

Arthur assumed Tobias felt doubly duped and that he was riding along inside the scene of a horrible emotional crime because Arthur had twice deceived him that day. He knew Tobias had seen him, and he went along with Tobias's perceived mistake that it was someone else.

As soon as Tobias got in the car, he stopped speaking.

So, Arthur talked. He begged for his life, for their life. He told Tobias a tale, about drunkenness and feigned homelessness and Century City and finding himself, with Tobias, strangely *because* of Tobias, who had rescued him that first night. He talked about love and real friendship and equality between partners and his soul and their souls and their purpose, together.

He described life in his hollow castle that was fed by his fifteen million a year, which had ballooned into a net worth of three hundred and fifty million barriers to connecting with anyone in a meaningful way.

He told of how he had lived on the precipice of disaster and had almost taken up permanent residence at the bottom of a bottle and drowned in whatever liquid it held and talked of how lonely he was and how no one treated him like an individual instead of like a sum of money. He talked happily about how when he found Tobias, he found a calling, a devotion, one morning in a tent, over a Styrofoam cup of coffee, shared with a friendly face and a kind, kind voice, a voice that had led to dreams of strange castles full of figures who sounded like Tobias and gave Arthur great comfort and took away his fears about everything, about an empty life.

Arthur tried to convince Tobias he had committed wrongdoings that were also, by their nature, the penance they demanded. Surely, his living honestly for the first time in years was the cure to the dishonesty in how he went about it.

He also talked of a displaced math teacher who had been born to help others and had so often thought about how to contribute, he hadn't remembered to take care of himself, and yet he hadn't blamed anyone else or lashed out. Instead, he had continued to reach out. He had reached out to Arthur and given him everything from so little that was worldly but from so much that came from his heart. That teacher learned he had the ability to make feeling and caring and a little bit of shelter enough to save another and fill up a man, until he overflowed with love.

He talked of how he hoped and dreamt they would live and love somewhere in the figurative middle, between the hardships of life outside the tent and the machinations of the castle that kept Arthur imprisoned, in a literal space they chose together, one that enveloped them and held and kept them close the way the tent had but that let them run free, from worry and fear and loneliness.

"We've changed," Arthur said. "Don't you see? Each of us carried the other to a place we couldn't carry ourselves. We can do it for life, if you'll let us."

Tobias didn't answer.

Arthur's phone chimed several times. He ignored it. He knew without checking that it was Kelly. She probably wanted a few details about where Tobias had been and how he fared before they settled into a long reunion that barred access. She had worried for ten days with Arthur, and she deserved to know that Tobias hadn't been harmed.

But Arthur was in the fight of his life, the same fight she had sent him into, from his corner of the relationship ring, waving a towel and yelling at him to stay off the ropes and throw punches at Destiny, which fought against him and Tobias, and she would have to wait until Fate rang the final bell and sent him back to his corner to find out if he'd won the fight. He let the phone ping.

After a while, though, faced with steady silence, he stopped talking. The only sound in the car were the chimes from Kelly's texts.

Tobias never said a word.

∞ **18** ∞

ELEVATOR TO EMERALD CITY

TOBIAS AND ARTHUR ARRIVED IN the driveway of Arthur's mansion. Tobias resisted saying, "You live here?"

He thought back to the night he stormed out of the tent for the tunnels and had compared it to living in a mansion and going to the other side of the house. He was mortified at how Arthur must have laughed at him, especially after Arthur had said the tunnels were much farther away, and Tobias had said, "Speaking from experience, and all."

They parked in a long garage, an out-building set away from the primary residence, that held five other cars, two luxury cars and three economy cars, each better looking than Tobias's old Honda—and one of the cars *was* a Honda. There was room for four more cars in addition to the Maserati Arthur pulled into the spot closest to the house.

His favorite car.

It took a full minute to walk from the garage to the front door of the house. An ivy-covered wrought iron fence that had thicker greenery enmeshed in the ivy formed a barrier between the garage compound and the rest of the back of the house so that the backyard was masked from view. Tobias could only guess what lay behind the million-dollar-looking iron-and-ivy "hedge". A larger wall bordered the front of the property, so that even the garage area was shrouded from view if approaching from the street.

With a nervous patter in his tone, Arthur pointed to a side door and said, "That lets into the kitchen. It's a quicker entry into the house, but the front door is actually faster for the few places I use.”

Kind of like the front and back zippers on my tent and how the front zipper gives me quicker access to the one corner of the tent that I use.

Arthur wore an apologetic face and stepped up his pace for the front door. “The, uh, staff is off today. Sunday, and all. We’ll have the place to ourselves.”

Tobias didn’t respond to the sudden good news of available privacy since he hadn’t expected the bad news of “staff” being around to watch him and Arthur.

At the ornate entry, Arthur pulled out a set of keys, *his* keys, and unlocked the door. A long, steady beep sounded. It was Arthur’s home alarm system. Tobias watched Arthur walk quickly to a keypad hidden behind a tiny door on the wall and punch in four numbers he could plainly see since Arthur made no attempt to hide his hand behind the little door. The tiny door lay flat open.

The numbers corresponded to Tobias’s birthday. Tobias didn’t feel any closer to Arthur seeing his birthday keep burglars away from him. He only thought that Arthur’s system was a lot higher tech than battery-operated rat repellent.

Arthur placed the keys on a small hook inside the alarm panel hideaway and closed the tiny door. The intricacy of the routine brought it home for Tobias.

Arthur had lived a double life.

Tobias witnessed the other half of it and tried to grasp Arthur’s explanation that not only was it not actually a whole, the whole of who Arthur was, but it was not a part of the space that made up the area or volume of Arthur’s life, other than the space the drunkenness and recklessness and loneliness had filled before he met

Tobias. Arthur had insisted that the tent and his life with Tobias were what his life was made of.

Tobias hoped to understand Arthur for a reason that surprised him. He was deeply in love with Arthur, or, at least with the man he thought Arthur was. The love wasn't the surprise, but that it still had any influence on Tobias, was.

He understood the power of that love on the drive along Sunset Boulevard. He listened to Arthur and, as he spoke, remembered how he looked that first night, when he had been mugged, and it had been easy to believe he had been headed for a dark place from there. It made sad sense that he had little in his life to keep him off the streets of downtown. Seeing his opulent life and how many places within it to escape that he did not or could not use only magnified that impression.

He stood in the large foyer in Beverly Hills and saw that there had been nothing in Arthur's life powerful or meaningful enough, nothing of substance in that large space that found Arthur worthy enough to tether him to the life he had crafted. There was nothing that had kept him from venturing into self-destruction. He had strayed all the way from Beverly Hills to a Grand Park mugging, and no one had cared. No one had missed him. He hadn't mentioned, in the tent the morning after the attack, anyone who would be worried about him, especially when they couldn't reach him on his stolen phone. Tobias hadn't thought to ask about anyone. Arthur's comportment hadn't let the thought cross Tobias's mind. Arthur had so easily appeared homeless and as alone as that tended to make one and *seemed* homeless because, emotionally, and maybe even actually, he was homeless, if one defined the opposite of homelessness as living somewhere that warmed and comforted and not just as living somewhere, period.

Arthur led them through the entryway, which had, to Tobias's eye, a square footage of a thousand. Tobias's condo had only been a few hundred square feet larger.

Several windows let in lots of light. Glass and mirrors and hard angles and long, open spaces set a formal tone. It didn't look like Arthur or remind Tobias of him, except for the clear appreciation for sunshine.

Based on the Arthur he knew in the tent, Tobias expected large, dust-colored ceramic tiles, rooms filled with soft leather or funky mid-century modern, bright-colored furniture, books, blanket-throws, magazines, jazzy art, and comfortable shoes.

Very little of that was present, although some of it was, as though Arthur had set out to achieve that kind of dream home and had given up somewhere along the way so that he lived in an abandoned building of sorts. There were paintings that would have fit well in the tent, if it were a sturdy home, and looked as though they had been stolen from Arthur's favorite corners of museums around town, so much did they exude Arthur's essence, but there were also dull marble fixtures that might have adorned a fancy restroom at a high-end hotel.

Mostly, Tobias felt as though he had wandered into a foggy nightmare dressed up as a dream in which he chased the *spirit* of Arthur, down fancy hallways and over shiny floors, while he couldn't quite find the man who held the spirit.

Then he spotted an older looking grand piano sitting on a thick, worn, but chic rug in a large living room. Its slightly beat-up look gave it an earthy charm that felt like Arthur. Arthur would have no way of knowing it, but the sight was a comfort to Tobias on an otherwise strange and sad day.

Tobias couldn't help himself. He migrated to the instrument and sat down on the bench in front of it. The overstuffed leather seat provided another hint of the Arthur Tobias knew.

Tobias played a little of Mozart's Piano Sonata No. 5 in G. His fingers rattled off the allegro movement with a speed and accuracy he had thought he had forgotten how to deliver.

He eased into the andante movement with a lightness that transported him to another time he had never told Arthur about. He had been too ashamed. It had seemed to belong to ways of being that he had tried to grow away from, with Arthur. He thought it better left in the past, his love for the instrument, anyway. He was relieved he still had his skill.

"You never told me you played," Arthur said. He listened a little longer. "You obviously went well beyond a few years of piano lessons on Saturdays. That's beautiful."

"I was a math-y kid." He continued to play. "That meant music for a lot of years. One of the few things my parents got right." His fingers glided into the presto movement. "I had a piano, but it was lost in the commotion. Not my childhood one. I left that one behind, but I bought another one, something else I was irresponsible about. I paid it off before I paid off my car. But at least I had it."

He stopped playing and stared at his hands resting on the keys. "This may make no sense to you, who can buy and sell what you want without a care about priorities," and he looked around Arthur's lavish living room, "but I needed it. I didn't just want it. I needed it."

"It makes sense to me. You're saying what I've been saying. It's not about things. It's about meaning." He was silent for a moment then said, "This is exactly how I see you cutting loose and unleashing. At a piano, using your mind. I wish you had told me."

"I probably would have, eventually." He looked up at Arthur. "I wouldn't have been able to resist." He looked down at the keys again. "In the end, I think I would have told you every bit of minutia about myself that I could remember."

"You can tell me now, about your piano, which I can tell is far from minutia, or about anything."

Tobias stared at the instrument. "Not much to tell." He tapped a few keys then held still. "It ended up in storage, the worst place on earth for a piano, and then they sold it. It was almost a relief to not have to worry anymore about it sitting there dying."

"I'm sorry," Arthur said.

With that, Tobias got up and worked his way around the piano bench.

They stood awkwardly staring at each other.

"Well?" Tobias said. "Is this what you wanted me to see?" He gestured around the room. "I could have guessed at this, Arthur. I'm not sure what seeing it changes."

"I'm sure you see a lot. But I wonder if you see what's not here. Come with me."

"Where?"

"To the elevator."

They took a long stroll down a wide hallway and boarded an elevator at the end of it. After a slow, quiet ride to the third floor, they exited the lift and stepped onto a landing that was decorated and desolate.

The hallway fanned broadly to the left and right, and farther down on each side, Tobias saw additional hallways and vestibules. Many of the accoutrements he had seen at the Biltmore adorned the corridors. He spotted a fountain down one gangway that had a gated entry. Another passage had large paintings on its walls and benches installed at intervals along the middle where guests could sit and admire the art as though they were in a museum. Tobias and Arthur had found such benches in desolate areas of real museums and gazed at lonely art and stolen kisses from each other. Tobias wondered if Arthur had thought at those times, "This painting would look great in my upstairs hallway."

They twisted and turned past several rooms and alcoves and even took what looked like a shortcut through a diagonal hall. Tobias could not imagine Arthur, who loved to return from the showers on Sunday mornings and climb into his sleeping bag and read the Times and nap under the breeze that traveled through the tent, living, really living, in and around the sterile rooms they passed on their way to the end of what Arthur called the upper east hallway.

In the distance, there was a door on the left. Tobias understood that behind the long wall they had passed was probably a huge room that lay behind that door.

When they reached it, Arthur said, "Don't underestimate what a tent can do for a person, Tobias. A man can feel himself," he reached up and stroked Tobias's cheek, and Tobias didn't fight him, "what matters, whom he loves, who's close to him, in a tent, unlike what I feel in the rather large hellhole you're about to enter."

Arthur opened the door to a great master suite that was four times the size of the room they had just been in at the Biltmore and far more elegant, which was hard to achieve.

But there was more, or rather less, Tobias noticed. There was no warmth, no humanness, no errors, no favorite-sweatshirt-on-the-bed mistakes or the familiar scent of Arthur that Tobias knew well from the tent. It had been sanitized away. Arthur wasn't there.

The atmosphere was stripped of feeling and being and the sense that anyone had been there and left some of themselves behind because it was theirs and removing signs of them would make no sense, and because they looked forward to returning to it and being greeted by familiar favorite things, as would happen in any home inhabited by people who loved in it and who loved being in it. Nothing was out of place. The bed was crisp. The large bathroom was pristine. Tobias wondered whether *anyone* lived there.

"It's the same everywhere in the house. I would show you my dining room table that seats twenty-six, or my so-called smaller kitchen table that seats ten, where I mostly eat Cheerios, but I think you get the idea."

They stood in the middle of the room.

"I don't doubt that some of this isn't as easy as most people would think, but it doesn't change anything, Arthur," he said.

Still, he was curious. He wandered to the large closet. Arthur followed and clapped his hands with no energy, as though he had attended a bad performance. Lights and overhead music came on. He then clapped three times quickly, and the music stopped.

Tobias searched above his head as though he were unstable and heard voices. He chuckled with no mirth and surveyed the room. He beheld what looked like a million-dollar wardrobe hanging all around him. The suits were made of exquisite material, and they hung on satin hangers spaced at intervals that kept them from touching one another and prevented one suit from disturbing the luxuriousness of its neighbor.

There were larger drawers and multiple thin drawers. Tobias pulled open a thin one, and it felt like it floated on air. Inside were many pairs of neatly organized expensive socks that had gold-toe sections. Several drawers held just six ties each, all royal looking. Still others—many—held just one crisply ironed dress shirt that lay flat to avoid wrinkles and poked-out shoulders created by hangers.

The underwear drawer was the only one that contained run-of-the-mill looking garments. Tobias recognized the boxer briefs that lay there. It was strange to see lying in a million-dollar closet underwear like what he had laundered and tucked into a duffel bag drawer in a tent on a city sidewalk. The underwear was the only thing recognizable in that labyrinth as being "of" Arthur.

In another area of the closet, there were rows of expensive footwear, with several places to sit down and put on one's shoes and multiple sizes of expensive shoehorns fashioned from different materials hanging on a wall.

There was an entire wall dedicated to a full-length mirror so that no matter where in the closet Arthur dressed, he could see himself and immediately jettison bad fashion statements. The carpet beneath Tobias's feet felt plusher and airier than the mattresses he used for his sleeping bags.

There was just one section that contained casual clothes that looked very out of place. The rest of the room—to Tobias it wasn't a closet—added up to three times the cost of his condo, he was sure.

"Heavens," he said. "A person could live just in here and be very comfortable."

He left the closet and spotted another door. He walked to it and assumed it was a smaller storage area, but it was a full second bathroom, complete with the double-sink arrangement he had seen in the first bathroom, the same luxurious shower-sauna, the identical Roman tub with Jacuzzi jets, a familiar linen closet, and the same extensive space for walking around from area to area. In that bathroom, he spotted a smaller door he hadn't noticed in the first bathroom. He pulled it open, and an ironing board unfolded. He shook his head.

He returned to the main portion of the bedroom.

"I see you shaking your head. I thought bringing you here would make it all make sense and that you would remember how happy I was in the tent and realize all of this couldn't mean much to me, but I see it just looks worse."

"Because it is, even if, somewhere inside, I see the disconnect you want me to see. I do. But this is fancier than a hotel or an expensive restaurant or even a museum. This is the fanciest place I've ever been in in my life, and you *live* here." He snort-laughed with disdain.

"I live with you."

"No, you visited me. You live *here*, and you came here every day and rode elevators, while I rode buses and walked miles to run errands. I searched for you for ten days. I was lucky to find a bus bench to rest on when I got tired. You say you searched—"

"I did."

"Maybe you did, but you had a helluva different place to take a breather."

"That's not true. I slept on the sidewalk some nights, looking for you. I walked till I dropped trying to find you." It was the first time that day, since he had confessed, that he had raised his voice, which also shook.

Tobias forced himself to ignore the emotion. "Sure. By choice." He shook his head again. "You've been unhappy, but do you know what it means to be foreclosed on? To lose it all? To feel like an ignorant failure because you're not sure you didn't give it all away with your stupidity and poor choices? To be so destitute, you're not sure what life will look like three hours later? They took my home, my belongings, and my car. I lost everything. Or gave it up. I'm not sure, but there was nothing to return to the way you could come back here every day. For two years I've lived in madness. You played at it. Camped out. You could always come home." He paused. "And home wasn't with me."

"It was with you. Why won't you believe that?"

Tobias laughed again with no humor. "How many times did you come back here? And shower and take a perfect nap in this bed or in one of two-dozen others we passed on our way here?"

He sat down on the foot of the bed and bounced on it a little. He turned around and looked at the head of the bed and spotted a strange remote.

"Is…is this a Sleep Number bed?" He got up and headed for the remote. He picked it up and toyed with the controls. "What are you? A forty-five? A fifty? A thirty-five on hard days, when you need an extra soft bed?"

Arthur closed his eyes. Tobias sat down again. "And what else? I can't imagine you don't have a pool. Did you come here and go for a swim on hot days while I traipsed back and forth to the tent in hundred-degree heat to make sure our stuff was still there? Stuff you didn't even need? Dime-store garbage?"

"Don't say that."

"Did you?"

"No."

"Or hit the sauna, when Spring Street got a little too dusty for your sinuses?"

"No."

"What else? Soothing lotions? Health food? Musical couches, depending upon which room you wanted to sit or fall asleep in on a lazy Tuesday afternoon while I was at the library trying to find a way to contribute and ease your temp-job load?"

"No."

"Maybe you streamed a little TV during a long lunch at home? Or in your office, where you're the boss?"

"Never."

"You must have thought my air mattresses and duffel bag were the worst thing you ever suffered."

"You're wrong."

"I don't know how you didn't laugh," he choked up thinking about their first time together, "that first night, with me fishing around in a *duffel bag* for some charity condoms. Maybe you did laugh later, after I fell asleep in your arms."

"I didn't. Don't say that. That isn't true. Don't say that." His voice broke.

Hearing the sound made Tobias feel wretched and sad. "Like I said, I'm an idiot." He sniffed and left the bedroom and tried to find the elevator but couldn't. He made several turns down hallways and finally spotted a staircase and worked his way toward it at a fast clip.

For the second time that day, Arthur chased him. He caught up to Tobias at the top of the staircase and pulled gently on his arm.

Tobias stopped.

Something came over Arthur, something Tobias hadn't expected: anger.

"Tobias, I love you, and I'll do whatever it takes to make it right, but stop telling me what you think I am when I'm in this house."

They stared at each other in the dim hallway.

"And don't tell me I don't know what it means to lose it all. I know exactly what it's like. It was how I felt when I came home and found you gone, and our home was gone, too. Everything, everything I love had been stolen or lost."

Tobias wanted to see only the pain in Arthur, for he could reach out to that and maybe find his way back. But they were surrounded in his deception, and it cluttered the road to redemption.

"This house has sheltered me a long while, but it means nothing. You say I played a game, but a game can be stopped at any time. I can cash in or flip the checker board, and that's it. This house was a game, and I stopped playing with it easily and happily when I found you."

Tobias swallowed hard.

"But tell me how to stop loving you. What are the rules, exactly, in this game I'm supposed to be playing, for letting me walk away from the only man I'll ever love?"

Tobias couldn't stand it. He ran down the long, long staircase. He had no idea where it led. It curved, and the bottom was out of sight, giving it the illusion of going on forever. He thought it had to have been fifteen feet wide, and the carpet on each stair seemed fifteen inches thick. The steps were shallow, so that he barely had to lift his feet to get from one step to the other. Moving down them felt like gliding on air.

Arthur raced after him, pleading his case. "This is the game, Tobias. Where we are right now. The way I've been living in this house. What I had with you was real life."

It had taken an eternity, but they reached the bottom floor and were close to the entryway of the house in a smaller foyer off the main one.

This house is absurd.

They were back where they had started.

Tobias sprang for the door. "I'll grab my bag from the car and hitchhike home."

"Tobias!" Arthur's voice echoed around the ground floor, as though Arthur had called Tobias a dozen times.

The voice surrounded Tobias and pulled him in. He stopped in the middle of the atrium and turned to face Arthur. He saw a raw pain in Arthur's eyes. He heard a painfilled strain in his voice. It kept Tobias from turning again and heading out the door.

"No one lets me in," Arthur said. "I'm not allowed to share for real. The minute they know about my money, it becomes who I am, and everything about me is sidelined. Do you know how devastating it is to be invisible everywhere you go? To catch someone checking their watch on a first date because the initial excitement of a date with money has worn off and they realize they've got to fake interest for three hours?"

"That's…hard to believe."

"It's true."

"No…I know. It's just that…you're so handsome and easy to talk to, I can't imagine checking my watch on a first date with you. I still had my watch on our first date, and I never checked it once."

Arthur looked grateful and so in love with Tobias and very sad. "The first real conversation I had in years was when I woke up with you in your tent, bruised and battered and cared for and talked to like a real person. I don't want this. I want that, I want what I had with you."

Tobias blinked back the moistness in his eyes and stared out a floor-to-ceiling window that looked onto a vast courtyard that hadn't been visible from the street or the garage. Doors on the far end of it appeared to lead to other areas of the house.

It was an intimate alcove that one could probably walk through naked without reserve, a shortcut added for the convenience of the homeowner who didn't feel like walking all the way around his square footage to get to whatever was on the other side. Tobias could have pitched his tent in the middle of it and still had plenty of room to romp around any side of it. A small swimming pool could have fit inside that courtyard, and yet it was cozy, pleasing.

I'm such a fool.

"I used to want to matter to someone, anyone. Then I spent that second night in your tent and left the next morning filled with loneliness and jealousy because I wanted to be invited back into your space, to be with you, and I was locked out. And I wanted to matter only to you. But it seems I don't matter to anyone, not even to you, anymore."

The words stabbed Tobias and hurt him in a strange way. They were the first foelike words Arthur had spoken.

They were enemies in love.

Tobias knew he had pushed them both to the ledge, with his pride and his rights. He peered over the cliff and into the abyss of a doomed relationship and felt terror, for he knew he had to jump. Arthur had given him no choice.

"I know you see me as a liar you can't trust, but I have a feeling you're also standing there talking to my money, which always steals the limelight, wondering what it thinks of you, what it hopes to buy you so that I may have my way with you, how it hopes to distract us both with its shiny objects, which room it'll sleep in tonight, whether it ever laughed at you. It didn't. It laughs at me. It mocks me. Constantly. It knows it's cleverer than I am, that I worked hard to earn my own jailer, that I can use it to buy everything but what matters." He laughed a bitter laugh. "Even my money knows that you, Tobias, can't be bought. It's one of the many reasons I love you."

Tobias closed his eyes. "Arthur, please," he said. *I'm about to tumble into a bottomless pit. Let me fall.*

"That virtue might even be how you ended up losing so much."

Tobias opened his eyes and regarded Arthur. *Please stop talking.*

"I wish I had known you for *five minutes* two years ago, just long enough to give you a little advice and help you stem your losses. I wouldn't have even asked you to love me if I could just avert disaster for you. And, yes, the piano would have been the first thing I saved."

He took a few steps toward Tobias but held up his hands to show he didn't plan to encroach.

"It turned out to be you who came to *my* rescue. It started with your voice, which mesmerized me the minute you offered me a cup of black coffee and has, at times, paralyzed me with its resonance and beauty and kindness. There's something about it."

He was resolute and calm. He seemed to Tobias to be desperate but determined, like the man who earned the house they stood in—and walked three miles with him to buy provisions at the cheapest store.

"I'm proud," he kept on, "of what we are together, what I've become with you. I'm sorry I lied. I've been destitute and vacant, in my own way, for a long time. I didn't know any other way to finally be human. I stumbled into it, literally, and then I lied to hang onto a truth and the person I really am."

Hearing those words, Tobias felt the old Arthur, *his* Arthur all around him. The feeling let him drop his defenses a little. "Why did you surround yourself with so many barriers?" he said. "Fancy cars and clothes and a damned castle?"

"The fact that you asked that question proves my point. You want to know why I didn't live somewhere less obvious and daunting, somewhere more approachable, why I didn't drive something that hid my wealth or dress on an average budget, presumably so that people could get to know me for me, am I right?"

"Yes."

"That's what I finally did."

Tobias looked away and shook his head, in defiance of himself, or a part of himself that understood Arthur. Something about Arthur's words disturbed him and made him want to run. A truth that lurked within those words tried to break out and pull him to a different ledge, one that overlooked a future with Arthur, but Tobias denied it its escape with obstinance and righteousness. He had been lied to, and he would travel that path.

"I met you while I was wearing three-day-worn sales rack clothes that appeared to be the only thing standing between me and all of outdoors," Arthur said. "I was pitiful and appeared to have lousy life skills, and you let me right in."

"It isn't that easy," Tobias managed to say, but somewhere in his mind, he wondered. He backed away from the edge of the cliff.

A fichus tree in the corner of the courtyard caught his eye. It had no other purpose than to look lovely and please the owner with its presence. It may have been a small playground to squirrels and provided a place for ladybugs to land, but its primary reason for being was aesthetic. Arthur had a courtyard with a tree in it, just because. For what that spare tree symbolized—the difference between frivolity and survival on a worn-out patch of city sidewalk next to some rutty grass—it could have been a mighty oak.

Tobias returned to the edge of the cliff. He knew it was where he belonged. He determined that he would make Arthur see the truth, and he would jump.

"I think back on every conversation," he said, "and I wonder who was listening to me. Were you some rich stranger filtering my words through what you know in this life? I saw a man who was down and lived like I did and really had to think about where his next meal came from, and whose feelings were born from the same fear and deprivation and exhaustion that mine were. But that wasn't you. And I shared things with you. Some of my worst humiliations," his head hung for a moment, "awful things that I never would have told you if I thought you were hearing me from so dishonest a place." He paused to be sure his last point got through and said, "From a place so different from mine. It's called relating for a reason. I *did* let you right in because of your sales-rack clothes."

He had said his piece, but it all overwhelmed him. The echoes and staircase and elevator and fichus tree were too much. He choked back tears of self-pity and raw anger. "I'm humiliated, Arthur. Don't you see that? And not because you're rich and I'm poor, not really. It's because I was giddy to share things with you, almost the way it is with children in school when they find a friend who is like them. That's what I found. A friend," he swallowed, "and a lover who was like me, someone who seemed to be happy to know me because of that bridge of commonality we built and that we used to easily reach each other, and you tricked me, as though I really were a child, which I guess I was to you considering I was so naïve I had lost everything," he glared at Arthur, "and believed you when you had lied and learned things about me because you gained false access."

"Tobias, please, I—"

"You sneaked in and let me believe you were a special safe space where I could really be me because, you know, we were in the same kind of mess, and it wasn't true. You robbed me of the right to relate to whom I wanted in the way I wanted. You intercepted messages that weren't really meant for you. And you made a fool of me in the process. I mean, you literally let me run my mouth in the tent about how I would spend the money if you really drove that Maserati and turned out to be rich, and *it was you in that car*. Do you see how awful that is?"

"I do see it." Arthur stepped a little closer. "I do, and I'm sorry, Tobias. I'm so sorry. I never saw it that way. I kept facts from you, but I was always me. It was the real me who listened to you and loved you and related to you. Those *were* my messages."

"I'd like to believe that. I don't know...."

"You can believe it. And I can only say that I'm humiliated too, by this absurd life I live. I brought you here to expose myself and show you you're *not* alone. Do you know what it's like to reach a point where basically nobody cares about you? *That's* abject failure, Tobias. I wrought that. And maybe *I'm* naïve, but I thought our love had no conditions and that you shared things with me because you loved me, and you knew I loved you and cared about you, but it sounds like you needed me to be only one kind of way, a poor man, to love me. That hurts."

At that moment, Tobias empathized with Arthur and still loved him. He wanted to embrace Arthur and say *I care about you more than about life itself. I will love you until I die, even if I'm not sure who you are and can't live that way.*

Instead, he spoke a different truth and knew he probably hurt Arthur worse. "I didn't need you to be poor to love you. I needed you to be honest about your poverty. I needed my sympathies for you and my worries about you to be real. That's all. When you don't have basic needs met, when you're not able to provide a meal for yourself or aren't worthy of the dignity of not smelling bad because you made some mistakes with money, when life kicks you down that hard and doesn't care if you ever stand up again, when you could crawl into a tent and die and no one would know until the smell overwhelmed them, *that's* abject failure. When you find someone, who gets it because they live it, too, that's…a blessing. But that blessing's been shattered. I mean, I ride a bus to take a shower. *You have a fucking elevator in your house!*" His voice bounced all around him, up to the ceiling, and back to the floor, where it lingered for several seconds before it faded away.

"And the fact that you just yelled, 'You have a fucking elevator in your house!' is why I didn't tell you that I have a fucking elevator in my house!"

They stood still and let the echoes dissipate.

Tobias ventured into the quiet. "I felt sorry for your situation and sometimes really hurt for you, and it was unnecessary. How do you use someone like that?"

"Because I *did* need every bit of that sympathy. And I guess it's in how you measure it. You lost possessions and a quality of life. It cost you your friends, unfairly. I was unable to build those personal connections. A different kind of poverty, but I was destitute, nevertheless, and in a way that I think is far more indicative of failure."

Arthur's words hurt Tobias, for his love for Arthur ran deep, and he felt tremendous sympathy for how lonely he really was. He even resented those absent, ghosted people in Arthur's life, who wouldn't materialize for him and be his friend.

He said, "I wish you had told me that from the beginning. I could have loved you just as easily. Really. You could have said after the mugging, 'Hey, thanks for the save. I'm embarrassed. I'm actually pretty well off. Guess I lost my head last night. Too much to drink. I appreciate the help. Wanna get dinner sometime?'"

Arthur kept his tacit promise to Tobias not to come too close, but he stepped a little nearer and spoke softly so that not a word echoed off the many, many walls or the high ceiling.

"Even though I didn't tell you, do you think I made up my feelings and sentiments?" He stood closer to Tobias than he had since they had arrived there. "That everything I said was scripted? That when I touched you, it meant nothing? That I didn't want to give you everything when I made love to you? That when you made love to me, I felt nothing? It wasn't heaven? I didn't care? I didn't treasure it as the gift that it was? It wasn't really me, so it didn't matter who you were?"

Tobias gathered himself and stared into Arthur's eyes. "No, I don't know. I don't know, Arthur."

"I told lies. But I didn't see it as lying to you. I saw it as keeping myself safe. Everyone, *everyone* holds something back in the beginning. Things that make them too vulnerable to another person. Things they're ashamed of, things they believe they'll be misjudged for. Maybe crimes they committed or past relationships in which they were a victim or a job they got fired from, and they don't want to carry that legacy into what they hope will be something good, in our case, for me, the best thing to happen in my life." He let those words hang a moment. In the silence and long wait that hovered between them, he kissed Tobias.

Tobias was trapped, by Arthur's kiss, Arthur's professions of love, and his own love for Arthur.

"Let me ask you. The night I came by and invited you for Chinese, you said you had been at the library looking for a job. Were you? Or were you surfing the Internet?"

"We know the answer. I wasn't as motivated then."

"Yet, you presented yourself otherwise, presumably to achieve a certain result in your interaction with me, right?"

Tobias weighed Arthur's words. "True," he finally said.

"You knew you were trying to get back on your feet and that you wanted to be job-hunting that day and that you had job-hunted on other days, and you conflated it all that night and gave me your *essence*. It's like when someone says they're dieting. It doesn't matter if they say they ate salad or cottage cheese for lunch. They're telling the truth about watching their weight. What I did is the same thing."

"On a very different scale."

"On the exact same scale. I put forth an image, and so did you. You wanted me to think you were an enterprising man who was simply down on his luck. It turned out to be true in a different way, just like it turned out I was destitute in a different way from what you thought, but you shaped the story of who you were to grab the essence of your truth if not the exact facts, to advance your cause in a way that made no difference. You didn't lie to me about who you were."

"So, you think it's okay for partners to lie to each other and fudge facts to keep things comfortable and easy?"

"No, not at all. I'm saying that at the beginning, we all hide something, like, if I really were a construction guy and we got married. If people asked us how we met, we would say we bumped into each other at the park, across from the Music Center, you know, hoping that the 'Music Center' reference would hide the rest of the story. We would never say, 'One of us was drunk off his ass, getting mugged, and the other one happened to see it while panhandling not too far from the tent he lived in.'"

Tobias almost smiled.

"Sometimes, keeping some things veiled is the only way someone vulnerable can protect themselves, especially in the beginning. I prolonged that phase a little, but the proof that I never would have withheld the real story forever is the fact that you're standing in this house. When I came clean, I revealed the ugly mugging, so to speak. I showed you everything. For the rest of my life, I'll tell you whatever you want to know. I'll share it all. Once you let someone in, because you trust them and it makes sense, the hiding is over."

Tobias didn't say anything. He realized he had no good answer.

"Can you honestly say that if I had handed you the five hundred dollars I had in my pocket the morning after I was mugged, you would have seen me as Arthur? The Arthur you know? Would you have bothered to get to know who I am? Would my money have daunted you into deference? Wouldn't I have become 'that rich guy' who thanked you with charity, like someone whose wallet is found and who hands over a ten or a twenty as a courtesy for the other person's trouble? I'd be the guy you didn't want to bother with too many details about your life because you figured I wouldn't care about your struggles moving around at my so-called fabulous heights. You said to me more than once that you didn't want my charity or my pity. Honestly, I don't think we ever would have gotten to know each other without my holding back certain truths."

Tobias took a step back.

"You had five hundred dollars in your pocket the night I rescued you?"

Arthur hesitated. "Yes," he finally said. He looked guilty.

"And I was feeling magnanimous and like a good host spending my spare change on a small coffee." He cradled his forehead in his hands. "I'm such a chump." He looked up. "And a loser. What a loser."

Arthur took Tobias's hands and held them. Their faces were close. "You're not a loser. I really don't like hearing that. I love you. And I'm asking you to answer my question. If I had come back the next day and asked you to dinner, wouldn't you have said no because you would have been worried about bothering a wealthy person with someone poor and thought it was a token gesture you should refuse? Wouldn't you have wondered how you looked and whether it was up to par?"

Tobias *had* worried, even under the actual circumstances, about how he smelled that night. Standing in that echo-chamber foyer, he had to admit that he wondered if Arthur's being wealthy would have caused him to refuse the dinner invitation. There was no doubt in Tobias's mind that if they hadn't gone to dinner, they probably would not have fallen in love. Arthur's lies might have been the reason they came together.

Arthur pressed on. "Wouldn't you have dreaded landing in some fancy place with fifteen forks and a different wine for every course and said no? If you had said yes, and I had taken us somewhere even a little more expensive than that Chinese place, you would have thought, 'Why are we here when he knows I can't contribute to the tab? How do I explain that when the check comes? Do I stand out? How am I dressed? Am I boring? Is this a waste of his rich time?' You know I'm right. It's me, and I know you. You're even doing it now. I mentioned the money, and now that's what matters. What we went through, even whether I lied or your doubts about whom you love, have been shunted to the side. The whole scope of this conversation has shifted to the money."

Arthur let go of Tobias's hands and walked away.

Tobias wasn't sure why, but he followed Arthur. He hated to accept it, but he *was* guilty of focusing on the money. He *did* wonder what the wealthy Arthur thought of him and not just because it was a different Arthur. It was that it was a rich Arthur. He hadn't even been peeved that Arthur had let him spend his last cash on coffee, the morning after the mugging, when he had his own money.

Arthur made his way through two long, wide hallways that traveled the distance of the house to get to a large set of French doors. The doors led to a covered patio in a backyard that was larger than the grassy section of Grand Park and had a great lagoon-like swimming pool about fifty feet from the patio and a second house situated at the farthest corner of the lawn, the guest house Arthur had mentioned, Tobias presumed. Thirty yards in the other direction stood a smaller structure that appeared to be a pool house. It was almost the size of Tobias's condo.

Arthur sat down on a patio chair with his head in his hands. Sitting there in that wonderland filled with clean grass for his bare feet—unlike the dirty grass they had in most places downtown except for the park—and large lounge chairs to sleep in by the water that lapped along the sides of his pool, he looked miserable, as though he didn't really know where he was or that any of what surrounded him was there and belonged entirely to him, to do with what he wished.

Tobias said, "If you hadn't been forced, when were you going to tell me the truth?"

Arthur looked at him. "You won't believe me, but I probably would have told you about a month after you started your job."

"Easy to say, now."

"It's true. I love you, so I'm going to say it plainly. Your situation was a vicious cycle. At first, it knocked you down. And then from the ground, you made hasty decisions that kept you there."

Tobias felt exposed. It was true.

"After we met, after a while, I noticed that changed. You slowed down. You made prudent decisions. You even said you felt inspired by what we could have that day you saw me in my car."

Tobias stared at the pool in the near distance. He knew Arthur was right.

"The more I saw you getting back on your own feet, under your own steam—"

"Not just my own steam. Having you mattered a lot." He stared at the pool again and said, "You showed me why it was all worth it. Just having you there. Don't discount that." It was a moment of honesty that, for an instant, put them back on the same side. It felt good to Tobias. He glanced again at Arthur, who smiled warmly.

"You call yourself a loser," Arthur said, "but you're not. You left home young, succeeded in school, and found a noble profession that you are good at and worked in for over a decade. You are impetuous, though. You got knocked down, and, while injured, you made some bad calls, some hasty ones, too. And you were finally coming off that popped Achilles heel and getting back in the game with workable plays. I didn't think it would be a good idea to interfere with the way you were turning your life around. Believe me, I know at least twenty people who would have hired your math-y brilliance on my say-so inside of fifteen minutes. And they wouldn't have insulted me or dared to alienate me with pesky things like work history and credit checks. They would have cleared some office space and handed you your benefits package. If I hadn't ruined us, you would have seen my firm and noticed it's small. I keep it simple. But that's because I've been at it a long time, and I don't need to exploit the skills of others and disguise it as big-firm pomp. I work fine with an assistant and a phone, but I would tell you don't let that fool you. I'm as powerful as this ridiculous house implies."

Tobias's jaw dropped.

"But I knew you wouldn't want that kind of help and, way more importantly, didn't need it because you'd get there on your own. And," he shrugged a little like he was about to state the obvious and wanted to acknowledge it, "I knew they would love you at your job. Once you were there for a while and knew they liked you and could draw on that earned success if I gave you doubts, I planned to tell you. I planned to tell you and beg for mercy, beg because, despite what you think, I know what I did is hard to accept. I've always known this day would arrive and maybe break us."

"Why did you confess this morning?"

Arthur became emotional and shook his head. "I don't know. There was something about you. When I saw you and realized how much you had already proven you can take, I couldn't watch it anymore. It no longer seemed to have a positive purpose."

After a moment, Tobias said, "Were there any other lies? I mean, are you hiding anything else?"

"Yes, there is one other lie."

Tobias shook his head and looked away. He was hurt anew.

"It's not what you think. There's nothing left to unmask, but…."

Tobias raised his eyebrows and turned his palms up as if to ask, "Well?"

"That first Sunday I showed up at the tent, I told you about a man who had been arrested. Do you remember?"

Tobias shook his head again in distracted irritation and with dread for whatever was to come next. "Yeah, I remember."

"I was so shocked by that, that I needed to vent, and I was so happy to see you and to be talking to you, and it was just my second day on the streets, and, as I said, I was shocked, so I blurted out the story."

"And?" He was impatient.

"What I didn't tell you was that I stepped away from that incident and called my civil attorney, a guy named Nathan Cresswell, and asked him to find a good defense attorney and send him or her to the police station to get the man out. The man's name was Terrence Godfrey, and they got him out that day and reunited him with his stuff. My attorney gave him five hundred dollars in cash."

Five hundred dollars, again.

"So, you just skipped that part."

"Yes, and I had immediate hindsight that telling you that story was a dumb idea, not only because I had to commit a lie of omission, but because I let you think that man was rounded up and maybe had to wait a long time to get out."

"I did think that."

"I know. And, it's a tired line, but I know you won't believe me when I say it also violated my principles. Yes, I kept my money a secret, but I worked very hard to be sure I was always truthful with you about life, about my day and whether it was good or bad, about who I am, as a person. I never talked about any of my so-called temp jobs because it would have forced me to lie. If you think about it, it would have added great layers to the story, all the crazy details about the weird places they sent me, but I couldn't do it. I never gave you the name of a place or a fake co-worker."

It was true, Tobias realized, but it wasn't enough.

"I set the stage with vague facts at the Chinese restaurant, when I had only known you four days, and I veered far from the topic after that, the way, as I said earlier, a person who isn't ready to share hard parts of their past will avoid subjects that could make them have to do that. A woman who has maybe terminated a pregnancy that was no one's business may have to blink her way through a conversation about kids and whether she has them or wants them. If forced, she may have to say, 'I've never been pregnant.' I didn't want to have to say untrue things like that, so I stayed away from those subjects. That's why I tell you, you really know me. Who I am was the only thing I could talk about truthfully, and us getting to know each other was all I cared about, so it worked fine."

Tobias had to admit Arthur had a point. He even admitted it out loud. "I hear you, a little. It's like when people talk about Father's Day or Mother's Day or going home for the holidays or family, in general. I chit-chat my way around the fact that I'm on horrible terms with my parents."

"Exactly. Or an atheist who doesn't want to explain themselves to a person of faith. They just allow the person of faith to express it and, by that, they maybe give the impression they believe in God, too, when they don't."

Tobias nodded a little, more to himself than at anything else or at Arthur.

"I was silent about my money, but if I opened my mouth to speak, I tried always to tell the truth. Even the day you saw me in my car, I never said it wasn't me."

Tobias thought hard about that day and realized Arthur was right. It didn't excuse the fact that he hadn't corrected Tobias when he said he thought it was a man who only looked like Arthur and that it wasn't Arthur, but on the technicality of Arthur trying to speak only truth as he lived his lie, he was correct.

"The one exception was telling you about Terrence and not admitting I had hired a lawyer for him."

"Maybe *my* line is tired, but I don't know, Arthur. I just don't know."

Tobias was resolute and very sad, about all of it. He gazed at the swimming pool again. After a while, he couldn't help himself. He walked to the water's edge and stared down at his reflection in what looked like a quiet alcove in a great sea.

Soon, Arthur's reflection appeared next to his and wavered a little as a gentle breeze stirred the water below them.

As he had many times since they had arrived at Arthur's house, Tobias shook his head and let out a puff of incredulous air.

They stared at each other in the water.

Finally, Tobias asked Arthur's reflection, "What's it like?"

Arthur's reflection looked up at him and asked, "What's what like?"

"Walking into your own backyard to go swimming in a lagoon. I'll bet the water's perfect." He bent down and swirled his hand in the pool. Their reflections disappeared. "Yep. Pushing eighty degrees, but still in the seventies, and saltwater not chlorine. No funny smell. Easy on the skin and eyes."

Arthur didn't respond.

Tobias glanced in every direction around them and noticed there were no other houses in sight. Trees and very high ivy-covered walls blocked out all spectators.

"I guess you can bare it all out here, and no one will know," Tobias said.

"I wouldn't know. I haven't tried it," Arthur said.

Tobias unbuttoned his shirt and tossed it on a nearby chaise lounge.

Arthur stared at him. "I get your point. My pool is also ridiculous." He turned to go back to the house.

Tobias loosened his belt. He kicked off his shoes and stepped out of his pants and tossed them onto the chair.

Arthur turned to him. "Tobias—"

Tobias added his socks to the pile of clothes. He stood in his boxer briefs in the bright, afternoon, Southern California sun.

It was Arthur's turn to shake his head. "You don't have to go swimming in your underwear to prove how absurd my life is."

"I wasn't going to swim in my underwear. Don't want it to get wet."

Arthur was struck a little dumb and didn't say anything. He only stared.

Tobias removed his boxer briefs.

Arthur glanced at Tobias's naked midriff and quickly looked up to meet Tobias's eyes.

"Don't worry, Arthur. Unlike you with me, I'm not aiming to hide anything from you."

They stood there, one fully clothed, one naked, and watched each other.

Finally, Tobias strolled to the side of the pool that had several shallow steps and waded in.

He swam to middle of the lagoon, where the water wasn't too shallow or deep. From there, he worked his way to the edge and pushed off and swam laps, freestyle, across the middle of the pool. Out of the corner of his eye, he spotted Arthur watching him. He ducked his head so that all he could feel above water was fresh air on his rear end. When he turned to take in a breath, he turned away from Arthur and no longer saw him.

He picked up speed. He thought about how he had never been alone with Arthur in a place that large. Everywhere they went—the park, the mission, the library—they shared with dozens of others. As always, he thought like a math teacher and realized the largest area he had ever been alone in with Arthur was his ten-by-ten-foot tent.

He was oblivious to everything except the fact that he hadn't had that much freedom in years. He had been hemmed in by the boundaries of foreclosure and poverty so long, he forgot what it felt like to experience abandon.

He made a hard, angry flip-turn and, as he came out of it and pushed off, almost bumped into Arthur, who was also in the pool, wearing no clothes. Tobias stopped swimming and stood near Arthur.

They stared at each other.

Arthur said, "It's breathtaking."

"What is?" Tobias said through water that dripped down his face.

"Your beautiful bottom, poking out of the water and gliding by me."

"Have you been there the whole time?"

"Yeah. You didn't see me get in? I've been watching you swim laps like your life depended on it."

Tobias was surprised. He treaded a little to his right and swam around Arthur.

Like a twin dolphin, Arthur swam alongside him.

Tobias stopped. "I asked you once before. Are you stalking me?"

"Yes."

Tobias didn't swim away.

Arthur moved closer. Tobias felt heat from his body.

"Tobias. Please don't take yourself away from me. Not in here and not out there. Don't leave."

The water was comforting. Arthur commanded gently, and Tobias knew if they touched one another, their skin would glide easily together, and Tobias would respond with an obvious reaction from a part of his body he thought he should keep under water for the moment. Arthur's dark, wet hair shone in the sun and contrasted against his barely tanned skin in a sexy way.

"It's getting late," Tobias said. He swam to the steps and walked out of the pool. The chill from exiting the pool distracted him enough to keep his lower-body reactions to Arthur, wet and sexy, in check.

Arthur wasn't far behind him. "Wait here," he said.

Tobias watched him walk to the pool house. He took in the image of Arthur's wet behind. The fine hair on his cheeks gave him an earthy look.

"It's strange," Tobias said.

Arthur turned and quickly looked up and down his own body and glanced around at his rear end as if to inspect himself for problems. Finding nothing, he looked up with a lost expression on his face.

"No," Tobias smiled. "Not your backside. That's beautiful." Without looking down, he felt himself grow.

Arthur smiled a little shyly, and Tobias saw him grow, too.

"It's just that it's the first time I've seen you naked from more than a few feet away. In the tent, I never got to gaze at you from across some private expanse. A perfectly normal thing, and we never got to do it."

Arthur stared at him for a moment and then moved to take a step forward.

"We can't," Tobias said.

Arthur stopped. He stared again, but Tobias gave him no encouragement. After a moment, he turned back for the pool house. He returned with two towels.

Tobias fought a strong desire to take his towel and caress Arthur with it all over his body and stand behind him and dry his back and kiss his neck and massage his ass and reach around to the front and stroke his manhood and turn him around and kiss him there, too, and take him, hard and easy and fast and slow again, on a chaise lounge, as in the tent, exposed but seen only by one another.

Instead, he dried himself as quickly as he could and got dressed. Arthur was soon dressed, too.

"I think I should leave. This is the first time I've been away from my tent on a Sunday in the new spot. And I'm just remembering that I never rolled the covers over the windows. I spotted your flyer and lost all perspective. People can see in if they get nosy and close enough."

"*Your* tent?"

"Yes, my tent." Tobias could only hold Arthur's gaze for a few seconds. The pain on Arthur's face forced him to look away.

"So that's it?"

"I don't know what else to say, Arthur."

"It's over? Nothing we had survives?"

"It isn't my fault."

"I know." Arthur cleared his throat.

"I have to leave."

"At least let me drive you. If you're determined to spend the night in the tent, I can get you there faster."

Tobias wasn't sure what to do. Despite his earlier bravado, hitchhiking from Beverly Hills was a nonstarter, and he wasn't sure how far away a bus stop on Sunset might be from the upscale stretch of the boulevard where they were.

"If it makes you feel better—I know I'll feel better—we can take a smaller car that'll be less conspicuous when we get near…your campout. I don't want to draw any attention that could put your safety at risk."

Tobias hesitated. "Sure," he finally said. "And Arthur?"

"Yes?"

"For what it's worth, part of your experiment worked."

"My experiment?"

"You wanted the you I knew to be loved, by me, you say."

Arthur stared and waited.

"I do love you, or him." He turned and headed for the house.

∞ 19 ∞

BULLETS, LIGHT, HEAVEN, EARTH

ARTHUR PARKED ON WALL STREET, near the corner of Seventh Street. It was just after four o'clock, and autumn dusk had settled. A grayness that fought with the last of the sun hovered, but darkness remained a little in the distance.

The dim tone emphasized Tobias's feeling of doom. He believed his life had just a few minutes left and that it would end as soon as he got out of the car.

The ride back to his new encampment was as silent as the ride to Beverly Hills and included the same occasional sounds from Arthur's phone. In the turmoil, Arthur had forgotten to silence it before he started the car, and Tobias had no desire to touch it to silence it for him. The heaviness of the quiet, made heavier by the contrast of the intermittent tin pings, bore down on Tobias.

Arthur turned off the motor and his phone chimed again. He ignored it.

"You don't have to pretend that didn't happen."

"I know. It's just someone I can't talk to, right now."

Tobias had been curious about who had pinged Arthur's phone all day. He caved to his own desire to know.

"Who would that be?" He tried to sound nonchalant, but he wondered who the people were in Arthur's other world. In some way, he wanted to know them so that he'd gather how much they shaped Arthur and made him who he was. And, he wondered whether they were people with whom he should be angry. Had they laughed at him, too?

"It's Kelly. The Kelly I told you about, my assistant, the one who was my temp agency. She doesn't just run my work life. She's been the only other friend I've had through this, and she's dying to meet you. She really likes you, you know?"

"She doesn't know me," Tobias said tentatively.

"Yes, she does. I talk about you constantly, and she worries about me…constantly, or at least she did worry about me some, until you and I met. Then she worried a lot less. Later, when she saw how much I had on the line, she worried more." He smiled a little. "It's funny. We weren't really friends until the mugging. And the tent. And you. She calls me Mr. Dewynter because she prefers that and gives me grief for not having a website and treats me like Methuselah, but she's just the second real friend I've made in the past four months and in the past fifteen years."

Tobias had to admit he was intrigued by Arthur's other life.

"When I got your yearbook photo, I texted it to her. She texted back, 'Wow! I get it, now.' " He held up his hands and flashed jazz palms to imitate Kelly's enlightenment. "There was a GIF of a girl fainting. Her way of telling me she thinks you're handsome. It's funny how fast she finds those things. She attaches one to every text. The ones about you. And the occasional snarky ones about rude clients." He laughed a little.

"You two text about me?"

Arthur sighed. "We do. But not like you think. And she was the only one in the firm who knew about my feigned life. I promise. Everyone else just assumed I was seeing someone I met somewhere. But Kelly's different. She's always wondering what we're up to. The day after my second night in the tent, that Sunday I showed up, when I knew," he paused and gathered himself, "that I loved you, as I lay awake all night and thought about you while I listened to the cars fly by below us, and thought it best to never see you again because," he paused again, "I didn't think you'd love me back," he inhaled with his eyes closed and held them that way, "it was Kelly who gave me the courage to go back, to wait for you outside the library and fight it out." He opened his eyes and looked at Tobias.

Tobias was silent. He didn't know what to say.

"After that," Arthur said, "she let me brag about you. I gave her an update every morning that I went into the office."

"Really?" Tobias wasn't annoyed. He was surprised to find that Arthur seemed to have held him in such high regard and that he had been almost like a giddy teenager, telling Kelly every day about Tobias and making him sound a little like the big man on campus with whom Arthur didn't want to blow it.

Why does that surprise you? Is Arthur correct? Do you see his money as something that elevates him beyond you, even when he said he doesn't feel that way? Aren't you 'thinking for him' the way he laments people have for years, projecting assumptions about his money onto him and presuming certain motives and feelings, based on those assumptions? Or is it that he lied, and you assumed it was to make a fool of you, which he didn't do? Or is it that this new information makes it harder to accuse him of seeing you as a loser?

Arthur smiled. "Yeah. Really. Every day that I woke up with you as my boyfriend was like a new bit of good news. I would tell Kelly what we ate the night before and what happened with other tents and just the goings on in our lives. She's still pissed about JoJo. I think she may have secretly reached out to him at the place I took him to."

Tobias was surprised. He had been part of a circle he knew nothing about.

"Even if we just played Frisbee in the park, she wanted to hear about it."

"I don't know what to say."

Arthur shook his head. "It's okay." After a moment, he said, "I'm probably sinking my own boat, but the day you saw me in my car, she almost took my head off."

Tobias shifted in his seat. The topic made him uneasy. In a way, for Tobias, it had been Arthur's most egregious moment of dishonesty.

"At first," Arthur said, "I thought she was just mad that our cover had been blown."

Tobias felt himself getting riled. "Arthur, you should drop it."

"No, please let me finish. It's not about me, it's about her." He touched Tobias's arm. "I wondered about her what you're thinking about me. That it was a game, something to be naughty about for the thrill of getting away with it. But the entire time she yelled at me for taking my car downtown, I could tell she was genuinely worried I was going to lose you. I knew then that she didn't want that to happen because she knew it wasn't a game for me and that my life and happiness were on the line, and I knew she didn't want that for herself, like the friend that she is. She didn't want to see me hurt. And she didn't want that for you. She bought into us, for real. I'm sorry I let you both down."

Tobias couldn't take much more. Arthur's hand on his arm gave him the worst feeling of dread, of ruin. It wasn't like in the pool, where the water and freedom cast a spell of suspension that held defeat at bay. In the car, with Arthur about to leave him there forever, the destruction was real.

He wanted to bolt from the car and literally run, even though he knew doom lay in any direction he might go. There was nothing for him outside the car.

"She sounds lovely, and like a good friend," he said. He hoped that ended the conversation.

"She is. Both things. My dream was to take you and her to dinner and let you get to know each other and pick on me a little in the process, you know, to bond." He smiled again, wistfully. "You don't know it, but you've broken up with both of us. She'll be crushed."

Tobias was sorry for the lost opportunity to meet Kelly. She reminded him of his wittier high school students who had aged into post-college as young adults wise beyond their years and able to keep pace with the grownups. He was sad for what would never be, for the tragedy he and Arthur had become. The day had shredded his nerves. He moved to exit the car.

Arthur squeezed his arm. He closed his eyes. "Please, Tobias. Please don't do this. You're taking my whole life with you."

No, I'm leaving my whole life with you.

Arthur opened his eyes. "I love you. Greatly. Almost tragically. You're…everything to me. An unexpected gem. A left-handed, right-brained, creative, piano-playing, math genius, who's sexy as hell and everything to me. I don't want to be without you. I'm so sorry I hurt you. I'll say that every day, if that's what it takes. I never aimed at deceiving you. I'm sorry."

Tobias pretended with not much success that he wasn't on the verge of tears. "I need to go. I want to see if anyone's hanging around who shouldn't be. I have to get out of this car."

"Okay, okay, but one more thing."

"Yes?"

"Look, I'm not trying to make excuses to be with you, but I never got to see what…we lost, what's left, of mine, I mean." The words, combined with the gentle way Arthur's hand rested on

Tobias's arm, with his hair still a little wet, wrecked Tobias. "Can I please come in and get my things?"

Tobias gazed through the front windshield at nothing. In front of him lay the length of Wall Street. In the near distance, he saw where the tents began to pop up toward the end of the lane, approaching Sixth Street. His tent was closest. He hated the sight of it, as he had hated it the day he moved into it, long before he knew Arthur.

He hadn't realized how much he reviled it until that moment. For four months, he had relished the instant, as he walked home from a day on the streets and worked his way up Spring Street, when the tent came into view, knowing Arthur would be there with him. Without Arthur, the tent was again a prison and a symbol of his abject failure. He remembered that Arthur had called his bedroom a hellhole. Tobias thought that was a fitting description for his tent. He no longer cared what happened next.

"Sure. Come get your things," he said. He pulled his arm away and jumped out of the car. He headed up the street without bothering to check whether Arthur followed, as though he still swam laps in Arthur's pool, unfettered. It had grown a little darker.

Arthur caught up to him and tried to chat. "Not too many people here," he said.

"No."

"The police probably won't monitor it too much."

"That's what I'm hoping."

They arrived at the front door flap. It suddenly felt strange to Tobias to invite Arthur into the tent once he knew that Arthur had other options. It seemed like a waste of Arthur's time.

He's right. He practically begged to come inside, and you still assume he doesn't want to be here because he has so much more than this tent available to him.

Neither of them moved to unzip the tent. Finally, Arthur said, "It's not my place, anymore, to just walk in."

"Oh. Yeah," Tobias said. He walked into the tent, and Arthur followed.

Arthur stood near the front entrance and looked around. His mouth fell open. "It's all gone." He blinked several times. "The table? The lamp? Our chairs?"

"Yes," Tobias said. He softened a little. "There was no time. I rolled the sleeping bags into their sacks and hooked them onto the tent. I deflated the mattresses and pillows and shoved them into the duffel bag." He gestured around the tent. "I grabbed some clothes and some drugstore stuff, the heater, the repellent devices. The rest is gone. Shoes, kitchen stuff, everything. I threw the tent on my back and walked away."

It was a weird kind of good feeling, sad but gratifying, to finally tell Arthur what had happened to him. He still needed Arthur's sympathy and secretly craved his comfort. The trauma of the previous ten days hadn't worn off. It had begun to, at ten o'clock that morning on Spring Street, but it had returned and worsened at the Biltmore and turned ghastly in Beverly Hills. In the semi-dark tent, Tobias wished he could lay next to Arthur and unburden himself.

Arthur went to the corner of the tent where Tobias had set up a makeshift nightstand out of stacked library books. He tapped the book at the top of the stack. "I was still reading this…and then I just forgot when everything went to hell and I couldn't find you…."

He picked up a pair of chopsticks that lay on the books. They were from the restaurant where they had had their first date. It was the set Tobias hadn't used. That night, he had jokingly tucked them into his shirt pocket, as though he would use them later, knowing he "sucked at chopsticks" and couldn't use them. It was the one nonessential item he took with him on the day of the raid.

"I can't believe it," Arthur said. "We lost so much." He cleared his throat. "I couldn't wait to get back to these things. To you. To us." He sniffed and cleared his throat again. "Our things. Our life. It's gone. Every, damned thing in my life is gone."

Tobias looked away. The words were true for him, too. The air became heavy and unusually cold. Darkness lurked. The tent closed in around him.

Arthur clung to the chopsticks. "I'm glad you were able to keep these."

"They were small enough."

"You have them on display."

"They kept me going," Tobias swallowed hard and repeated his first words, "they kept me going while you were gone."

Arthur returned the chopsticks to their place on the books.

They stared at each other in the dimmed light that came through the mesh tent windows.

"So, you're gonna do this? By yourself?"

Tobias was silent.

"I'm serious about this, Tobias. Don't struggle out here. You have nothing to prove. If you get pushed up against it," he choked back tears, "call me." He pulled out a high-tech gadget and pressed his thumbprint on it. It opened, and Tobias realized it was a combination wallet and phone case. The phone wasn't in it. Arthur took a business card from a thin compartment.

"Here."

Tobias took the card. He stared at it. In the shadows, he just made out the words on it. The card said, THE DEWYNTER FIRM, ARTHUR DEWYNTER, OWNER, LEAD ADVISOR. Arthur's e-mail address and cell and office phone numbers were listed. The Century City address was one that Tobias recognized as posh. The only logo was an embossed gold square, a muted gold, not a flashy one.

Arthur grabbed the card. "Wait," he said. He pulled a tiny pen from the wallet and phone case. His hand shook as he wrote down a number on the back of the card. He handed the card back to Tobias.

"This is the number to the landline at—"

"Your house."

"Yes." Arthur looked self-conscious.

Tobias contemplated the card. He wasn't sure whether to tear it up or sleep with it under his makeshift tent pillow. For the moment, he shoved it in his pocket.

Arthur handed him another card. "Would you please write your e-mail address on that? And your work information? You may not want to hear from me, but I don't want to lose contact. I need to know you're all right. If it's okay."

Tobias stared at the second card and then took it. "It's okay." He accepted the small pen and wrote down his information.

"Tobias, please."

"Don't." He handed Arthur the pen and the card.

Arthur put the pen away and pulled his phone out and greedily typed into it Tobias's contact information. He typed a little more. "I just sent you an e-mail. We're connected online, now." He tucked the card into a safe place in his gadget. "And, I'll subscribe you to my, well, it's barely a newsletter. It's, uh, just called *Dewynter*. Just some investment updates. Once a month. It's…dull. I…keep my firm dull."

Nothing about you is dull. I love you so much, right now.

Tobias took comfort knowing that, even if some evil force raided him again and took everything, including Arthur's card, and he forgot the information on it, and forgot how to find Arthur's house, Arthur had ensured they would never again be lost to one another. Tobias would always be able to find Arthur, and Arthur would be able to find him.

"If you need me…."

I do need you.

Arthur laughed a little and cried a little. "You know, I'm still the rudest guy in downtown." He knelt and reached for the sleeping bags. "The least I can do is help you with the mattresses and the bags. And I won't take no for an answer. You know I could always figure out this weird zipper combination better than you."

"Sure," Tobias said. "I'll roll down the windows." He stepped outside and closed the tent windows. A moment later, he returned and joined Arthur on the floor. He opened the nozzles on the air mattresses and let them self-inflate.

He watched Arthur. Arthur fumbled with the zippers. He couldn't get them to connect to one another. He hung his head.

And Tobias knew it was over.

His standing his ground, his rejection of Arthur, his insistence on tearing them apart. He couldn't do it. He wouldn't make it, emotionally. He wouldn't survive without Arthur. He didn't want to, and, somehow, no longer felt he needed to.

Kneeling on the tent floor with Arthur as they had done every night and all the days they stayed in the tent and relaxed and shared books and life and love, he didn't care about Arthur's money. He didn't love it or hate it. Tobias wasn't even sure Arthur's money was an interloper since it hadn't come between them. Arthur's lies had.

Somewhere in Tobias's mind, one dot connected to another. He realized he had no opinion of Arthur's money because he didn't know it. He was unfamiliar with it. Until that day, he had never seen it. It was a stranger to him, and as with any stranger, it felt like contact with it would be so fleeting, it deserved no serious consideration beyond polite acknowledgment because it would have no real effect on his own life.

And that was when it dawned on Tobias.

That was why Arthur did it, why he lied.

Tobias stared at Arthur, who still fought with the zippers, from across the mattresses and through the dim tent, and had a great epiphany: Arthur had been right to hide, to lie even. By doing so, he had shrouded his money from Tobias's psyche, his line of thinking, his approach to his own problems, *and the way he loved Arthur.* Arthur's money had never factored into Tobias's life or his love because it wasn't in the equation. And the fact that Arthur knew, and Tobias didn't, wasn't about one man duping the other. It was simply a fact that existed, without further meaning, because the money existed without further meaning.

And what Arthur had tried to tell Tobias all day finally became clear to Tobias. Arthur could take or leave his own money. It didn't make him happy. He didn't lie as much as he created an ideal world for himself and Tobias and them as a couple, without the money because lifelong love had nothing to do with money or any other material possession. It was like not telling someone what kind of car you drove or whether you owned a vase or kept a piano in storage. The presence or absence of the thing had nothing to do with love, especially not his and Arthur's, which survived on four dollars a day, sometimes, and had no sturdy walls around it.

Arthur gave Tobias his truest self, stripped bare, to be sure Tobias loved that person and to be sure he made Tobias happy, only as himself, as Arthur, both for his own sake and for Tobias's, out of love for him. Arthur knew money toyed with people in an intrusive way. It had toyed with Tobias all day in Beverly Hills and right outside the tent door. He wanted Tobias to be free of that influence as he considered whether he wanted a life with Arthur.

And not just for you, Tobias. He's human and hurts, too. Just as you're leaving to protect yourself, he had a right to be sure you could love him and want a life with him. And I do want a life with him because he does make me happy, in the tent, with only the spare change in his pockets. I don't need his money because I never have. I only need him.

Those realities hit him so hard, he felt the force of the blow in his chest and almost fell backward in the tent, for he knew it had come to him too late. He had accused Arthur of possessing the worst motives, and he didn't see a way back from that.

Tobias was suddenly terrified that he had pushed Arthur too far away to get him back, the right way, with Arthur not resentful of the accusations.

He used his knees as feet and inched closer to Arthur. He made Arthur let go of the sleeping bags.

Arthur looked at him.

Tobias brought his arms around Arthur and pulled him close in the dark. He spoke three words into his ear. "Stay. Please stay."

Arthur pulled away and looked at Tobias. He seemed caught off-guard. He looked afraid. "To what end? What do you want?" he said.

"It's what I don't want. I don't want you to leave. I love you. I need you. Seeing you here, I see *you*. I look at you and I can't even remember you have money, or maybe it's that I don't see your money. I just see what the last four months were like, here with you, in our home." He gave Arthur a very soft kiss. "I think about you in your other house, and the picture isn't right. I suddenly see that the distortions aren't the lies you told to protect yourself and give us a chance. They are that you don't really belong where we just were. It seemed easy to accuse you of being false in that big, strange place that was so different from here, but, here, I see the truth. And…I owe you a huge apology. I'm the one who's sorry for not trusting you and seeing why you did what you did. I'm sorry."

In the very last light the day would give, Tobias sensed that Arthur wanted with everything in him to give himself over to Tobias, but he wasn't sure that Tobias hadn't experienced a weak moment he would rescind.

"You don't believe me," Tobias said.

"I'm not sure. I trust who you are, but I'm scared."

Tobias leaned in a little. "So am I. But in here, in our home, without elevators and courtyards to distract me, and maybe too late, I think I understand why you did it. I think you were after the best kind of truth there is. Real love. And it worked. And I'm glad for it."

His mouth almost touched Arthur's.

"Did it?" Arthur said. "Did it work?"

Tobias brushed Arthur's lips with his own. "Yes. And I would be a fool to reject that kind of love. I'm sorry I let pride cloud my judgment. If you stay, I pledge to be better and have more faith—all the faith there is in the world—the next time we face trouble. I'll show the same faith I did that first night, when I brought you as a total stranger into this tent because I knew I could trust you."

Arthur was still too afraid to say anything.

"I love you, Arthur. I want you. Here or there. I just want you with me. I need you. Will you marry me?"

Arthur's surprise left his mouth partly open, and his warm breath on Tobias's face was comforting and sensual and intimate and private and sexy. Tobias barely held back.

He moved his mouth closer to Arthur's, without touching it. He stared into Arthur's eyes and asked the question again. "Will you marry me, Arthur?" He gave into desire and need and kissed Arthur, just with his lips. He withheld his tongue to keep control of himself until he got his answer. "Will you marry me?"

"Yes, yes, yes. I'll marry you," Arthur whispered, and once he had given his answer, they held back nothing.

They stripped in the dusky tent as they had done many times, and everything else fell away too—the distance between them, the horrors of their ten-day nightmare, doubt, pain, and longing. It was a reunion of lovers who had been torn apart twice, by separation and sorrow, and their first desperate fits of touching and reaching and caressing and hugging and kissing had as much to do with banishing forever those terrible events and reassuring one another as they did with making each other feel good physically.

It took Tobias back to their first night together, when they made love over the freeway and sailed higher than either of them ever had, and he realized on that strange evening after a stranger day in Beverly Hills that nothing was different between them, that Arthur's truth hadn't changed how he made Tobias feel as he made love to Tobias and as Tobias made love to him. They longed for the same connections they always had and melded in familiar ways to achieve them. They made deep love and slow love and reminded each other of the ecstasy of hard love and segued into the wonder of tender love. They felt the familiar thrill of giving themselves to each other fully, with their nakedness on display for one another but cloaked from passersby by the cloth of the tent.

Arthur still spanked with quiet perfection.

Tobias still cried out while holding Arthur's face close so that only he heard the joy.

Arthur drove forward with a steady rhythm that needed no voice because the feelings he experienced were on his face.

Tobias led them into steady streams of deep kisses and kept the juices flowing between their mouths to make the journeys of their lips and tongues and teeth that took teasing bites from making a sound.

Arthur whispered, "Who loves you?"

Tobias mouthed, "You do," and they rocked harder with more quiet intensity and murmured over and over to one another, "God, I love you."

When they were spent and reunified and reassured, they talked in whispers and planned their life together and apologized a final time for all the hurts and agreed they wouldn't dwell on any injuries. They had forgiven each other everything.

They slept a while, but anxiousness woke Tobias in the late hours that were the first hours of the next day, and he found Arthur was awake, too.

"Hi, Babe." Arthur said.

"Hi."

"Worried?"

"A little."

"About us?"

"Never." Tobias pulled Arthur close and kissed him. "Never."

"It's going to be fine. It'll take some time to get used to not having to worry all the time."

Tobias kissed Arthur's cheek and settled in closer to him. They lay face-to-face, each with an arm around the other. "You read my mind. I'm feeling strangely panicked, but not about us. It's about…I don't know."

"I think I do. You've been running for two years, and almost too abruptly, it's over."

"Exactly. I mean, if we really do this, if I really go back to Beverly Hills with you—"

"Only until we move to a place we both choose."

"I know, and I'm looking forward to everything we've planned, but it feels strange to know that when I step onto that sidewalk, I can walk in any direction and explore whatever's there and be safe and indulge, too. Feels like cheating the life's lessons I still hadn't learned."

Arthur was quiet.

Tobias pulled him closer. "Before you think I'm talking about money—because I love you and I *did* hear every word you said about it stealing the limelight and everyone giving it all the attention and treating you like you're not separate from your money," he kissed Arthur, "that's not what I mean."

Arthur kissed him back. "I know, but it helps to hear it. It means everything to me that you understand what hurts me and that you don't laugh at me for almost complaining about having money."

"Never. I get it. And what you said at your house was true. There's no way you would have left all of what surrounds you in that world to live in this tent if you weren't really looking for something more, something different."

"I love you. I almost can't believe we're here and this is real."

They kissed for a longer moment, and Tobias nearly forgot what he had been trying to say, but he remembered.

"No, I'm talking about proving to myself that I could find a way out of this hole with bus rides to a job that helped me crawl out. What I hadn't counted on was you."

Arthur rubbed his back, and Tobias felt better than he had, he thought, maybe in his whole life.

"The irony about me screaming about elevators in your house is that it's not your money that's coming to my rescue. It's you. It's loving you and needing you and having the grand fortune—pun intended—of getting to be with you and you loving me back. I said it once. It's a miracle, and it will always be the thing that saved me. I guess it just feels weird that my path of hard lessons learned was cut off so suddenly. By you, not your money. It happened way before yesterday. I was panhandling and you were getting mugged and I was suddenly madly in love and my life has changed wildly for the better because of you. I hope I don't sound silly."

"No, with me, you can talk forever, especially when you say things like this."

They kissed again and hugged each other tighter.

Tobias spoke softly. "The minute I met you, the hard lessons had eased, and I see that now. The physical changes around me are just driving it home. I see what you mean about money being distracting and a detractor. It's there, so we'll use it, and by virtue of that, everything now looks different. My mind hasn't caught up to my new reality, yet, is all. That's all it is, Babe. But make no mistake, I'm very happy. And I just hope I can make you happy."

"Are you kidding me? You're kidding right?" They kissed. "It's the same for me, in reverse. I was traveling along blinded by wealth and objects and a lifestyle, and…you were panhandling, and I was getting mugged, and you brought me to this tent and changed my world, for life. It was a shock to me, too. I went back to work that first morning I left here and stared at downtown out of my window it seemed like all day. I was trying to figure out where you were. I wanted to be out there, wherever you were."

Again, they kissed for a long while.

Arthur finally said, "My guess is, you're also feeling a little guilty that you're getting out before others have and like you didn't do all your time, but no one should have to live outside, as you say. Every day out here, for anyone, is too much time, and, anyway you earned your way back in."

"Really? Do you think so?"

"Yes, exponentially, Babe. Yes. You found a job under the most difficult of circumstances. You've survived three foreclosures. And you did it honorably and soberly and with dignity. You kept your wits. That's not easy out here. Where a lot of people would have given up, you rose up, and even took in others because that's who you were before your troubles, and that is who you stayed. It's what I love. It's why I'm so proud of you."

"Thank you for saying that. I have a hard time seeing it that way, and I need to be reminded. I think I got too used to this existence to have perspective."

"Believe it because it's true. And now I can tell you what I never could, which is that there's so much I learn from you every day. I mean, I was stumbling around over loneliness and boredom, with my security not even on the line, and you held it together literally by the threads of a tent and saved another person. *I admire you tremendously.* You're the strongest person I know."

"I love you, Arthur. I will love only you, forever."

"I'm the numerator to your denominator?"

Tobias laughed. "My prime number, divisible only by me."

"Your—"

Tobias pulled him close and kissed him.

"Yes, my...."

They made quick, hot love and fell back onto their makeshift bed and talked over each other with excitement about their new life.

"I know you have a new job," Arthur said, "and so much on the horizon, but because of you, so do I. I mean, I want to show you off, for real, and introduce you to everybody I know. I want to travel to places where the sun sets with more beauty because the language it's setting on is foreign and we're there together to watch it. I want orchestra seats at the theater, with dinner someplace fabulous beforehand and dessert afterward, not to say we ate somewhere fancy, but to be together and talk about everything. I want to experience everything with you. I want the world to see you, to see how wonderful you are. And you can decide it all. I'll go wherever you like."

"I'll go wherever you are," Tobias said. "I think that first time I followed you through the park was a sign of me wanting to be where you are."

"And money's not all bad." Arthur laughed softly and pulled them into another cozy embrace. "I mean, I'm a little traumatized, too. These last ten days have been a horrible odyssey. I'm looking forward to easy, predictable communication, through phones we use to flirt with each other during our mundane days. Starting today, you drive the car of your choice so you can go wherever you want and volunteer and see friends and re-enter the atmosphere."

"Wow. I hadn't even thought about a car or anything like that."

"You'll get it back, the thinking about ownership and fun possessions and spending money and doing frivolous things like streaming a movie for three ninety-nine. You'll get there."

Tobias chuckled. "Three ninety-nine on a movie is a fortune. And it's gonna feel weird driving again."

"But, far more importantly, from this second on, we eat for real, whenever and wherever we want. I get that it's obvious we can afford it, but even when I had fake temp job money, you were always watching every morsel and bargaining breakfast for bus fare. I commend it, but that's over. Hear me well because I mean this, Tobias. One of the first ways to put the trauma behind you is to have your basic needs met. I need you to eat with abandon. I mean it. For your own mental health, from this second on, never again stop to think about cost when you eat, or tradeoffs. You can count calories, cholesterol, carbs, whatever, but not cost. If the hamburger on the menu is some fancy twenty-two-dollar thing, and you want it, *order it.*"

Tobias's heart was full of love for Arthur. "Okay."

"And it applies to me, too, but it's going to be fun. We've travelled through narrow corridors of survival. We love each other, but our outlook has been confined. You said it. We haven't even seen each other naked from across the room. It's time to roam the world and be spontaneous and see how we grow and where it takes us."

"Can we roam naked?"

They laughed.

"Yes. Indoors."

"Well, until we leave the castle, outdoors, too. That lagoon is fabulous. I want to get naked with you in it again."

They laughed and kissed.

"Okay," Arthur said. "For you, lagoon nakedness."

Tobias said, more seriously, "Do you think where this all takes us will be anywhere bad? Are we going to find out we can't survive outside this tent?"

"No, no, *no*. Never. I have no doubts that where we're going is wonderful. I just can't wait to see what it looks like, to live it, with you."

"You had me nervous there, for a minute, talking about 'seeing where it takes us.' " After a moment, he said, "But what's gonna happen when…?"

"Say it, Babe."

"When…you realize you've come home another day and it's still just me there. I don't mean because I'm not rich. Just because life gets dull."

Arthur pulled Tobias closer. "I'm gonna feel lucky I get to be the one who loves you, and I'll love you harder for being there with me and loving me. You're an extraordinary man, Tobias. I'll be thinking, 'Wow. I can't believe he's *my* husband.' "

Their lips touched softly.

"And please don't say no to things my money can buy. It's not the things I want. It's the experiences with you that I crave. I want a whole, huge life with you."

Tobias was the happiest he had been, for he understood that money would never be why Arthur did anything. Tobias, and their love, would be the reasons, and money was merely the gateway to more life.

"Have I told you I love you?" he said.

They made love into the early morning hours, and, after dawn, for the first time, Arthur pulled out his real phone and called Kelly, instead of the other way around.

Tobias couldn't hear Kelly coming through the nice phone. He just heard Arthur say, "We're good. More than. I can't wait to tell you about it. I'll see you tomorrow, though. It's moving day on this end."

Kelly spoke. Arthur boomed with laughter. "Yes, yes, yes. For real." He nodded a few times. "Everything, yes."

And Tobias understood that Kelly knew that Tobias knew it all, and that she seemed very happy about that fact. Their glee was contagious. Tobias had a huge smile on his face.

"Let Frank and Charlie know I'll be back for good on Tuesday." He nodded again. "All the details, I promise," he said.

Arthur was just about to hang up and remembered something. "Add this to your lawsuit file," Arthur said, and he looked at Tobias with a face that said, "I'll explain later." To Kelly, he said, "What are you doing next Sunday evening? Tobias and I would love to take you and any friend you choose to dinner."

His phone chimed. Kelly had switched from phone mode and texted, as quickly as Arthur had claimed she could, a GIF of a sassy comedian snapping her fingers three times with the words *I'm there!* at the bottom.

Arthur laughed and went back to phone mode. "Great! See you then and see you tomorrow."

After he hung up, he said to Tobias, "I promise, that will be the last time I make plans without asking you first. I just thought we owed it to her. We've put her through the ringer."

"Are you kidding? I can't wait to meet her."

They kissed and made love one last time in the tent.

∞

Later that morning, they dismantled the tent and brought it to Melinda with the sleeping bags, mattresses, pillows, heater, and repellent devices.

"Please give these to whoever you feel can best use them," Arthur said.

"Thanks, Art. That's really nice."

"One more thing." He took out a business card and handed it to her. "This is me."

She looked at the gold square logo, and her eyes moved as she did a quick comparison of the name of the firm and the name on the card. She nodded. "Wow. Who knew?"

"If you ever need anything, *anything at all*, if the City is giving you trouble or your pipes bust and you need some help or you want to expand your services or the police are bothering your patrons or anything, you call me."

"Wait. That day they snatched Terrence, you were here. Bobby told me a man got him a lawyer. Was that you?"

"Yes, and I mean it. You will not be bothering me if you hit a wall and call me. I want you to pick up that phone."

She smiled. "Okay, Art. I appreciate it. Thanks. And don't be surprised if your phone rings." She laughed a little.

He laughed, too. "I won't. And *you* don't be surprised when you see a large donation come your way."

"Wow, Art. I don't know what to say."

"How about, 'Take a cookie.' "

"You bet." She slid the plate of cookies on her counter closer to him.

"Bye, Melinda," Arthur said. He used both hands to shake hers and said, "Take care. And call me. I mean it."

"Okay. I will. I promise. You take care, too, Art. Bye, Tobias."

"Bye," Tobias said.

Arthur bit his cookie and left with a huge grin on his face.

"You are such a flirt," Tobias said when they were outside.

"I know." He smiled wider. "Home?"

Tobias stopped and gazed at his surroundings and took a deep breath of downtown air. The word "home" made him feel strange. For two years, any time anyone spoke the word, he thought of the fight he was in to keep his condo. He hid from people that, for him, it was the back seat of a car. He convinced himself that a tent being the only thing that stood between him and the world was a legitimate abode. And, finally, he looked forward to returning to a dwelling space that he would share with the love of his life.

He knew it would take time for the survivor's guilt he had about getting off the streets so suddenly and leaving JoJo and others behind to fade, but he leaned deliberately, and not on impulse, into his new life, after months of tent life and shared lemonade and talking over a newspaper while falling in love, and couldn't wait to start it.

"Home," he said. "I'm dying to try the sauna."

They both laughed loud, and, for once, the car ride was full of chatter and laughter and music.

They arrived in Beverly Hills, and Tobias was relieved Arthur's mansion seemed far less ominous and alien that time.

He moved the few things he owned into a couple of regular-sized drawers inside Arthur's large closet. Somehow, that he had moved in with so little told him everything he needed to know. It said that possessions had nothing to do with his and Arthur's love. Arthur had tried to tell him that, and seeing his meagre belongings resting in two drawers while knowing he would come home from work every night and talk with Arthur and sleep next to him and love with him reminded him that Arthur was right all along. What they owned was immaterial. Their effects possessed volume but no meaning beyond the sentimental. What they shared, what they couldn't touch but what they felt, always, was everything, would be everything.

As agreed, Tobias chose one of Arthur's modest cars because he felt better driving to work in something reasonable and spotted freedom down the road, freedom to run to the store for tortilla chips, to give a coworker a ride home, to stay late anywhere and not worry about whether a bus would get him home.

And although Tobias teased Arthur about the elevator and the six-head shower and the Brioni suits, he never ridiculed him. He even confessed he enjoyed the Jacuzzi and the expensive shower gel and Arthur's huge bed, where they expanded their lovemaking repertoire—with the space and privacy they had to make noise—and slept late and watched foreign films and listened to opera, piped in on an extravagant sound system.

There were whole sections of the house Tobias rarely explored, and they had agreed they would move on from the mansion, but while they waited to downsize a little, Tobias had fun watching Arthur share the things he had kept hidden, like his home theater and his light sensors and the drinking fountains carved into walls that one might encounter on their way to some far end of the house.

Tobias had spent the first few weeks marveling at facets of the castle and chuckling in good-natured disbelief, like when he got lost on the second floor and had to ask a staff member he bumped into in a hallway how to find his way to the staircase, and he giggled, or when he went to take out the trash and laughed at himself when he saw that it was gone, or when his dirty clothes reappeared clean, crisply ironed, on hangers and in drawers, and he laughed again at the seeming miracle of it, or when he hid from Arthur at the bottom of the stairs and then jumped on the elevator to the third floor and shouted, just as Arthur arrived downstairs, "Hide and go seek, and you're it!" and his laughter traveled around the house, or when he played show tunes on the piano, not having to care about how loud he was for the neighbors, and Arthur sang along and they laughed.

Those moments aside, though, he took seriously their existence, whether they cooked in the ginormous kitchen or they read in the private library or Tobias played quieter melodies on the piano to soothe Arthur's mind after a hard day. He transitioned to their new existence and took it at face value.

And, most importantly, he took Arthur seriously. And he admired him and all that he had accomplished. He told him so, often. And he unabashedly appreciated the outward signs of Arthur's success.

One morning, Arthur came down to the breakfast nook wearing more than ten thousand dollars' worth of clothes.

"Damn," Tobias said.

"What?"

"You are *fine*."

"You like me like this?" Arthur grinned.

"I do. You look…powerful." Tobias smiled. "Like a boss. In fact, you better leave now, or I'm going to make you miss your meeting."

And they had had dinner with Kelly, who helped Tobias make Arthur's life miserable throughout the meal, just as Arthur had wanted. Arthur confessed later that he had never been so happy to be the butt of so many jokes.

The teacher in Tobias related well to Kelly, a young adult who expressed herself with less inhibition than Arthur and Tobias's contemporaries. Where it sometimes threw off Arthur, Tobias easily responded to Kelly's enthusiasm.

He liked her. She was funny and offered a glimpse of Arthur that revealed a softer side, a magnanimous boss who willingly ceded authority to those around him because he saw them as equals, a genius not only with numbers but with ideas for growth—of money, business, entrepreneurial plans, and charitable concepts. It helped Tobias understand how Arthur could be down-to-earth enough to not merely accept tent life but embrace and even enjoy it. He had told the truth. He had been, in many ways, more suited to that environment.

In fact, Tobias picked up from Kelly's tidbits that Arthur had shown more change in her world. Tent life had informed him and shaped his opinions and altered his approach to his business.

At dinner, Arthur asked Kelly to be his best person at their wedding when the time came, and she texted him, right at the table, a GIF of an entire wedding party disco dancing their way up the aisle to the altar as a "yes".

Several months later, on the anniversary of the night they had met in Grand Park in the strangest of ways, Tobias and Arthur had a June wedding, and Kelly had kept her promise to stand up for Arthur. Michael, the one friend who had stuck with Tobias through his turbulence, had been Tobias's best person.

By the time they became Tobias and Arthur Pelletier-Dewynter, they had moved away from the castle and Tobias had rehabilitated his resume with his tutoring job and found a position teaching at a secular private school. The hours were better, and he was home every evening.

Most nights, he and Arthur shared modest dinners in their new home, something smaller than the mansion but still tucked away in a secluded corner of Beverly Hills and with a flare that recognized how hard Arthur had worked to achieve success.

Tobias had promised Arthur he would never make him apologize for his accomplishments or feel guilty about enjoying the fruits of his lifelong efforts. So, they had a swimming pool, smaller than the lagoon, but good-sized, in an expansive backyard, a standalone building that functioned as a gym, elegant bathrooms with saunas, a dedicated library with high walls decorated with loaded bookshelves, a patio that became a sun room, a snug home theater, and a kitchen that let them spread out and cook together. And their piano.

They had no elevator or fourteen main-house bedrooms or courtyard with a tree, but they lived in comfort and in the degree of elegant, unique, and specially tailored style Arthur had earned. Their driveway was long. Their garage was large. Their hallways were wide. Their guest rooms were mini-havens with fireplaces and big-screen TVs and chic bathrooms. Their furniture was custom-made. Their carpets were plush. Their art was original. Their neighbors were not "right next door". Yet, the scope and scale of the property were reasonable and far more manageable than the intricacies of the castle had been, with its complex water lines, elaborate lighting, and mazelike configuration that hid thousands of crannies to dust.

Still, they kept life simple. They each had a car, and they kept a third one for staff, but they donated the remaining three to three different charities whose primary purpose was helping homeless people downtown.

After life downtown, and the razing of the encampment, and Terrence and JoJo and Melinda and so many others, and so much else, Arthur adopted Tobias's volunteer spirit and felt strongly that with their money came the responsibility of doing what they could for others who couldn't make it on their own. He and Tobias said often, "Even we didn't make it without each other, Babe."

They agreed Arthur would not change the name of his firm and include "Pelletier" because THE DEWYNTER FIRM was its own brand and institution that clients relied on. Change made investors nervous, and for the financial security of Arthur's staff, they kept all things at the firm consistent.

Arthur did commandeer Tobias's paychecks to teach him how to invest in case anything ever happened to Arthur. He wanted to be sure Tobias knew how to manage money well so that he would never again be destitute. Arthur explained that even large fortunes could disappear if not properly handled, and he made sure Tobias had his own funds to work with, learn from, and even tap into, if necessary. Neither of them cared about whose money was whose or prenuptial or postnuptial agreements because they knew divorce was not in their cards. They had been separated, and they would never again allow it to happen.

They traveled and took in local entertainment, but they still played Frisbee in the park and enjoyed free events downtown. They stayed connected to Michael's foundation, to which Arthur had donated the most expensive of the cars. Michael was the head of his organization and knew people from every echelon. He had seen greats who had been felled by drugs and bad choices and worse investments. He was surprised to learn about Arthur's money but not stunned. Mostly, he had been relieved they had survived the raid.

He had lost track of several people who relied on him the day they cleared out Spring Street.

Most enriching for them both was that Arthur expanded his firm to include a charitable foundation whose sole focus was downtown homelessness. The organization refurbished buildings for shelter space, found and funneled donations, and set up a legal clinic not far from San Julian Street that helped people deal with harassment and arrests.

Arthur tapped Kelly to oversee it. She had balked, out of fear of an inability to do the job, but Arthur had said, "You're the best person for the job. You manage difficult people well, you're analytical, you juggle multiple tasks expertly, you dig where others give up, you're like Charlie in that you work your guts out, you've had some exposure to the problem, and you *care*. Even without the other qualities, that alone makes you ideal for the job. The deeper into it you get, the more you'll see I'm right about that fact. I lived it, and I know. A person who doesn't care can't do this job. I need you."

And, so, she assented. She coordinated with Charlie and Arthur's attorney Nathan Cresswell at the beginning, but she eventually staffed up with her own crew and managed a team of six. As a group, they partnered with many members of the homeless community. The attorneys at the clinic earned very high salaries paid for by the foundation and defended their clients with the weight of a high-powered law firm. Michael and Tobias sat on their board, and the job gave Kelly regular contact with them. Over time, they all became fast friends, and Kelly had finally transitioned to calling Arthur by his first name so that those days of "Mr. Dewynter" seemed long ago and far away.

And Arthur continued to tell one lie, with Tobias's permission and on his behalf: He never revealed to anyone else in his firm how he had faked being homeless. He didn't want anyone to judge Tobias, and the specifics of why Arthur's fake life had worked for Tobias and Arthur were hard to explain and no one's business. Kelly was fiercely loyal to Arthur—and Tobias—and would never reveal what she knew.

Tobias taught tenth grade and twelfth grade and, being left-handed, sometimes became sidetracked by the sight of his wedding ring as he wrote theorems on the board. At times, he still couldn't believe Arthur was his husband, that they had graduated from a mugging to matrimony, that he was loved as much as he was, that there was a person out there who meant more to him than anyone or anything else in his life.

Tobias waited for them to fall into that stage where they took each other for granted and worked a little less hard at being together and loving each other, but it hadn't happened. Their ten-day separation had shown them what a gift their relationship was and how fragile any two people could be, and the tight quarters of the tent that had helped them bond had also taught them immeasurable cooperation. It was forever embedded in how they related.

Their worst argument, other than the day Arthur had confessed, had remained the one they had had the night Tobias went to the tunnels. Their disagreements tended to last just one round. One of them might say, "This is why we should have left at six o'clock," to which the other answered, "I know." Or maybe Tobias said, "Next time, if you shoot me a text, I'll know what the deal is," and Arthur answered, "You're right."

The tent hadn't permitted angry recriminations, stormy tantrums, or long silences. There just wasn't enough room. They never learned to relate to one another in those difficult ways. They had always looked for and assumed the best in each other and searched for a peaceful resolution that would maintain equilibrium in the tent, and that system had stuck, helped along by their compatible temperaments.

Life had gone well.

∞

Then there came a black day. One of death and the end of two lives.

An AR-15 traveled into Tobias's school on the arm of a man whose disgruntlement no one ever really defined. They only knew that he had made his way up a hallway where the school's trophy cases were displayed and posters for school events adorned the walls, fired scattered shots, and turned down a corridor with doors, all shut. He walked along the passage in search of nothing and everyone.

At one door, he lingered. He shot at the handle and kicked in the shattered door.

He fired more shots.

Sounds from his weapon echoed around the corridor and across campus.

He retreated from the door.

He headed up the hallway. He took twisted mercy on other doors, on other classrooms. At the end of the hallway, he reached a dead end. Cornered, he shot and killed himself.

And in the classroom where he had kicked in the door and fired with abandon, Tobias lay on the ground. He bled from a gunshot wound on the left side of his chest.

An ambulance rushed him, barely alive, to the nearest hospital. From the roof of that hospital, connected to a steady supply of blood, he was airlifted to another, one that could handle the devastation to his body.

In Century City, Arthur appeared in the doorway of Kelly's office, with the blood drained from his face. He stammered and staggered. He held up his cell phone.

He had just received a call, he said.

Tobias, he said.

Shot, he said.

And Arthur and Kelly and Michael and others waited down the hall from the operating room.

In the operating theater, a surgeon, one of three, cursed. The machine that monitored Tobias's heartbeat let out one long beep, telling the cursing surgeon that Tobias's heart had stopped.

In the waiting area, Arthur's chest beat hard, as though something had been trapped inside it and had fought to fly out. He didn't understand it, except that he knew his soul was gone from his body, and there was an inexplicable heat emanating from no clear source, on his left side. The warmth was prickly, ominous. It bore down on him like a threat.

He fell to his knees and sat back on his own legs, close to the ground, and hung his head low as it came rushing back to him—the mugging, the Chinese restaurant, that first Sunday in the tent when he knew he loved Tobias. He muttered, on his knees, "Come with me, Babe." His voice sounded strange to himself. He didn't understand why he said those words.

He only knew that Tobias had died and that both their lives had ended.

Tobias knew, too. He heard the machine sounding one, long note of death. The noise sounded like the beep of Arthur's alarm in his mansion, which baffled Tobias.

He also didn't comprehend why there was a bright light in the room and how it was that he walked toward the light. He was sure he had been shot teaching geometry to his third period class. He knew he couldn't walk.

He moved closer to the light to see if he could solve the problem.

He was near the light.

Arthur appeared on his left. It felt wonderful to see him.

He was naked, and Tobias looked down and saw that he, too, was naked. He remembered a question he had once asked Arthur. "Can we roam naked?" *Maybe that's what the light is for, Babe. A place for us to roam naked. You look beautiful.*

The light and Arthur were almost the same distance from Tobias, but Arthur was a little farther. With the light at high, bright noon and Arthur at nine o'clock, Tobias and Arthur and the light formed a right-triangle, with Tobias at the center of the clock.

Clock hands appeared. The short hand pointed to twelve o'clock. The long hand led to Arthur to make it quarter to noon. Or midnight, when bad things happened. Tobias thought if the long hand moved and hit twelve, it would strike midnight and Tobias would be struck dead in an irretrievable way.

The light glowed bright and lit up the left side of Arthur's being, his nudeness a vague impression with no definition, but

Arthur ignored the light. He looked only at Tobias, whose own nakedness seemed more like a feeling than a truth.

Tobias wanted to know more about the light. He needed to explore it, define its area, explain its volume, but he felt he should make a left turn toward Arthur and help him keep the long hand from moving toward twelve.

There was a problem, though. Arthur was so far away. Tobias didn't think he could reach him. The light was closer. It beckoned him.

He headed toward the light.

"This way," Arthur said.

Tobias stopped and looked at him. "I can't. It's too far."

"Let me carry you, Babe," Arthur said. "I've got you. Come this way."

"The light. Do you know what it is?"

"I do. It's why you must come with me. Now. Just like I came with you, back to Spring Street. Back to the tent."

"The tent? Oh, yeah. Our rebirth, like naked babes, destined for a new life."

Arthur nodded. "Come with me, Babe."

The light held mystery, warmth that didn't comfort, indefinable breadth. Arthur held love. And Tobias had learned that the short way was often the wrong way. The long way, distant places that could only be reached with perseverance, were where the true light lay.

And Tobias turned away from the strange light and toward deep, knowable love that enveloped and comforted and warmed more completely than the light could.

Slowly, he walked to Arthur. "Yes, carry me, Babe."

He reached Arthur and lay a palm on his chest. Arthur's bare skin was warm to the touch, but not because of the light. It came from inside Arthur. His heart beat was palpable.

"Steady, Babe," Tobias said. "I made it. I'm here."

And the deadly, flat, shrill beep became an intermittent one of life.

And Tobias knew that the journey inside the lighted passage had ended. He was with Arthur, on a different path, walking toward a different light, one less brilliant and blinding, one more loving and inviting.

A doctor emerged from the operating room and told Arthur and Kelly and Michael and the others that the round from the AR-15 had entered Tobias's body through his shoulder and had tumbled around inside before blasting a tennis-ball-sized hole in Tobias's back on its way out. It had nicked a brachial artery on its way by.

Tobias had died for seventeen seconds, as they worked to patch his torn body, but they had revived him and mended the area near his heart and closed the chasm in his back and the one that had almost opened between Tobias and life and Tobias and Arthur. The next several hours would be critical, the doctor said, but Tobias could make it.

Arthur had known when those seventeen seconds had ticked by on the clock. They had brought him to his knees and killed him. Tobias's revival had given Arthur life again.

∞

Tobias made it, through the next several hours and the next day and the next several days and weeks and their June wedding anniversary and the long, hot summer.

He told Arthur about the choice he had made standing before the light during those seventeen seconds, and Arthur said he had already known somehow and had sensed their lives depended on his fighting to keep Tobias from walking into the light.

With three more surgeries, Tobias made a full recovery, except for an ironic twist: for the rest of his life, he would feel the occasional shoulder pain that Arthur had claimed to have on his first date with Tobias.

When autumn arrived, Arthur begged Tobias not to return to work.

Tobias explained why he had to. He said the students had no choice but to return if they wanted to finish school, and Tobias thought it only right that he not take the escape hatch an independent adulthood gave him. He agreed none of them, not the students or teachers, should have had to bargain with unknown threats every day for a little more time to carry on with life, but he would bargain every day anyway, along with his students.

Gradually, Arthur understood, and he knew that no matter what misfortunes they faced, they would always have waited for one another and walked toward one another, and whoever was strongest would carry the other. Arthur had carried Tobias away from the light that time, but Tobias might be the one to carry Arthur the next time, as he had carried him back to the tent the first time.

Tobias added it up his way: He knew that they may have been just two people, may have each carried just one other, but he understood that as they did that over and over, and as the boon that arose from that redounded to their union again and again, the breathtaking results of that sum, of the love of his one and his one, over a lifetime, would be exponential.

A lifetime later, he learned he was right.

I hope you enjoyed *Carry the One*, a story set in a town I love. Alas, my hometown isn't perfect. I'm a native Angeleno who lives near downtown, and, over the past decade, I have witnessed throughout the city a startling increase in the popping up of enclaves like the one in which Tobias and Arthur live in *Carry the One*. These encampments are found in the downtown area and are also peppered throughout the environs. They border grocery store parking lots, parks, and rows of fully functioning businesses, among many other locations where they can be found. The dwelling spaces in most encampments range in size from a large tent like Tobias's to makeshift shelters, such as the shopping-cart-and-tarp arrangement in which JoJo "lives".

While *Carry the One* is not based on any real person, living or dead, or any real-life incident or encampment—all events, depictions, places, and persons are fictitious or used in a fictitious manner—I did witness a few years before publication the disappearance of a vast tent city not far from where I live. I had driven by it often, and watched it grow over time. The sidewalk there is wide, and, as I recall, many tents in the encampment were as large as Tobias's. Then one day, every tent was gone, replaced by a long chain-link fence running down the middle of the sidewalk.

In a way, it wasn't a surprise, even if it was shocking and very sad. One could "feel" that result building, as more people moved in, and the encampment, on its own side of the street, crossed over a large boulevard and continued down the road. One said to oneself, "I think someone is going to shut this down." And they did.

Witnessing that mass-displacement; my time spent as a tutor for homeless teens; my experiences volunteering in homeless shelters; and my daily exposure to the dichotomy of what lies to the west of Main Street (businesses, government agencies, expensive lofts, the Music Center, Grand Park) and what lies to the *immediate* east (Skid Row—not a large area compared to greater Los Angeles but crowded and growing more compact due to gentrification of nearby areas squeezing Skid Row into a reduced space) inspired me to set this M/M romance in the world of homelessness, or "houselessness", a term I recently heard that I think gets right to the heart of the issue.

Of course, the sources, causes, and geopolitical layers of homelessness—or houselessness—are many and varied. Thus, in *Carry the One*, I took a micro approach and focused on what this life could look like for just two people—a math teacher and a financial advisor—falling in love for the first time, under these circumstances. The love was the thing.

THE UGLY POST

A love story that will grab you and not let you go until you know how it ends.

Charlie and **Bryce** have been together seven years. They don't have it all, but they have all they want—each other and the only relationship that's ever meant anything to them. The week they met, they didn't flirt with seduction to see what would happen. They fell in love and proved it the only way they knew how. They've never been apart since that first tumble into life as lovers, playful partners, best friends, and soul mates.

Charlie has no reason to believe arriving home ahead of Bryce on a random Monday night will change everything between them. But when Charlie logs onto a computer he shares with Bryce, he stumbles into the devastating truth about their relationship.

Or does he? Charlie is sure he's discovered a secret Bryce has kept for seven years, but Bryce swears Charlie is wrong. Blindsided by lies, mistrust, and shattered faith, the two are swallowed into a vortex spinning so fast, it tears them apart. Can they reveal the fiction in the truth and find their way back to each other, or will the black-and-white portrait one man's words paint destroy them forever?

For fans of stories where you're the fly on the wall watching two people who love each other madly "go through it".

THEN CAME MICHAEL

Galen had no idea a weekend trip during his senior year of high school would be the reason he escaped the people who murdered his parents. Years later, he just wants a life he can count on, and, miraculously, he has it. His job as a police officer has treated him well for eleven years and lets him work on his own terms. He's happily married to an androgynously sexy woman. His best friend works on the force.

On the night he arrests a man in the park for vagrancy and throws him into the holding cell at the police station, his life begins to unravel. For one thing, even from behind bars, the man draws in Galen and intoxicates him into forgetting how to do his job. For another, after Galen releases the man, Galen's troubles don't end. He can't get the man out of his head, and he has an even harder time keeping his distance from him. Soon, all he can think about is **Michael**.

With the night of the arrest behind them, Michael warms to Galen, who strangely came to Michael's rescue just minutes after Michael was released from the police station's lock-up with no charges filed. As their unexpected friendship grows, feelings Galen hasn't experienced in years, ones he thought had been the youthful yearnings of a boy in need of friendship after tragedy had struck his family, awaken in Galen. But as the answers to Galen's questions about his feelings become clear, Michael retreats. Will Galen give in to a longing for a man who doesn't want to have anything to do with him and enter the fight of his life? Will the object of his affection, the man preoccupying his thoughts, fight with him…or against him?

Can Michael resist the man whose tragic history and quiet toughness have attracted him the way no other man has? Will he risk loving a man who may not be able to love him back?

About the Author

Sailor Penniman lives in Los Angeles and writes modern literature short stories, novellas, and novels. Born in the heart of the city, Sailor enjoys featuring Los Angeles in a story's narrative, wherever possible, and using the city's diverse palette of life circumstances to weave tales of love, perseverance, and equality.

Follow Sailor Penniman on Twitter: @sailorpenniman

(http://www.twitter.com/sailorpenniman)